"What am I going to do with you?"

Tia brushed away the juice on his chin with her fingers. Her hand lingered, caressing the long column of his neck before moving lower.

"Keep me." Chris placed his hand over hers, holding her hand against his skin. His thumb stroked the back of her hand.

Tia's skin tingled and grew warm under his hand. She gazed into his eyes, and her heart nearly stopped in her chest. Barely checked naked desire glared back at her from his pale blue eyes. Something deep and primal stirred within her. Tia did something she'd never done before. She took the lead, leaning forward and lightly kissing his lips.

Surprise crossed Chris's face. The heat in his gaze warmed Tia's cheeks. "Do you know what you're doing?"

"I think so," Tia answered honestly, leaning in for another kiss. This time Chris met her halfway.

YOU'RE All
I NEED

KAREN WHITE-OWENS

Kensington Publishing Corp.
http://www.kensingtonbooks.com

DAFINA BOOKS are published by

Kensington Publishing Corp.
119 West 40th Street
New York, NY 10018

All Kensington Titles, Imprints, and Distributed Lines are
available at special quantity discounts for bulk purchases for
sales promotions, premiums, fund-raising, and educational or
institutional use. Special book excerpts or customized print-
ings can also be created to fit specific needs. For details,
write or phone the office of the Kensington special sales manager: Kensington Publishing Corp., 119 West 40th Street,
New York, NY 10018, attn: Special Sales Department, Phone:
1-800-221-2647.

Dafina and the Dafina logo Reg. U.S. Pat. & TM Off.

ISBN-13: 978-0-7582-2960-1
ISBN-10: 0-7582-2960-7

First mass market printing: October 2010

10 9 8 7 6 5 4 3 2 1

Printed in the United States of America

YOU'RE All I NEED

1

Monday morning at 7:45, Adam Carlyle stepped out of his Renaissance Center office and stood next to Tia Edwards's workstation. With a laptop in one hand and his chocolate suit jacket in the other, Tia's boss placed his computer on the edge of her desk before sliding his arms into the suit jacket.

"I've got a meeting at eight with Reynolds. After we're done, I'm holding a staff meeting with the legal department in the fifteenth-floor conference room."

"Do I need to be there?" Tia brushed a wayward curl from her eyes. Silently, she hoped Adam would say no. She had plenty to keep her occupied until he returned from his meetings.

Her boss folded his arms across his chest, considering her question. "No." He glanced at his wristwatch. "I should be back around noon."

Tia nodded.

"I'll need drafts of the Swinson, Jamison, and

DeVry's briefs when I return." He straightened his tie and smoothed the front of his shirt.

"Got it." She tapped her to-do list with the point of her pen. "It's on my agenda for this morning."

Adam picked up the laptop and tucked it under his arm. "Hold down the legal department. I've got my cell phone, and the computer will be on if you need to contact me. See you around twelve."

He hurried down the hallway, then turned and disappeared down another corridor. Tia smiled. After two years of working for the vice president of Legal Services at Gautier International Motors, she still believed she worked for a great guy. When Adam offered her the position, Tia hesitated in accepting it. He seemed so demanding and forceful that she questioned whether she'd be able to meet his requirements.

It was never an issue. There were days Adam expected everyone on his team to go full force, kick butt, and work as hard as he did. On other occasions, if he knew she had a school project due, he sometimes gave her the afternoon off. He was a kind, considerate boss who understood her busy school schedule and offered compassion and support for her educational pursuits.

Since Adam would be away for a while, Tia settled back in her chair and finished her cup of coffee before tackling her work. She spent the next few minutes tracking a freight ship slowly cruising down the Detroit River toward Grosse Pointe while sipping a mug of caffeine elixir. Once she swallowed the last mouthful of coffee,

Tia started her daily routine of returning phone calls, retrieving voice mail, making appointments, and sorting incoming mail. After those tasks were completed, she concentrated on the legal documents Adam requested.

A little before noon, Tia placed Adam's briefs, mail, and messages on his desk. Head down, she made her way to the door, focused on the remaining tasks on her to-do list.

"Whoo! Watch out," Adam called, barely missing a head-on collision with Tia. He sidestepped her lithe frame with a guiding hand on her arm.

"Sorry. I wasn't looking where I was going."

"Obviously." He grinned, taking the sting out of his observation as he crossed the floor to set his laptop on his desk. He turned to her as he removed his jacket and placed his cell phone on the charger.

Tia asked, "How did the meeting go?"

"Very well." Adam hunched his shoulders and then stretched. He pinched his chin between his thumb and forefinger. "Some information came out of my meeting with Reynolds that I need to share. Let me grab a cup of coffee while you get your stuff." He reached for his mug. "I'll be right back."

Tia watched him leave the office. *Something's up*, she thought. Adam's body language revealed important information. She'd seen him like this before. Something important happened at the meeting.

Heart fluttering in her chest, Tia swiftly returned to her desk, grabbed her computer, and switched on voice mail. Adam always returned from his meetings with Reynolds with a boatload of work to do. Work didn't worry him, so this had to be something different.

By the time Adam made it back from the executive lounge with his cup of coffee, Tia had settled in a chair in his office with her computer opened to a new document, ready for whatever new assignments he was about to share.

"Let's get started." He shut his office door and took his place behind the desk. "The legal department is going to expand."

Oh, man! This is huge, she thought, typing this into her document. Since opening his U.S. office in the GM Renaissance Center two years ago, Reynolds had been very cautious about his hiring practices. The president of Gautier International Motors lectured his staff on erring on the side of fewer, instead of more, employees. But why was Adam concerned?

Her boss hit the power switch on his laptop and opened a file. Glancing at the screen, his forehead crinkled as he reviewed his notes. "Reynolds wants me to cross-train an attorney from the home office in France. He'll be working here for a while."

That doesn't sound so bad, Tia thought. "How long is a while?"

"Um"—Adam shrugged—"that hasn't been determined. I do know that he'll be in this office for at least six to eight months. What happens after that is Reynolds's decision."

"When will he start?"

"He's here already."

"Oh!" Tia sat up straighter in her chair. "That was quick. Where is he?"

"In Reynolds's office. He'll be down here in a bit." Adam pointed to the door. "We're going to put him in the office on the other side of your workstation."

Okay. She didn't have a problem with that. "What about staff? Is he bringing anyone with him?"

Amazed, Tia watched Adam shift uncomfortably in his chair. That wasn't like him. What was going on?

"This is where things get a bit dicey," he announced.

"Oh?" Tia uttered cautiously. *What's going on, Adam?* she wondered.

Nodding, Adam answered, "Mmm-hmm." He leaned forward in his chair. "Look, I hate to do this but I don't have a choice. I need your help."

"For what?"

"I need you to help acclimate Christophe to the office."

Not liking the sound of this request, she asked, "What does that mean, exactly?"

"You'll be his admin like you are mine. We'll increase your salary. Don't worry about that," he added hurriedly. "Tyler Hudson's admin will be your backup."

Tia brushed a curly lock from her forehead and then held Adam's gaze with her own. "You haven't answered my question. I'm stuck on the word *acclimate*. What exactly do you expect from me?"

Adam sighed. "Christophe Jensen is from France. He's going to need a little help beyond the office."

"Am I going to be dealing with a language issue? Problems with English?"

He shook his head. "No, not at all. Chris is very fluent in English."

"Then what's the catch?" Tia asked. Her eyebrows lifted questioningly, and her voice dropped. "What does 'outside the office' really mean?"

"Okay, you got me." Adam held up his hands in a gesture of surrender. "I'm sorry about this. But Christophe is going to need a little direction in finding an apartment, getting around for the first few weeks, and learning the office routine. You'll have to go over his briefs and show him how we structure things here. It wouldn't surprise me if you end up in court with him. There's just so much that he's not going to know and will need help learning. Think of him as a first-year attorney." He offered Tia his most engaging smile. "Please. I truly need you on this one."

"Adam!" she whined, gearing up for a major rant. The last thing she wanted to do was play nursemaid to a company transplant.

He halted her tirade with a slice of his hand through the air. "Tia, help me out."

Unmoved by his pleading, Tia crossed her arms over her chest and sat back in her chair, considering all of the options and implications of Adam's request. "What do I get out of this?"

Adam swung into negotiation mode. "I know you are finishing your degree and that you want to make a move in a different direction. That makes sense. You didn't go to school to be an executive assistant for the rest of your career. I'll tell you what. Do this for me and I'll move you into a law clerk position once you're admitted into law school."

Lips pursed, Tia considered Adam's offer. *He'll give me this promotion for showing some French guy around town?* she thought. *There's got to be more to it.* She examined Adam's poker face but found nothing. There were times when Adam played his cards close to his chest until he found the best possible moment to reveal them. She had to keep in mind that there might be more to this deal than she already knew. Was she willing to do whatever it took to get that promotion? Short of going to jail for killing someone or taking Mr. Frenchie to bed, she could handle this assignment.

She did a mental debate while her hopes soared. This may well be the opportunity she needed. But she didn't want any gray area. Tia needed the offer to be as clear as possible to avoid any misunderstandings or mistakes later. "I know you'll keep your word. If something happens to you, I want everything clear and tight. Here's the deal. Bear with me. I'm going over our agreement one more time. If I get into law school, you'll find me a law clerk position at Gautier's." She reached out her hand. "Agreed?"

Adam leaned back in his chair, mentally reviewing the agreement for any loopholes that might cause him problems later. His lips pursed, and then he lifted his hand, taking hers. "Deal."

On cue, there was a knock on the door.

"That should be him." Adam rose and strolled across the office. He opened the door and greeted the newcomer. "Hey, come on in."

The man entered the office and shook hands with Adam.

Tia rose, allowing her professional smile to drop into place. She straightened her skirt and jacket and ran a hand through her wavy hair, waiting for her first glimpse of the French attorney.

Adam led the man toward the desk.

Christophe had the well-toned physique of a man who worked out regularly. His oval face and blemish-free skin would have been considered pretty on a woman, yet he wore them well. It made him appear more alluring and attractive.

Golden locks lightly brushed his shoulders. For a moment, Tia had a flashback to one of the romance novels she'd read during her high school years. The hero stood tall, blond, and handsome on the book cover, just like this man.

Adam touched her arm and drew her closer. "This is my executive assistant, Tia Edwards."

Fascinated by the sheer beauty of the man, Tia stared, tongue-tied. As tall as Adam, Christophe moved forward. Casually dressed in a blue and white striped poplin shirt with the cuffs rolled back, he revealed a set of long, muscular arms sparkled with blond hair. The man completed his outfit with a pair of tan Dockers and sandalwood-colored snakeskin boots.

Tia gazed into a pair of pale blue eyes that twinkled with humor and intelligence. She nodded at the man.

Adam made introductions. "Christophe Jensen. Tia Edwards."

"Nice to meet you," he stated in an accented, musical voice. The deep tone resonated within her. He captured Tia's hand and shook it. A spark of something sizzled between them. Christophe's eyes widened and his gaze settled on their intertwined fingers.

"You too." Flustered by the contact, Tia pulled her hand free and rubbed her hands together.

"I'm going to leave you in Tia's very capable hands," Adam said. "She'll take you to your new office and get you settled. If you need anything, Tia will be your contact person."

Christophe's eyebrows rose, questioning. "Oh? With anything?"

"Work related," Tia clarified swiftly, wanting to make her role as clear as possible. She waved a hand toward the door and then retrieved her computer. "Let me show you your office."

Christophe hesitated in the doorway. "Adam?"

Back at his desk, Adam glanced at the pair, shifting through a dozen or so pink message slips. "I've got a few things to sort out. Let's meet back here after lunch, around two-thirty?"

Nodding, Christophe replied, "That sounds good."

"See you then." Adam picked up the telephone and began to dial. "Tia, did my wife call?"

"Yes, Wynn called around nine-fifteen."

"Thanks." He focused on his phone call. "Good morning, Helen. Can I speak to Wynn?"

"Your office is this way." Tia shut Adam's door

as she led the way with Christophe on her heels. She stopped to deposit her computer on her desk, and grabbed a pen and notebook and a set of keys from the drawer before continuing to a dark door on the opposite side of her workstation. "We've had this office as part of our suite but never had a need for it. It's yours now." She unlocked and threw open the door, reaching for the light switch on the wall. Instantly, light bathed the room. Tia waved him inside.

Christophe slowly strolled around, examining the workspace, touching the desktop, opening empty file drawers, and peeking into the closets. After a moment, he stopped at the floor-to-ceiling windows, taking a look at downtown Windsor's shoreline. Nodding approvingly, he gazed directly at her. "This is nice."

"Good. I'm glad you like it." She moved closer to the man, drawn by the combined scent of his tangy aftershave and unique scent. "There's an attached restroom," she explained, crossing the floor and turning on the light to the washroom. "Let me know if you'd like anything changed. We can have maintenance move the furniture or add anything that you believe you'll need."

"A log-in and password so that I can access Gautier's databases would help."

Nodding, Tia said, "I'll take care of that immediately. Anything else?"

Christophe tapped a long, tapered finger against his lips. "Supplies—pens, notepads? Telephone? I have my laptop, but I do need Internet access."

"Internet, phone. They'll get taken care of when

I get back to my desk. Until you're up and running, you can use my computer for the Internet."

"Thanks. I appreciate that."

Tia jotted a few notes on her pad. "For supplies, there are a couple of ways we can go. We have an office-supply closet down the hall on this floor. You can raid it and find most of what you need."

"Or?" He raised an eyebrow.

"I have a catalog at my desk." She jabbed her thumb at the door. "Anything that you don't find in the supply closet can be ordered from that book."

"Merveilleux!"

"Let me show you a few other things, like the executive dining room. Then I'll introduce you to the rest of the legal department."

"I appreciate that."

"Where are you staying?" Tia asked.

"The hotel."

Eyebrows raised, she pointed a finger toward the floor. "Here?"

"Yes. I believe it's called the Marriott."

"That's the one. What about a car? Will you need a parking card?"

"I don't have a car yet, but I do want to get out and away. I want to see more than downtown Detroit and the Detroit River. Can you arrange for me to have a car spot?"

"Certainly. Parking space and card for you." Tia added this to his growing list of requests.

An hour later, Tia returned to her desk and sank into the chair. Together, after she and Christophe raided the office-supply closet, they returned to his office and set up his desk. She took him on a tour of the Gautier executive branch and introduced him to his colleagues. Christophe's pleasant personality was a huge hit with the legal department. The attorneys welcomed him enthusiastically. That wasn't all. Tia suspected it was his good looks that also won over the female staff.

Tickled, Tia turned aside, hiding her smile when several of the executive assistants began to giggle like tweens when Christophe flirted lightly with them. She couldn't blame them. From the moment that charming and handsome hunk of male perfection had entered Adam's office and turned his pale blue eyes on her, Tia's heart had thumped wildly in her chest while her body quivered in response.

Her immediate reaction and attraction to Christophe was a major surprise. She had never before reacted to a white man or a colleague in this fashion. There was definitely a spark of something she hadn't felt since high school. The sensation was stronger than any she had felt after meeting Darnell.

Calm down, she warned herself silently. *That white boy is not for you. Remember, you're in a relationship.*

Smiling, she swiveled her chair from side to side. *I think I've made a good deal with Adam. I'll get my promotion and a chance to work as a law clerk. This Christophe assignment doesn't seem like it will be difficult at all.*

Tia grabbed her purse from the bottom drawer of her desk and rose. The next few months would be interesting. She hoped that she would not regret agreeing to this deal.

2

A week later, Tia tapped on Christophe's office door.

"Yes?" came the accented reply.

She poked her head inside the room. The surreal lyrics of Enya filled his office. "Hi, Mr. Jensen."

"Come on in." Chris rose from the desk and met her in the center of the room. He moved close to Tia, entering her personal space. "Let's not be so formal. After all, we work together. Please, call me Chris."

She smiled. "Okay. Chris."

He looked handsome in a crisp white silk shirt, a floral multicolored tie, and navy trousers. His hair had that rumpled, just-out-of-bed look that movie stars sported. One wayward lock fell across his forehead. Tia shoved her hand inside the pocket of her suit jacket, ignoring the urge to smooth the blond tresses into place.

Instead, she handed Chris the stack of pages.

"Take a look at the motion and brief. Let me know if you need any changes."

"Thanks, Tia. Will do." He flipped through the pages and then gently patted her shoulder.

Chris's soft touch made Tia's skin tingle and her heart race. "You're welcome." She struggled to keep her voice light and professional.

Was it just Chris's way? A cultural habit? Tia didn't remember Reynolds ever acting so familiar. She doubted Chris was flirting with her. He seemed far too professional to jeopardize his career over a light dallying. Yet, she found herself remembering that spark that had surged between them the day they met. Tia also noticed that Chris always maintained physical contact with other staff when he spoke with them, too.

Tia put a step or two between them and waited.

He flipped through the pages. "You're very efficient."

"Thank you. That's what I aim for." Tia started for the door and called over her shoulder, "I'll be leaving for lunch around one. Let me know if you have any changes."

"Will do."

Tia returned to her desk. She typed in her password, unlocked her computer, and opened a new file. Her fingers rested on the keyboard as she considered the past week. Doing double duty for Adam and Chris hadn't been as difficult and merciless as she had expected. Adam kept his word, finding help from other staff when needed.

To make life easier, Chris typed his initial documents and then e-mailed them to Tia for the proper formatting and proofing. He displayed a high level of self-sufficiency and didn't require a lot of hand-holding.

If she had any concerns about their working relationship, it would be that the heightened physical awareness contributed to her nervousness. No matter which way Tia turned, Chris stood near her, watching with his intense stare that made her wonder if she had forgotten to comb her hair or brush her teeth that morning.

The object of her thoughts came out of his office and stopped at her desk. "You're going to lunch at one?"

"Yes. Do you need something?"

His suntanned skin turned a light shade of red. *What the heck is going on?* Tia wondered, fascinated by the transformation.

"Can I ask you for a favor?"

Uncertain, she hesitated before answering. "I guess so."

"I hope you won't take this the wrong way."

Tia's curiosity grew. Butterflies fluttered in her belly. *What could he possibly want?* Tia wondered. *Maybe he needs me to delay my lunch to finish some work.* "What can I do for you?"

"Where do you think you might go?"

Oh! She relaxed. *He wants me to pick up a meal for him. I can do that.* "I haven't decided. Do you want me to pick up something for you?"

He chuckled nervously. "No, thank you. Actually, I'd like to come along with you. *S'il vous plaît.*"

With me? What is this? Confused, she gazed at the man. "Um. Sure. I guess."

Chris brushed blond hair away from his eyes. "I don't think you understand. I'm always alone. I live in the hotel here and eat here every day. It would be nice to share a meal with a friendly face and get away."

He surprised her. But she understood the feeling of being away from friends and family and bored with your own company. "I don't know where I'm going for lunch, but you're welcome to tag along." She nibbled on her bottom lip. "Let me think for a minute. Have you been to any place outside of the RenCen?"

"Sweet Lorraine's, Tom's Oyster Bar, and the Marriott restaurants." He shrugged. "That's it."

"We won't go to any of those places." Tia twisted from side to side in her chair as she considered several eateries for lunch.

Chris shoved his hands into his pockets. "If you don't mind, I'd like to get out and see a bit of the city."

"No, I don't mind at all. It makes perfect sense. Oh!" Tia sat up straighter as a spark of an idea surged through her. She waved a finger in the air and said in a confident tone, "I know where we'll go."

He eagerly took a step closer to her desk. "Where?"

"Traffic Jam. Students around Wayne State call it TJ's. They have a pretty diverse menu. I'm sure you'll find something you'll like. Plus, we'll take the scenic route so that you can see some of Detroit." Tia shrugged apologetically. "Some of it's not so nice."

"*Merveilleux!* But what is TJ's?"

"It's a restaurant on Wayne State University's campus. After we eat, I'll take you around the Fisher and the old General Motors buildings so that you can check it out. Plus, it's a colorful area. It's part of the cultural center. The Detroit Institute of Arts, the main public library, and the medical center all surround the campus. We'll do a road trip." Excited with this adventure, Tia reached for her telephone. "Let me put something on voice mail and call Ruby to let her know that we're going to lunch. She can cover for me if Adam needs anything while we're gone. And I'll leave a message for Adam. I'll meet you at the elevators in ten minutes."

"*Merci beaucoup!* I appreciate it." Chris grinned and checked his watch. "See you in ten minutes."

"No problem. You're welcome. This will be fun."

Chris slipped into the olive-green-vinyl-covered bench opposite Tia and glanced around the restaurant. "This is TJ's?"

Nodding, Tia glanced at the menu offerings. "Pretty much. This is the place. It's a hangout for the local Wayne State students and a trendy locale for the surrounding businesses."

"Nice." He picked up the paper menu and studied it. "How is their vegetarian lasagna?"

"Oh! It's heavenly!" Tia shut her eyes, envisioning the delicious mixture of spinach, three cheeses, and pasta noodles.

A tall, lean man with silver facial jewelry

approached their table. "Welcome to Traffic Jam. I'm Sunshine and I'll be taking care of you today." He placed a white beverage napkin in front of each of them. "Can I start you off with something to drink?" Sunshine pointed to a section of the menu listing beers and wines.

Pursing his lips, Chris gave the question his complete attention while he studied the wine list. "You make your own wines here?"

Smiling proudly, Sunshine nodded and pointed toward the Second Avenue entrance. "Yes. The brewery is across the street, beyond the parking lot."

"*Très intéressant.*"

"We do some very flavorful wines and beers. Traffic Jam operates a bakery on site. After your meal, take a moment to check out some of the goodies we sell in the lobby."

"We will," Chris promised.

"Would you like to try one of our house wines?" asked Sunshine.

"Yes." He looked directly at Tia and held her gaze. The intensity of his look flustered her. "I already know exactly what I want."

Her heart skipped a beat. *There goes that flirting note in Chris's voice again.*

"I'd like the pinot noir."

"Excellent choice, sir." Sunshine turned to Tia. "And for you, ma'am?"

"Lemonade."

Sunshine scribbled their orders in a small spiral notebook. "I'll get your beverages while you review our menu."

After Sunshine left, Chris said, "Tell me about yourself, Miss Tia Edwards."

She shrugged, hiding her surprise. Questions about her were the last thing she expected from him. "I'm an employee of Gautier."

"That I already know." He crossed his arms, placed them on the table, and focused his pale blue eyes on her.

Her heart thumped erratically in her chest. She found herself fidgeting nervously with her beverage napkin.

"But there's more to you than work. What about your family? Are you married? Do you have children?"

"Goodness no! I'm single. No kids."

"Boyfriend?"

A twinge of apprehension slithered down her spine, but she answered the question anyway. This was none of his business. "Yes. Darnell."

"Lucky man." Chris's eyebrows rose suggestively. "Really. Does he work for Gautier?"

Tia shifted uncomfortably. These personal questions were unexpected and made her feel awkward. "No. He's an insurance agent for Buckhouser Life."

"Sounds like fun."

Tia shrugged. "I don't know. Darnell seems to enjoy it."

"Interesting."

She decided to turn the tables and ask a few questions of her own. "What about you? You came from France. Moving to Michigan had to be a major life change. Do you have a wife, children, or a special someone who's waiting for you to come home?"

He shook his head. "No wife. My friend and I split before I left home. She didn't like the traveling part of this job."

"I'm sorry." Instantly, Tia's heart went into sympathy mode. Without thinking, she reached across the table and squeezed his hand reassuringly. A muscle leaped to life under her fingertips as he held on to her hand for a second longer than necessary.

"Some things are meant to end. Patrice and I were one of them."

"Do you have children?"

"No. Not yet. But I want a big family. I believe it's my turn. Are you from the Detroit area?"

Tia nodded. "Yes. Born and raised here."

"What about your family?" Chris asked.

Sunshine returned with their drinks, placed the glasses in front of them, and then took their food orders. He added a small basket of bread before making a quiet retreat.

"I come from a medium-sized family." Tia took a sip from her glass. The lemonade tasted tart and sugary, just the way she liked it. "I have three brothers and one sister. My twin."

"Twins! That means there's another one out there just like you?"

"No, nothing like me, except for our looks. Nia's very different." Tia laughed softly, getting a mental image of her twin with her soft bob and tight, colorful clothes.

Chris took a sip, rolled the wine over his tongue,

and then swallowed. "I have a large family also. Big Catholic tribe. There are nine of us. I have five sisters and three brothers."

Tia blew out a puff of air. "Wow! I thought we were a large group." She tore off a piece of bread and buttered it. "Where are you from? Adam didn't say much about you. Do you live in Paris?"

He took another sip from his glass. "I know you probably won't believe this, but there are other cities in France."

"I know," Tia admitted bashfully. "But Paris is the one that comes to mind first."

"Shame on you." He strummed his finger at her. "Not enough geography while you were in school."

She laughed. Chris joined in. The rich, warm sound filled the room.

"I grew up in the city of Nantes. It's on the west side of France," Chris explained.

Leaning more comfortably against the vinyl seat, Tia asked, "How did you end up at Gautier?"

"Reynolds recruited me during my final year at the university."

"Adam said the same thing. Reynolds is a very clever man."

"Yes, he is." Chris broke off a piece of bread and chewed on it. "Reynolds is a major benefactor for the university."

"Did he go there?"

"Yes. But he's more than a pretty face with a checkbook. He spends time on campus and conducts entrepreneurial workshops for students and faculty."

"Very nice. I didn't know that." *Definitely more than a pretty face,* Tia thought.

"Reynolds doesn't brag. He likes things to be quiet." Chris smiled.

It captivated Tia. She found herself in a momentary daze.

"What?" he questioned. "Is there something between my teeth?"

Tia snapped out of her trance and decided to admit the truth. "Sorry. You have such a beautiful smile. I couldn't help admiring it."

"Thank you. So do you."

His compliment filled her with pleasure. Tia sat watching this interesting and very different man.

"Tell me, how do you know about this place?" Chris waved a hand around the room.

"I'm a Wayne State graduate. My study group came here for meals sometimes."

"We're going to see this campus after lunch, correct?"

"Sure."

"Merveilleux!"

Sunshine hurried to their booth with an entrée in each hand. He placed a dish on the table in front of Tia and the other before Chris. "These look really good. Enjoy," he said, then left the table.

Tia glanced at her vegetarian lasagna and inhaled the aroma of Italian seasonings and garlic. Sunshine was right. It did look wonderful. She picked up her fork and glanced at her lunch partner and laughed out loud.

Chris sat, studying his burger. "This isn't funny. I didn't expect the burger to be this big."

"It's a Jam Burger. It's half a pound of ground chuck. They are huge. You can always take some of it back to the office and have it for a late-afternoon snack."

He held the burger in both hands and took a bite. Nodding approvingly, he returned the burger to the wooden basket and wiped his mouth with his napkin. "I think I'm going to finish this."

"It looks pretty good. It's too much food for me, so I never order it. But I always wanted one."

"Here." Chris took the burger in his hands and held it out to her. "Have a taste."

With the bun in her face, Tia didn't know what to do. She shook her head. "Oh, no. I can't take your food."

"Of course you can. It's just a little bite. Come on. Enjoy!"

Tia wanted to say no. Eating his food seemed so intimate and personal. It was something you did with a partner, a lover, or a close friend. Tia was none of these, at least not to him. Again, this may be another cultural thing that she needed to learn.

With the burger in her face, she sank her teeth into the juicy beef. It was heavenly. She shut her eyes, savoring the taste. "Mmm!" Tia moaned. Opening her eyes, she found Chris's gaze on her. He smiled knowingly. Disconcerted, she drew away and grabbed her napkin, wiping her mouth. "Thank you."

"You're welcome." He placed the burger in its basket and pointed at her plate. "May I have a taste?"

"Oh! Sure." She pushed the plate in his direction.

"No, no. Just give me a forkful."

"Oh." She wasn't sure she wanted him using her fork.

Smiling at her, Chris said, "You don't have to worry about germs. I'd never hurt you that way."

3

Monday morning, Tia stood in the doorway to Adam's office. "Okay. I'll take care of it," she assured Adam before shutting his door and crossing the office suite to Chris's door. She tapped lightly on the wood surface and waited.

"Entrez."

Tia opened the door and entered the office. Chris sat at his desk with the daily newspaper spread across the surface. Excitement rippled through her. Instantly, guilt assaulted her. That feeling should be reserved for Darnell.

What is Chris up to now? She pursed her lips, moved across the room, and stopped in front of him. "Good morning."

After a quick glimpse in her direction, Chris returned to his paper. "Bonjour," he muttered back. *"Vous avez besoin de quelque chose?"*

She shook her head. "English!"

"Sorry. Do you need something?"

"Yes." Tia ran her fingers through her hair and

said, "Adam wants you at a meeting with Reynolds at two o'clock."

"What are we discussing?" Chris glanced at her. "The legal department's annual budget."

Grimacing, he dropped the paper and picked up a pen, jotting the information on his calendar. "Oh, *oui*. Two o'clock. Reynolds's office. I'll be there. *Très bien*. Thanks."

Reluctant to leave, Tia lingered, watching Chris for a moment. Absorbed in the paper, he failed to notice her. She stood, admiring the beauty of this handsome man as he turned the pages of his paper. Below the rolled-up sleeves of his shirt, she watched the ripple of muscles as he moved.

He glanced up unexpectedly. She covered by asking, "What's all of this? You're not looking for a new job, are you?" She waved a hand across the desktop, noting that the newspaper sat open to the classified section.

A bit frazzled, Chris shrugged. "No. I'm searching for a place to live."

Tia's eyebrows shot up. She struggled to keep the note of surprise out of her voice, but failed miserably. "You're apartment hunting?"

"*Oui.*" Brows furrowed, he pointed at an ad in the newspaper. "I don't understand. This is so complicated. Where is Beverly Hills? In California?"

Laughing softly, she circled the desk and stood beside him, leaning close to his shoulder to read the classified ad. The warmth of his body caressed her skin. "Yes and no. There's a Beverly Hills,

California, and a Beverly Hills, Michigan. So you were right. But not completely."

Eyes squeezed shut, he massaged his temples. *"Expliquez, s'il vous plaît.* Explain please."

Chris focused his pale blue eyes on her with a lost-puppy-dog expression that made Tia crumble. His need for help sucked her right in and tugged at her heart.

"I'm lost! Can you help me? I don't know this city." He chuckled without humor. "Or country."

Tia patted his arm. "Poor baby. Of course I'll help you. Let me see what you're doing here."

Annoyed, Chris pointed at an apartment ad. "Is this a good place to live?"

"Mmm. That's Chesterfield. Why don't you look for something closer?" Tia pulled a chair around the desk and placed it next to Chris's. "I thought you liked the Marriott."

"It was okay until this weekend. That place was a madhouse." He ran a hand through his blond hair. "People were up and down the hallway Friday, Saturday, and most of Sunday. They partied and made all kinds of noise. No sleep all night."

A closer inspection revealed Chris's eyes were red-rimmed, and his face looked haggard. "Did you call security?"

"Oui, a few times. They'd quiet down for a while and then start up all over again. It was nearly four o'clock on Sunday before things settled down. I can't have that. When I spoke with the manager, he said that it gets like this during play-off season."

"That's rough."

"It's time for me to get my own place."

"Do you have an idea where you want to live?"

"No. I'm baffled. What do you suggest?" He turned an earnest gaze to her. "I trust you."

She pressed her lips together, considering the options. "Chesterfield is so far away. Have you thought about staying closer to the office?"

He thought about it for a moment and then shook his head. "No. I've been living down here for a few weeks. I want to see more than downtown Detroit."

"Do you want to go east or west?"

"Which is nicer?"

Sighing, Tia answered, "Both sides of town have good and bad areas. It depends on what you want."

"What do you mean?"

"You've got a lot of options."

Frowning, Chris said, "I don't understand. I want to live in a place that is quiet and safe."

"That's important. Your apartment is where you'll be spending most of your free time. Do you want to be near a mall? Go to the movies? What about a gym? Are you a person who likes to cook or eat out a lot? All of those things matter when you're deciding where you want to live."

He leaned back in his chair and rubbed a hand over his face. "This is more difficult than I imagined."

"It's time to explore," Tia suggested. "You need to decide on a city and then check out the apartments in that area."

Slowly nodding, he answered, "That makes sense. Will you come with me?"

"Sure. How about Saturday around ten?" *Darnell is not going to be happy about this,* Tia thought, envisioning his rage when she told him about this assignment.

"Sounds good."

"Great. I'll pick you up at the hotel entrance." Chris took her hand and squeezed it. Physical awareness sizzled between them. An electrical current zinged its way down to her toes. "I appreciate you so much. Thank you for everything."

"You're welcome." Tia quickly put some distance between them as she rose from the chair and dragged it back to its place on the opposite side of the desk.

For most of the week, Tia and Chris spent their free time debating the merits of living on the east or west side of town. After many explanations, Tia finally convinced Chris to make the east side of town his first search location. Her rationale: going east would make it easier for him to get back and forth to work. Plus, she assured him that if he didn't find the type of apartment he wanted, they could continue their search on the west side.

On Saturday morning, Tia and Chris stood in front of a sprawling, two-story, brown brick apartment building that sat on a well-manicured lawn. Red, violet, pink, and white flowers sat beneath freshly trimmed shrubs. White shutters decorated the exterior of the windows at the front of the building.

Chris glanced at the ad in his hands. "'Two-bedroom apartment located in the heart of Grosse Pointe Farms; easy access to downtown Detroit; safe, quiet neighborhood; park within walking distance and secured parking.'"

Impressed by what she saw, Tia turned to Chris. "What do you think?"

Nodding, he pressed his lips together for a moment and then answered, "I like the outside."

"Me too." She nudged her companion. "Come on. Let's take a look at the inside."

Together they strolled up the curved walkway, pushed open a wooden door with an etched figure in the center of its frosted glass pane, and entered the foyer. Brown tile covered the floor, which contrasted with the tan and cream tiles decorating the walls. Metal mailboxes with apartment numbers and buzzers were secured into the wall that lined the tiny room. Without delay, Tia located and then rang the manager's apartment.

Minutes later, the door swung open and a plump, middle-aged woman in a floral housedress and flip-flops greeted them. Her sharp, assessing eyes latched on to Chris, widening a fraction as she did a slow perusal downward. With an approving nod, she grinned back at him, ignoring Tia. She could tell the woman liked what she saw.

"You are?" she asked him, regaining her professional posture.

"Chris Jensen." He captured her hand between both of his.

Flustered, the woman blushed and giggled. "I'm Mrs. DiAngelo, the landlady and manager."

Trying not to laugh, Tia turned aside. It didn't matter what age or race of woman, Chris had a way of charming the ladies.

"Pleasure," Chris added, dropping her hand. "We're here about the apartment."

"Oh, yes. It's on the second floor." The woman opened the door wider and waved Chris into the apartment building. "Come, come. I've got the keys with me."

Tia slipped through the door before Chris. For the first time, Mrs. DiAngelo noticed Tia. The older woman's eyes narrowed. She glanced at Chris.

"This is Ms. Edwards."

Mrs. DiAngelo nodded toward the younger woman. The warmth she exhibited toward Chris quickly shifted to cool wariness. Tia got the same once-over that Chris had received. It was instantly clear that she fell short of expectations. She smiled sweetly and trailed after Chris and the manager/landlady.

They climbed a series of stairs to the second floor. All the while, Mrs. DiAngelo chatted amicably with Chris while excluding Tia, who felt fine with this turn of events because it gave her a chance to take a better look at the building as they ascended the stairs.

The building was quiet, and every floor looked clean and well kept. As they headed down the hallway, the rubber soles of Mrs. DiAngelo's flip-flops slapped against the polished wood surface. She halted at an apartment door marked 201. Extracting a ring of keys from her pocket, she quickly found the one she wanted and turned the key in the lock.

"This is one of my favorite apartments. The previous tenant was transferred to Texas, so they had to move."

The trio halted inside the apartment. Like the hallway and staircase, the apartment's highly polished hardwood floors were beautifully maintained. A narrow foyer led into the living room. Large bay windows overlooked the front of the building. Tia could see her SUV on the street below. Slowly, Chris strolled around the room, examining everything. He moved into the dining room and then checked out the kitchen.

Tia hung back, waiting in the center of the foyer near the entrance. She wanted Chris to establish his first impression of the apartment alone. She believed it was important for him to form his own opinion of the place without her input. After all, if he decided to sign a lease, he would be the one living here. Landlady and potential tenant slipped in and out of her view as they moved though the living room, dining area, and kitchen, asking each other questions and making comments. The pair returned to the living room where Tia watched them from her spot in the hallway.

"What are the move-in costs?" Chris folded his arms across his broad chest.

"First and last months' rent, plus a security deposit that equals the first month's rent," Mrs. DiAngelo answered promptly. "A letter from your employer confirming your position will also be needed. Where do you work?"

"At the Renaissance Center."

"Oh, this location is perfect for you." She pointed toward the front of the building. "Shoot straight down Jefferson Avenue to downtown."

"I see."

The landlady perked up. "Are you French?"

"*Oui.*"

Mrs. DiAngelo pursed her lips. "Who is your employer?"

Chris paused as if debating whether to answer her question, and then he shrugged. "Gautier International Motors."

"Mmm." She nodded slowly. "I think I spoke with you. You're here for an indeterminate length of time, right?"

He nodded.

"I've heard of them. They're from France, right?"

"Correct." Chris turned away, searching for Tia. He found her at the door and waved her to him. "Tia. What are you doing there? Come see."

She sauntered down the hall and stood next to Chris. He touched her arm lightly and smiled down at her. "What do you think?"

"I like it. But the real question is, do you?"

Shrugging, he muttered, "Maybe."

Tia moved across the living room to the fireplace.

"This is beautiful." She turned to the older woman. "Does it work?"

Frowning, Mrs. DiAngelo focused an unfriendly gaze on Tia. "And you are?"

Chris took a step closer to Tia, wrapped a protective arm around her shoulders, and grinned down at her. "We're friends."

"Oh. Well, you do know that we only accept married couples. No living together or shacking up."

Chris's pale gaze narrowed and he said, "That's not a concern of ours or yours."

"Well, you do know that we don't tolerate a lot of loud noise. I don't want that loud, vulgar rap music seeping into the halls."

"I don't listen to rap."

Alarmed by the verbal attack, Tia took a step away, but Chris pulled her closer to his side.

The landlady's eyes narrowed and a sneer of disgust appeared on her face. "This is a quiet building. No fooling around or loud noise. The tenants who rent from me live here, but they take their partying elsewhere." Mrs. DiAngelo stared directly at Tia as she spoke.

"Well, Mrs. DiAngelo, I think Tia and I will talk about this; then we'll be in touch." Chris took Tia's hand and started for the door. "Thank you for showing us the apartment."

The woman followed them out. "Why don't you take an application with you? That way when you come back, you'll be all set."

He shook his head. "No. I'm fine. Thank you."

They headed down the stairs and made their

way out of the building. At her car, Tia turned to Chris and touched his arm. "What do you think?"

"Not for me."

"Why? It looks pretty nice and clean."

"I don't like the way that woman treated you," Chris stated.

Tia shrugged, wanting to give Chris the impression that it didn't bother her. "It's not my business. I won't be living here. You will."

"It matters to me." Chris touched her hand and squeezed it. "We're together a lot with work and you're helping me get used to Detroit. I won't have anyone treat you that way." He cupped her elbow and steered her away. "Let's go."

Surprised, Tia followed him out of the building. *That was interesting,* she thought. Chris had taken her feelings into consideration. She hadn't expected him to care. Tia hit the car remote and smiled. It gave her a warm feeling to think that he cared about her feelings.

4

Tia glanced at her watch and picked up her pace. *I'm late! I'm late! Man, this has been one crazy day.* She hurried into her town house and dropped her portfolio and purse on the sofa before continuing to her bedroom. Tia stripped off her clothes and then ran into the bathroom, turning on the shower. If her luck held out, she'd be able to let the water hit her for a few minutes before Darnell arrived.

When Tia had left home that morning, she had fully intended to be home by four so that she'd be dressed and waiting for Darnell to arrive for Eminem's concert tonight. A rap concert after a day of work didn't appeal to Tia's sense of fun. But since she had been so involved with school and work for the past year, she wanted a few nights with Darnell that focused exclusively on them.

However, apartment hunting with Chris had proven to be a fun but time-consuming experience that ate up many hours instead of the two she had initially planned. After she and Chris had finished looking at apartments, he had insisted that she share a short meal with him. They had ended up at Panera's for a sandwich and lemonade. It would have been rude to refuse his kind offer, so they sat and chatted about the pros and cons of each building they had visited.

As Tia showered, her thoughts turned to Chris. She laughed out loud at some of his outrageous remarks. He proved to be a fun companion as they joked together. Tia had to admit that she really had a great time.

After finishing her shower, she returned to her bedroom and searched for something sexy to wear that would please her boyfriend. Finally, she decided on a turquoise layered pantsuit. A shimmering silver sheer jacket covered the strapless top. A pair of silver sandals completed her outfit.

The doorbell echoed throughout the house, catching Tia off-guard. *Oh, man! Darnell's here! I thought I had a few more minutes.*

"Just a minute," Tia called, slipping her arms into a teal-colored robe as she hurried down the stairs in her bare feet. Tying the sash, Tia took a second to compose herself. A storm was brewing on the opposite side of her door. Darnell would raise hell when he saw her. She planted a smile on her face and opened the door.

"Hi." His eyes narrowed into angry slits as he took in her attire. Lips set in a stiff line, he added in a dry tone, "You're not dressed."

Well, that's pretty obvious, she thought. Immediately, she chastised herself. Darnell had a right to expect her to be dressed and ready to go out. After all, they had made tonight's plans weeks ago.

"I know. I'm sorry." Tia beckoned him into the room. "Give me a minute. I'll be right back," she promised, scurrying across the floor to the stairs.

Five minutes later, she emerged fully dressed and ready to leave. "I'm all set."

Darnell sat on the couch as he channel-surfed with the remote. He glanced up and frowned. "You're wearing that?"

She looked down. "Yeah."

"Hmm," he muttered. "Okay."

"What's wrong with it?"

"It looks like something you'd wear to work."

"It does not," Tia snapped, feeling anger rise inside of her. She planted her hands on her hips and said, "You were with me when I bought it. You said it was hot and begged me to buy it."

"Yeah, you're right. Forget I said anything." He dismissed it and then patted the cushion next to him. "We've got a few minutes. Why don't you sit? We need to talk."

Tia's heart flipped in her chest. The annoyance in Darnell's voice spoke volumes. For him to delay leaving was not a good thing.

"Okay." She drew her tongue across her dry lips and sank into the spot next to him. "What's on your mind?"

"I've got an issue that we need to settle," he said.

She hated it when he put her on the spot like this. Why did everything have to be such a big deal with him? "Okay. What's wrong?"

Darnell's right eye twitched, but his voice

remained calm. "When you decided to finish your degree, I tried my best to be supportive. I left you alone when you needed to work on your homework or finish a paper."

Tia raced right in, trying to defuse this situation before it could go any further. "I know. I appreciate your patience. It made completing my degree easier."

"But"—he raised a finger—"you're out of school now. I think the least you could do is be on time when we've got plans."

Tia turned to him and reached for his hand. He quickly moved away. Hurt by his rejection, she tried to hide her feelings and control the tremor in her voice when she spoke. "Darnell, I'm sorry. Things weren't supposed to happen this way."

Ignoring her apology, Darnell continued in a sour tone. "I've been patient . . . tried to understand what you were going through. That's all over. Now things are different. I'm not staying on the back burner anymore."

"You were never on the back burner. Darnell, I love you, and you're an important part of my life."

"Yeah, right." He leaned back against the sofa cushions and folded his arms across his chest. "When you decide to look my way."

"That's not true. Remember your company's holiday bash in February?"

"So?"

"You may not have known this, but I was in the middle of three papers and a presentation. I didn't hesitate to drop everything and go to the function even though I had to stay up practically all night for the next two days to get things done.

"That's what a relationship is about. You do things even when they're inconvenient, because you care about the other person. There's no doubt in my mind that it's the way things should go. Look, I planned to be home on time today. But I got caught up with Chris."

Frowning, he blinked as if he were caught completely off guard. "Chris? Who's Chris?"

"Christophe Jensen. He's a new attorney from France. I'm trying to get him settled, help him find an apartment."

Shaking his head, Darnell said, "I don't understand. Why are you taking responsibility for this man? Where did he come from? Is he working with Adam? Doesn't Gautier have people to do this kind of stuff?"

"Yes, me."

"No. This makes no sense to me. You busted your butt finishing your degree to play nursemaid to some French guy? Come on, Tia. Think! Use your brain!"

Indignant, she stated, "I do use my brain every day. But you don't understand. It's more than playing nursemaid to Chris. Adam and I have a deal going that will put me where I want to be in the future."

Jumping to his feet, Darnell scoffed, "Adam! It's always got something to do with that jerk."

"You're being unfair. Adam's a great boss."

"And there you go sticking up for him again. He's an arrogant SOB. You just won't admit it."

Tia gasped. She had no idea that Darnell disliked her boss so much. "No, he's not. What possessed you to say something like that?"

"I can say that and a whole lot more. You just won't open your eyes and see the man for who he is."

"Okay, tell me." Now Tia folded her arms across her chest. "Who is he? Who do you think he is?"

"Adam is a man who takes advantage of your good heart. He uses you like some dollar-an-hour typist. You're the executive assistant to the vice president of Legal Services. You should have some clout in that office. Instead, you do all of the grunt work. That crap should be handed down to some lower-level peon."

"That comment is uncalled for." Tia's voice dropped an octave. She glared angrily at Darnell. "Don't ever talk to me that way again."

Darnell took a step back and composed himself before mumbling begrudgingly, "I'm sorry. I probably shouldn't have said that."

"No. You shouldn't have," Tia agreed.

"Sometimes I wonder what's really going on at that company."

"Nothing that you have to worry about. Please, listen. If I help with the new guy, Adam will make it possible for me to move into a clerk position in the legal department. That's the direction I want to go. Eventually, I want to become one of the corporate attorneys. That's what I want."

"This is about your going to law school, isn't it?"

A bit embarrassed and feeling on edge, Tia muttered, "Partly."

"See, that's what I'm saying." Darnell jerked his finger toward the floor, gesturing wildly. "Adam takes advantage of you at every turn and you let him."

"It's not like that. This is my stepping stone to a better career."

"To what?"

"I—"

"Next you'll be doing his laundry."

"That's ridiculous. Adam and I don't have that kind of work relationship. Calm down and listen. Please."

"You know what? I've had enough." He glanced at his watch, fished inside his pocket, and produced his keys. "I'm tired of talking. Let's just go."

With nothing more to say, Tia held back tears as she grabbed her purse, obeying Darnell. Her heart heavy with questions and concerns for their future, Tia turned out the lights as they headed out of the apartment. Every time they were together, their conversations turned into an argument. These days their relationship felt so incredibly volatile. They disagreed on just about everything. There were days when she wondered why they were still together. They weren't happy. A line from one of Gladys Knight's tunes popped into her head: *Neither one of us wants to be the first to say good-bye.* That one line summed up their relationship to date.

Tia shook off those thoughts and decided to concentrate on having a good time. They had history and love between them. They could weather this storm and come out of it stronger and happier. She just had to do her part to make things better. Be on time and listen to Darnell when he needed her.

She locked her door. They moved down the hallway. Silence seemed to be a constant companion between them. These days she didn't know how to talk to Darnell. What was she doing in this relationship? She hadn't been happy in a long time, and she was certain Darnell felt the same way. Were they together because there was no one else or out of habit? Whatever the situation, they needed to sit down, talk honestly, and hash out their issues.

Five hours later, Darnell parked outside Tia's apartment. They sat for a moment, listening to Darnell's CD of Eminem's greatest hits. The night had been long and difficult. The concert was loud and filled with young people who stood up throughout the entire show. Their actions baffled Tia. Why pay good money for seats if they didn't plan to use them?

Unfortunately, Darnell's basketball buddies had accompanied them with their current bedmates. Now she understood why Darnell questioned her wardrobe selection. Dakai's and Lamar's chicks of the hour looked as if they had been poured into the crevices of their clothing. Tia wondered how the women could walk in such tight outfits. Both of them practically spilled from their tops, displaying an ample portion of their breasts. For some reason, Darnell expected Tia to dress the same way.

The night had been filled with catty remarks and loud cursing. By the time the concert ended, all Tia wanted to do was go home. But there was more fun to come. Dakai, Darnell's high school friend, suggested dinner. They all jumped into their cars and headed to the International House of Pancakes on Woodward Avenue in Royal Oak.

The food was delicious, but the company was not. The men acted like juveniles, laughing loudly and treating the server like their personal slave. Their dates talked to each other in soft whispers, excluding Tia. She didn't mind, but it did make her feel like a third wheel. Thankfully, dinner ended and the couples went their separate ways.

Now Tia was headed down the hallway to her apartment. Darnell trailed behind her. She halted at her door and removed the key from her purse. After unlocking the door, she asked, "Are you coming in?"

Darnell shook his head. "No. It's late and I have a couple of calls to make tomorrow morning."

The relief she felt by his answer shocked her. She still had a question or two. "On Sunday morning?" she quizzed.

"Breakfast meetings. My job depends on when customers are available. I have a valid reason for working on the weekends."

"I'm not trying to start a fight." Tia shrugged. "I'm surprised. That's all."

"Well, now you know."

"I'm sorry." This was her boyfriend, and she wanted to be close to him. Tia stood on her tiptoes and wrapped her arms around Darnell's neck, trying to entice a response from her man. She kissed his lips, waiting for a response.

It came, short and not very sweet. He brushed his lips across her and then loosened her hold on his neck.

"I got to go. Once I'm done, I'll call you. Maybe we'll catch a movie in the afternoon."

"Sure. Okay."

Darnell tilted his head toward the door. "Go on in. I want to make sure you're safe before I leave."

Nodding, Tia entered her townhouse and turned on the hall light. Darnell shut the door after her.

With a sigh of relief, she moved farther into the room and dropped her purse on the sofa. For the second time that evening, Gladys Knight's haunting lyrics sprung to mind. Only this time, Tia began to wonder if she should be the first to say good-bye.

5

Darnell never called. Tia never called him when he was making cold calls. She learned a long time ago to not disturb him while he worked.

Sunday dragged by without a word from him. After waiting most of the morning, she decided to get on with her day by doing a little grocery shopping. To top off her evening, she selected a light dinner of tuna salad, wheat crackers, and sliced tomatoes. She planned to watch a movie and then head to bed.

While preparing her meal, Tia debated calling Darnell. At least three or four times, she picked up the phone but returned it to its cradle without dialing. She glanced at the clock on her nightstand and doubted Darnell was working this late.

Besides, she really needed time to consider what she wanted to do. Should she and Darnell stay together? Were they at the end? Or did they still have some life in their relationship? Were they worth saving? Tia didn't have any answers.

She just had this nagging feeling that they were close to splitting.

Monday morning presented a welcoming distraction from the troublesome issues of Tia's personal life. A surprise waited for her when she arrived at the office. One long-stem yellow rose floated in a vase with a fresh, steaming cup of Starbucks Cinnamon Dolce Latte and a strawberry croissant.

A note sat under the coffee:

Thanks for giving up your Saturday to help me. I really appreciated and enjoyed the afternoon. Chris.

"That's so sweet. Chris is such a gentleman," Tia cooed softly, taking in the gentle fragrance of the flower. He didn't have to do this.

She locked her purse inside her bottom drawer and headed for Chris's office, tapping lightly on the door. After several seconds without a response, she peeked inside and found the room empty. The lights were on. A briefcase sat open on his desk. It looked as if he had dropped everything and hurried away. Tia shrugged. He must be in an early morning meeting.

Unable to thank him properly, Tia returned to her workstation and enjoyed her impromptu and delicious breakfast. *I'll thank Chris later,* she thought, biting into the buttery croissant. After finishing her meal, she got to work.

The morning flew by as she focused on her assignments. Near noon, Chris stepped out of Adam's office. He approached her desk with a warm smile on his face. "Good morning," he greeted in that sexy, accented voice that never failed to stir her blood and make every nerve ending tingle with awareness.

"Good morning to you. Thank you for my breakfast and the flower." She smiled broadly.

"You're welcome. I wanted to give you a little something special. I know your life is busy and your time is precious. I don't want you to think that I'm ungrateful for your efforts on my behalf."

"I didn't mind. Actually, I had a good time. You're a lot of fun. That wicked sense of humor of yours really tickles me."

One blond eyebrow arched into a flirtatious curve. "Does it, now?"

Giggling softly, Tia answered, "Yes."

"Since you enjoyed my company so much, what about this Saturday? Do you have time to look at a couple of apartments with me again?"

"Certainly."

"For all of your efforts, I promise to feed you again. Maybe I'll provide a little dinner this time."

"A full meal! Wow! Be still my beating heart." Tia patted her chest.

He winked at her. "Stick with me. There's more to me than you know."

Laughing softly, she touched his hand. Something warm and inviting sizzled between them. For a moment, the endless possibilities flashed through Tia's head, paralyzing her. Instantly, she shook off the sensations. "I don't doubt it. How was the rest of your weekend?"

"Uneventful."

Pretending to be surprised, she opened her eyes wide. "What? No late-night hallway parties?" Tia enjoyed this little flirtation with Chris. It meant nothing, just a way to pass the time. It was fun and harmless.

"No. I don't think I could take two weekends back-to-back." He perched on the edge of her desk and picked up her pen, twisting it between his fingers. "What about you? What did you do with the rest of your weekend?"

"I went to a concert Saturday night. I spent Sunday grocery shopping and watching a movie." Tia shrugged. "Nothing big."

"Concert?"

"Eminem."

"Rap."

"Correct."

"Sounds like fun," Chris replied with a sarcastic edge to his voice.

"Part of it was," Tia replied. "There were way too many people, which made it difficult to see anything. Plus, the people seated in front of us stood on their chairs throughout the whole show. We couldn't see a thing." Tia opened her mouth to add more when her twin turned the corner and headed straight for her desk.

Nia strolled up to Tia's workstation dressed in a dramatic, white off-the-shoulder crepe dress. The fabric cupped her body and emphasized the curve of her breasts. Slits in the long sleeves revealed trim arms. White stiletto heels adorned Nia's feet, and she carried a matching white leather clutch under one arm. "Hey, Tia-Mia."

Surprised, Tia rose from her desk and met her sister in the center of the room. "Hi. What are you doing here?"

"Don't look so surprised. I do know where you work. Want to do lunch?"

"Um. I don't know. Let me check my schedule." Frowning, Tia returned to her desk and checked hers and Adam's calendars.

Chris stood and watched the pair. He smiled and then said, "*Oui.* Two for the price of one."

"Cute, Chris." Tia waved a hand in his direction. "This is my sister, Nia Edwards. Nia, this is Christophe Jensen. He's an attorney from France and working in this office for a while."

Turning on the charm, Nia sashayed across the floor and stopped in front of Chris. With a smirk on her face, she gave Chris a thorough once-over before offering her hand. Chris took it and kissed the back of it.

"Nice to meet you," Nia said.

"Pleasure," he replied in his lightly accented voice.

Nia looked past him and gazed inquiringly at her twin. "What about lunch? My treat."

Surprised, Tia blinked back at her sister. She placed the palm of her hand on Nia's forehead. "Wow! No fever. This must be important. You never pay."

"Ha-ha! You're so funny." Laughing, Nia sank into the guest chair next to Tia's workstation. "That's not true. I just let you pick up the tab when we're out because it makes you feel important."

"I'll remember that the next time we're out

together," Tia promised. "It's a little early, but I can swing it. Give me a minute to let Adam know that I'll be out of the office for a bit and to turn on my voice mail. Then I'll be ready to go." Something was brewing inside Nia's head. She rarely dropped by the office. Tia could count on one hand the number of times her twin had bought lunch.

She headed for Adam's office, ready to knock on the door, when it opened unexpectedly and Adam and JerrDan Hill, the director of Engineering Operations, stepped out. The two men stood in the doorway shaking hands.

"Let me have one of the clerks do a little investigation and research. I'll get back to you with the results," Adam promised.

JerrDan folded his arms across his portfolio. "Sounds good. What time frame are we working with?"

Adam stroked his chin. "Give me a couple of weeks."

Nodding, JerrDan added, "I'll send you all the info I have."

"Good." Adam glanced past JerrDan. "Excuse me." He strolled to the trio standing at Tia's workstation. "Nia! How are you?"

Nia turned to Adam with a smile of pleasure on her face. "I'm good. What about you?"

"Fine. I'm fine. Oh, I'm sorry." Adam turned to the other man. "This is JerrDan Hill. JerrDan, Nia Edwards."

From the sideline, Tia watched JerrDan reach

for Nia's hand. Her twin smiled shyly back at the man as they shook hands.

"Nia," JerrDan said as if he were savoring the taste of a fine, expensive wine. He smiled, revealing even white teeth that must have cost the world. "It's nice to meet you."

JerrDan's smile must have flustered Nia, because she stood there without a comeback. Tia's twin was never without a sassy phrase or comment.

Awestruck, JerrDan stared. The strong, silent hunk of a man stood riveted to the spot, staring starry-eyed at Nia. Tia felt as if she were in the middle of one of those teen sex farces where hormones ruled and common sense flew out the window.

Although Nia would never admit it, she had the same expression on her face. Tia lowered her head, hiding her face from JerrDan and Nia. She didn't want either person to see her laugh at them.

Interesting, Tia thought. *It will be fun to see where this goes.* Nia shielded her heart from emotional bumps and bruises. She never allowed any man to get close to her. Yet, the chemistry that sizzled between JerrDan and Nia was unmistakable. JerrDan seemed like an upstanding, honest, hardworking guy who knew what he wanted from life and went after it without hesitation. Would he take the same approach with Nia?

At Coach Insignia, the hostess escorted them to a table overlooking the Detroit River and the distant downtown Windsor shore. Nia ordered a shot of cognac straight while Tia requested a glass of cranberry juice. They perused the menu and settled on their meals. When their drinks came, Nia sank back into her chair and watched sailboats crawl down the river.

Tia waited. After a moment, she said, "You didn't bring me here to spend your time looking out the window."

Nia asked softly, "So how's Darnell?"

"Okay," Tia answered. This didn't feel right. Nia disliked Darnell with a passion that surprised Tia. "Why?"

Nia shrugged. "Just wondering how things are between you two. You didn't seem all that happy the last time I saw you together."

Tia wet her dry lips and brushed her damp palms against her skirt while trying to come up with an appropriate answer. "Wait a minute. You hate Darnell. Most times you want him to drop off the end of the earth. Why the concern?"

"You're right. I don't like him," Nia snarled. "Trust me, my concern isn't for him. My concern is, and always will be, for you. Not him. Never Darnell."

"You're not the only one." Tia's hand flirted nervously around the bottom of her glass. "Junior can't stand him."

"I'm not surprised. Older brothers tend to be protective of their sisters." Nia reached for a slice of French bread and buttered it. She tore off a corner and chewed on it. "The difference between Junior and me is that he doesn't try to hide it. I always did for your sake."

Tia chuckled sadly. "No. Junior doesn't, and neither did you."

"True." Nia sat quietly, nibbling on the buttered bread and munching on her tossed salad while Tia enjoyed chicken and pasta soup. If Nia was waiting for additional info, she'd be waiting a long time. Tia planned to keep her problems to herself.

The server arrived with their next courses. Relieved to have something to do, Tia dug into her crab and shrimp salad, glad to focus on her meal. "Mmm. Good."

Nia took a bite out of her club sandwich and slowly chewed. After several sips of cognac, she leaned back in her chair, tented her fingers, and said, "A couple of the stylists from the shop invited me to Sips last night."

"Really?" Tia muttered politely, wondering where this conversation was headed.

"Have you ever been there?"

Tia shook her head, spearing a cherry tomato with her fork. "No. I heard about it on the radio."

"It's pretty nice. Great dance floor. Entertainment. Good food. Fun place to go. It's a safe, comfortable crowd. A lot of black professionals hang out there on the weekends."

"What's this got to do with anything?" Tia sipped her cranberry juice.

"You know I love you? That you're my girl?"

"I know you're making me nervous with this." Tia ran a shaky hand over her forehead. "Say what you have to say and then I'll deal with it."

"Okay." Nia sat straighter in her chair but

focused on the tablecloth. "I saw Darnell at Sips last night."

Tia's limbs stiffened. Darnell had been partying while she sat at home waiting for his call? No. There had to be some mistake, some logical explanation for the situation. "It *may* have been him."

"No." Nia rolled her eyes and stated firmly, "It *was* Darnell."

Still in denial, Tia added, "He had a couple of clients he needed to see on Sunday. They might have met at the club."

Nia shook her head and added, "He was with a woman. I didn't see anyone else."

"Again," Tia rationalized, although her voice wobbled a bit, "it was probably a client."

"I don't think so." Nia swallowed the last of her cognac, and then captured and held her sister's gaze.

"How do you know?"

"They were all over each other, on the dance floor and at their table. They never noticed me because they were getting busy."

Suddenly, Tia's belly twisted into a thousand knots. She tried to breathe but failed miserably. Tia knew deep in her heart that Nia was telling the truth. Tia always knew when Nia was lying. She couldn't hide from Tia her little telltale gestures that others overlooked or failed to notice.

What could she say? There wasn't an excuse she could make for Darnell or his behavior.

As if Nia needed to close the deal, she added, "It's not the first time I've seen him out and about, Tia. Darnell is never alone."

Tia pulled herself together, and over her pounding heart asked, "If you've spotted him out with other women at other times, why haven't you said something before now? What were you waiting for? What made you decide to tell me this time?"

"I'm sick of him thinking he can do what he wants." Nia reached across the table and took her sister's hand. Tia tried to pull her hand free, but Nia refused to let go. "He's a no-good piece of crap. I hate the way he treats you. Tia, you are a beautiful, intelligent woman who deserves a whole lot better than this idiot can give you. I want that for you. I'm sick of him messing over my sister."

Tia's head was swimming with images of Darnell with other girls. Nia's confession supported the idea that things were not going well between her and Darnell, but she never really expected him to be involved with another woman. Infidelity never entered her head. She'd always believed they would talk things out and then agree to go their separate ways. Theirs would be a cool and civilized breakup. Damn him! Now he's put her in a position where she'll have to confront him and put her emotions out there for him to tramp all over.

"Tia-Mia, I'm sorry." She swallowed hard and then continued. "At first, I wasn't going to say anything, but the more I thought about it, the madder I got. I realized you needed to know what was going on around you. Enough is enough."

"You're right. It is enough. Thank you for telling me."

"What are you going to do?" Nia asked. A worried frown had taken over her face.

Tia shrugged and answered in a dead tone, "Confront him."

6

Lunch ended on a low note. With her appetite shot, Tia pushed the plate full of salad away.

"I'm done." Tia rose from her chair and started for the door. At the restaurant's exit, she waited while Nia settled the bill. A chill iced Tia's skin. She wrapped her arms around her middle and turned away, heading out of the restaurant and through the Renaissance Center to her office. Nia raced along beside her. Deep in thought, Tia barely heard her twin's insistent chatter.

"Do you need me to be at your place when you talk to Darnell?" Nia asked as they strolled through the GM Wintergarden.

Tia shook her head.

Normally the glass, chrome, and greenery that lined this portion of the Renaissance Center provided a sense of beauty and peace for Tia. Today, nothing soothed the feelings of betrayal and embarrassment Darnell had sparked.

She pressed her lips together and concentrated

on moving up a series of escalators to the tower elevators. She smiled at the security person guarding the entrance to the executive wing of Gautier International Motors. Tia flashed her badge before turning to her twin. "Thanks for lunch. I'll talk to you later."

"What? No. We're not finished." Nia turned to the guard and picked up the pen from the clipboard. "I'm coming upstairs with you." With an exaggerated wave of her hand and a flirtatious wink at the guard, Nia signed her name across several lines. If the situation hadn't been so grave, Tia would have laughed. Her twin was such a diva. Nia loved every moment of it.

"Don't you have a home to go to?" Tia asked wearily.

"Of course. But right now I need to help my sister." Nia strolled toward the tower elevator.

"Suit yourself. Remember, I'm at work and I have things to do. I can't entertain you for the rest of the afternoon."

"I don't need you to amuse me."

Tired and wanting a little peace, Tia turned to her sister. "Then why are you coming back to my office?"

Waving a hand in the air, Nia answered, "To talk with you. To make sure you settle things with Darnell."

A sudden and almost urgent thought made Tia halt in her steps. Her head began to throb with the stab of a coming migraine. Did Junior know? Was that why Junior disliked Darnell so much? Had her oldest brother seen Darnell in a compromising position? Was he aware of something that he wanted to protect her from? If Junior knew, had he confided in their parents? Tia shut her eyes against the humiliation of having her family so involved with the most intimate parts of her life.

"Did you tell anybody about Darnell, Nia?"

"No. I came directly to you."

A sigh of relief escaped her lips. Thank goodness. The last thing she needed or wanted was a call from her mother, digging for details.

On the elevator, Nia's watchful gaze was constantly on Tia. Nia bit her bottom lip. Tia could tell that she wanted to say more, push a little further, but didn't know how her twin would react.

The pair made their way across the carpeted floor to Tia's workstation. Once they arrived, Tia sank into her chair after dropping her purse into the bottom drawer of her desk.

Nia rounded the desk, perched on the edge of the Formica surface, and folded her arms across her chest. "If you need me, call."

Shaking her head, Tia rubbed a weary hand across her throbbing forehead. "Thanks for the support. I'm okay."

"You can't let this situation go on any longer."

"I don't plan to."

"So you're going to kick him to the curb?" Nia asked with a happy gleam in her eyes.

"After I talk to him."

"For what? So that he can lie and sweet-talk his way back into your good graces?"

"Okay. I've had it. That's enough."

"No. It's not. I won't let you throw your life

away on that lying sack of crap. He doesn't deserve you."

Nia gently caressed her sister's arm. "I know you are tired, hon, but we've got to work this situation out."

"I've got a lot to think about. I plan to get through the rest of the day, and I'll worry about Darnell later." Tia noticed the blinking light on her telephone. Someone had called.

"You're not going to keep seeing that ass, are you?"

"I don't know what I'm going to do yet. Please, let it go."

Nia took her sister's hand. "I can't."

"Do the words *personal business* mean anything to you?"

"Yeah, but you don't get personal business when I'm the one who saw the jerk out with other women."

Tia sighed and studied her sister before asking, "What part of 'I need time to think things through' don't you understand? Why can't you let me do what needs to be done my way?"

"I can't, Tia. You are one of the smartest, most caring women I know." Nia's tone held a note of pride and then a touch of scorn. "But you are tenderhearted. You care way too much for that buffoon. You gave him your heart, and Darnell danced away with it."

"How about this? I'll call him and ask him to drop by my place tonight. Will you leave me alone then?"

Nia's head tilted to the side as she considered Tia's request. "Maybe."

"Thank goodness." Tia reached for the phone. She left a message on Darnell's cell phone before dialing his office. All the while, Nia watched and listened with an unblinking stare. His administrative assistant answered on the second ring. Sorry, but Darnell was out of the office. She expected him back around four. Yes, she'd have him give her a call. After a moment, Tia added that if he was too busy, he could just drop by her place on his way home.

Tia hung up, turned to Nia, and asked, "Satisfied?"

"Not really but it'll do."

Chris rounded the corner and strolled toward the sisters. "Hello."

Nia turned to face Chris, giving him one of her most engaging smiles. "Hi."

For a reason Tia didn't want to consider, she didn't like the expression on her sister's face. Nia was way too enthusiastic with Chris.

Smiling, Chris focused on Tia. The smile vanished. He rounded the workstation and sat opposite Nia. He touched Tia's hand. "You all right?"

"Yeah. I'm fine. There are a couple of things I have to resolve."

Watching her closely, he added, "If you need me, I'll do anything I can for you."

Almost in tears, Tia muttered, "Thanks. I appreciate it."

"I'll take care of her," Nia volunteered.

"Okay." He rose from the desk and strolled to his office.

"What now?" Tia asked, although she really didn't want to know the answer.

"I'm leaving. Going home."

"Good."

Nia stood and snatched up her purse, giving her twin a hard, intense glare. "Tia, don't let him off the hook. Darnell is a rat. You've got too much on the ball to let that lowlife stay in your life. Plus, if he's messing around with other women, there's a chance he can pass diseases to you that could end your life. I don't want that to happen. Besides, I'd be in jail because I'd kill him."

That's not a problem, Tia thought. They hadn't been intimate in six months or more. There always seemed to be a reason why he needed to leave or had something more important to do.

Tia watched her sister sashay out of the office. With a sense of relief, she sank into her chair. Finally, some peace. Nia meant well. She had made some good points, and in the very near future, Tia would consider them. But right now, she needed time to think, evaluate the situation, and come up with a plan.

For an hour, Tia sat on the sofa in her living room as the images from the six o'clock news flashed before her. Nia's words were embedded in her brain, rolling around in her head like a song she couldn't forget or ignore.

He was with a woman. They were all over each other. Nia's words continued to echo.

It's not the first time I've seen him out and about. Darnell is never alone.

Never alone, another woman . . . How many women were there? Her head pounded as questions swirled inside. Darnell was and had been cheating on her for some time. He lied Saturday night when he said that he planned to meet a client on Sunday.

Tia shut her eyes, searching for the strength to handle this situation with dignity while keeping it from digressing into an accusatory shouting match. She needed to hear the truth from Darnell's lips. No more lies.

Darnell's knock on the door came sooner than Tia expected. Like a zombie, she moved down the short-carpeted hallway to the front door. At the entrance, she paused, drawing in a deep, calming breath.

There was a moment when she thought about pretending she wasn't home and avoiding the whole sorry mess. *Courage,* her mind cautioned. *Take care of this and then you can move on.*

I can do this, she thought. Darnell stood on the opposite side of the iron security storm door. She opened it with a shaky hand.

Entering the house, Darnell leaned close to kiss Tia on the mouth. "Hey."

"Hi." Tia drew back, avoiding his lips, then led the way back to her living room and offered him a seat with the wave of her hand. She sat as far from Darnell as possible, choosing the chair near the patio windows instead of the sofa.

"I got your message." He reached for the remote on the coffee table and began to channel-surf. "What's up?"

"There's something we need to talk about."

Grinning like an idiot, he said, "Everything all right? You look all serious and stuff. Unload. Tell your daddy."

Tia cringed. "I had lunch with my sister today," she responded in a dead-calm tone.

Unconcerned, he said, "Yeah. How's my girl doing?"

"She's fine."

He must have noticed the lack of emotion in her voice. Frowning, Darnell asked, "Is the family okay?"

Tia nodded. "Nia was at Sips in Farmington Hills last night."

Darnell's grin slipped a tiny bit. He ran his hand across his face. "Mmm. Really? I was there last night. What time did she show up?"

"I think she was there most of the evening."

"Oh." They sat quietly together for several minutes. Deep in thought, Darnell tapped out a toneless tune on his knee.

Tia stared straight at him. "Nia told me that she saw you."

His head snapped up. A suspicious spark glared back at her, but he kept his tone light. "Did she, now?"

"Yes. And you weren't alone."

Instantly, Darnell swung into persuasive salesman mode. He smiled innocently and said, "Oh, yeah.

Sunday. There was a couple I met at the club. Old couple. It cracked me up when they suggested we meet there."

"Do they have a daughter?"

"What? Daughter?" He shook his head. "No."

"That's what I thought. Nia didn't mention an older couple. Just a young woman."

"What are you trying to say?" he demanded.

"It's pretty clear. You've been cheating on me."

Darnell jumped to his feet and approached her. "Oh, babe, come on. Nia must have gotten everything wrong."

Tia waved him away. "I don't think so. My sister finally admitted that last night wasn't the first time she's seen you with other women."

"I'm telling you this is all a mistake. Nia has got me mixed up with someone else."

"So you haven't been at the Motor City Casino on Grand River or the Dirty Dog Jazz Café in Grosse Pointe?"

"If she saw me at all of those places, why didn't she say something before now?" He sat down, crossed his leg over his knee, and smirked back at her. "That doesn't sound quite right."

"Nia kept her mouth shut because she didn't want to see me hurt."

He sat up straight on the sofa and shot back, "And making accusations like this is hurting you?"

"Yes, it is. But she had a better reason for telling me."

Grunting, he asked, "What?"

"My health."

Frowning, he stared back at her. "Health?"

"By messing around with other women, did you ever stop to think about the diseases and germs those encounters bring to me?"

Darnell opened his mouth to speak and shut it without saying a word. Tia could tell that he hadn't thought about that.

She snorted. "That's what I thought. I'm sure you didn't. Here's the deal. We're done. I want you to get your stuff out of my place." Tia pointed a finger toward the first-floor bathroom. "I won't call you. Don't call me. It's over."

"Come on, Tia, baby. It's all a huge mistake. I was wrong and I admit that. I shouldn't have done it. Things got out of hand, and I did a few things that were wrong. But I still love you. You're my girl. We've been together too long to let one little mistake tear us apart." Darnell gave her one of his sheepish, persuasive smiles. He leaned forward, pressing soft kisses to her cheek and lips. He took her hand between both of his and said, "I can make it up to you. We can make things better than ever."

"No, we can't." In a voice devoid of emotion, Tia continued, pulling her hands free from Darnell's. "It's over between you and me."

"I can't believe you're willing to let us go this easy. Think about all that we've shared. How can you walk away from that?"

"How could you cheat on me? *You* destroyed our relationship, not me."

"It's your job. That's what caused all the problems. You never had time for me. If you'd paid more attention to me, we wouldn't be in this position. Every time we had things to do, your job and Adam Carlyle got in the way."

Tia sighed. "Regardless, we're done. My job won't be coming between us anymore." She rose, went into the kitchen, and returned with a white plastic garbage bag. She held it out to Darnell. "You can put your stuff in this. Make sure you take everything. I don't want you back here again."

Nodding, Darnell snatched the bag from her hands. His first stop was the bathroom, where he removed all of his shaving items. Next, he climbed the stairs two at a time to retrieve his toothbrush and a set of clothes, which he stuffed into the bag. All the while, Tia followed him, making sure he picked up every item that belonged to him. She meant it when she said that she wanted him to take all of his things. She didn't want to see him again. They were completely finished.

7

I smell coffee, Tia thought, slowly waking from a fitful night with little sleep and horrific dreams. She turned onto her side and glanced at the radio clock sitting on the nightstand. Seven-thirty. Hovering between sleep and waking, Tia's eyes drifted shut. *Wait a minute!* Her eyes popped open. That must be wrong. Blinking repeatedly to clear her vision, Tia rubbed the sleep from her face and reached for the clock. The red LED display was correct. *Oh, man! I've overslept.*

Why hadn't her alarm gone off? Had she slept through the squeal of the alarm? *Oh, yeah.* Tia returned it to her nightstand. *I turned it off before I was finally able to fall asleep.*

Tia reached for the telephone and dialed the office. She was going to be late this morning. She left a message for one of the other executive assistants to keep an eye out for Adam and anything he might need until she made it to the office.

Tia felt incredibly sluggish as she swung her

legs off the mattress and let her feet hit the floor. She sat on the edge of the bed for several minutes, gathering her thoughts and energy. Normally she was a morning person who enjoyed the start of a new day. By this time, her morning regimen of exercises followed by a quick shower was usually complete. She'd be dressed and ready for a cup of coffee and bagel before heading to work.

Not this morning. Last night had been brutal. After making sure Darnell took all of his belongings with him, she had sat down for a good, long cry. The tears had restored some of her balance but took all of her energy. She felt hollow and empty. Like she'd lost a part of herself, and in some ways, maybe she had. After all, she'd been with Darnell quite a few years. They had shared many things, and now that had ended. Fresh tears sprang to her eyes. *Stop this,* Tia chastened silently. *You've got to go to work, and you can't excuse yourself each time a fresh batch of tears starts to fall.*

After leaving a message on Adam's cell phone telling him that she'd be in around ten, Tia stood and headed downstairs to make that imaginary coffee she believed she smelled earlier. Turning the corner to her kitchen, she halted. "What are you doing here?"

"I've come for breakfast," Nia Edwards answered, stirring a bowl of batter.

"I don't remember inviting you."

Nia shrugged delicately in her diva way. "Doesn't matter. I know you wanted and possibly needed me to be here. After all, you're my twin." She turned her attention to the meat sizzling in the

pan. "Coffee's ready, the table is set, and I'm
making waffles with Canadian bacon. I know it's
your favorite."

Surrendering to her sister's knowledge of her
favorite breakfast foods, Tia entered the small
kitchenette and removed a mug from the cupboard. After filling her cup, she headed for the
tiny dining room off the kitchen. The table was
indeed set. Nia had placed a vase of wildflowers
in the center and used the good china and silver.
Tia sank into a chair and sipped her morning
elixir, watching her sister prepare breakfast. A
thought occurred to her after a moment. "Don't
you have hair appointments scheduled for this
morning?"

"My first customer comes at eleven." Nia
glanced at the microwave clock. She removed a
bowl from the cabinet and began to slice strawberries into it. "I've got plenty of time. I can
always reschedule my appointments if need be.
Besides, you come first."

"And it was a nice way to make sure Darnell
wasn't here."

Grinning, Nia pointed a finger at Tia and
winked. "That, too. How are you?" She paused
for a moment. "Really."

"I'm okay. Tired. A little depressed." On the
edge of tears, her voice quivering, Tia added, "I'll
get over it."

"You're right. You will. And the rest is to be expected. You and Darnell have been together a
long time." Nia rinsed off her hands, grabbed a
paper towel, and took the chair next to Tia's. A

kind and concerned expression filled her sister's perfectly made-up face. "How did things go? What happened?"

Tia laughed. The sound was harsh and brutal. She blinked rapidly, surprised that such a horrific noise had actually come from her. It reminded her of the cry of a wounded animal. In some ways, Tia felt like one. "You know it's my fault that he cheated."

Surprised, Nia's eyes widened. "What?"

"Oh, yeah. Darnell blamed everything on me."

Nia grunted. "I'm not surprised. That's why I can't stand him. He's a rat and a typical man. Somebody else is always responsible. Never him. Don't buy into that bull."

Tia nodded. "I know. There's a part of me that wonders if I should have done things a little differently. Maybe we could have gotten past this."

"Sure there were. There's not a relationship out there that couldn't use a little tweaking. A little help in one way or another. But I do believe it was Darnell's responsibility to talk to you. That was his job as a partner in your relationship. Not go off with the next best thing. How can you work things out if he doesn't tell you what's wrong?"

"I know." Tia lifted her cup and took a long pull. "It's always easier to question yourself after the fact."

Nia patted her sister's hand and then headed back to the kitchen. "Men refuse to take responsibility for their actions. It's always someone else's fault. In Darnell's case, you're the fall girl. All he had to do was keep his junk in his pants and talk to you, and things would have been fine, but no. He had to show his jewels around town. What an ass."

"I feel really bad," Tia admitted, brushing away a tear. "Like I let him down or didn't do enough." She shrugged. "I don't know."

Nia watched Tia from the kitchen. "That's why I didn't want him to come back here. I knew he'd lay a guilt trip on you."

"I thought I was helping to secure our future by making a place for myself at Gautier's that no one could take away."

"Hello!" Nia tapped her twin on the forehead. "It takes two to make or break a relationship. You didn't do it alone."

"Darnell tried to tell me it was Adam's fault."

"Let's be honest about a few things. Darnell has always been jealous of Adam." Nia laughed. "Your boss has it going on. The looks, the career and lifestyle; Adam has all the things people like Darnell can only dream of. Don't take on his guilt. This is his way of wiggling out of his share of the responsibility."

"Everything sounds good in theory, but I'm the one by myself."

"No, you're not. You have family. And I'm going to tell you something. There are other men interested in you. There always have been. You were so involved with pleasing Darnell that you couldn't see what was in front of you."

"Yeah, right," Tia dismissed. "Like who?"

"That hottie at your job is very interesting and interested."

"Who are you talking about? Adam has a girlfriend."

"I'm not talking about Adam. That new guy. What's his name? Um . . . Chris." Nia waved the spatula in the air. "I know. Chris Jensen."

A jolt of something unique went through Tia. She almost choked on her coffee. "Have you lost your mind? I don't know him. He's been in our office about a month."

"What's that got to do with anything?" Nia placed a platter of Canadian bacon and waffles topped with fresh strawberries and whipped cream on the table before returning to the kitchen. "He likes you, Tia."

"There's a couple of flaws in your thinking. First, he's white and French. What am I going to do with that?" Nia opened her mouth, but Tia continued, ignoring her sister and refusing to let her say a word. "Second, I don't know how long Chris will be in the States. There's no specific timetable set up for him. Why would I let myself get involved with someone who could be gone in a matter of days? And third, our mother would have a fit."

Standing at the refrigerator, Nia stated defiantly, "Let her. This is your life, not hers. One thing I know about our mother: She would never allow Daddy to treat her the way Darnell has treated you." Nia returned to the dining room and placed a pitcher of orange juice on the table and then sat across from her twin.

"That's easy for you to say."

"No, it's not. But I do understand how Mother controls you and won't let go. She wants to turn you into her own personal mini-me. Remember this: Mother has a man. Why shouldn't you have one? You deserve someone who'll be there for you when you need him and who will love you and care for you just the way Daddy does for Mother."

"Some days I feel as if it's not in the cards for me. I think about Momma and it's too hard to deal with."

"Mother will have to get used to the idea. And, yeah, that would be interesting to watch. She's not a bigot. You're her favorite child, and whether you realize it or not, she wants you to be happy, no matter what color the man is."

Tia added waffles and bacon to her plate and then dug into her food. "I think you're wrong on all of it."

"I'm rarely wrong. And in this case, I believe I'm right on track."

"I'm not Momma's favorite."

Nia snorted. "Yes, you are. We've never gotten along, and I don't think that's going to change."

Tia held her sister's gaze with her own. "You could work a little harder at developing your relationship with her."

Waving away Tia's suggestion, Nia answered, "It's too hard to please Mother. Things always go way wrong when I try to do that. I'd rather live my own life."

"Well you do that."

"Yeah, I do." Nia twisted her shoulders in a sassy way before focusing her attention on her breakfast.

They ate in a comfortable silence for several minutes, and then Tia said, "Talking about men at the office, what was that I saw going on between you and JerrDan?"

Frowning, Nia asked cautiously, "What are you talking about?"

"Hey, I was there. I saw sparks flying all over you and JerrDan like Fourth of July fireworks. You two could have lit up a room with your chemistry."

Although a faint stain of red flooded Nia's cheeks, she maintained a strong, confident tone. "Obviously, this situation between you and Darnell has dulled your senses. I don't know the guy. He could be married with children for all I know."

"He isn't," Tia responded, watching the flicker of interest flare in her sister's eyes and quickly die. *Oh, yeah. Nia wanted more.* "JerrDan graduated from the University of Michigan. He came out of school at the top of his class. He's been with Gautier for about five years. The man works hard and is really focused."

"Why are you telling me all of this?"

Smiling sweetly, Tia answered, "Because you want to know."

"Okay. Maybe I do. He's some big dog at your company. I'm not his type."

Tia shot back, "How do you know?"

"Oh, come on. Do you really think he'll consider being in a permanent relationship with a hairdresser?"

"Maybe. I don't know. Why not? You're beautiful, talented, cultured when you choose to be, and you own your own business."

"Sweetie, I know and understand my place in the world. I'm perfect for the bedroom. Nothing more."

Tia silently studied her sister. Until today, she'd always believed Nia was the strong one. Maybe not. She had a bunch of insecurities. "Nia, don't do this. There's more to you. Don't sell yourself short. You've got a lot to offer any man."

"I don't want to talk about this anymore." Nia pushed her plate away.

Tia grabbed her sister's arm. "You can't avoid it."

"Yes, I can." Nia shook off her hand. "Besides, I'm not going to change for some man I know nothing about."

"No one's asked you to."

"Let's drop the subject, okay?" Nia perked up. "Anyway, that's not why I'm here."

"Why are you here?"

"To make sure my twin is okay." Nia's gaze swept over Tia. "From what I can see, you're going to be okay. It'll take a little time, but you'll do just fine."

8

Like radar, Chris zeroed in on Tia once she arrived at work. He emerged from his office and ambled up to her workstation. Concern etched his handsome features as he studied her.

"Hi," Chris greeted with a soft smile and wave of his hand. "I missed you this morning. Is everything going well?"

Why did he always have to be so gentle and caring? His concern called to her bruised feelings and made her want to confess all of her problems. Not trusting her voice, Tia shut her eyes and willed her crazy emotions to stay in check. After a moment, she felt more in control, but she nodded and swiveled her chair to the telephone, away from his probing gaze. "I got a late start this morning."

"That's not what I'm trying to say." Chris perched on the edge of her workstation. "You're the first friendly face I see in the mornings. Your smile starts my day. I look forward to seeing you. I got worried when you weren't at your desk."

Her breakup with Darnell had left her numb, but Chris's concern and compliment sparked a moment of pleasure inside of her. "Thank you."

"No thanks needed." He studied her for a beat and then asked, "Late night? Did you oversleep?"

"Little bit. Excuse me." Ready to avoid additional probing questions, Tia dialed the code to retrieve voice messages and picked up a pen, poised to scribble down information.

Chris silently watched her with a keen eye that bordered on intrusive. Tia felt herself go hot all over as she fought to maintain a dignified, professional presence in front of this man. At the same time, her insides quivered as Chris studied her. What did he see? What was he searching for?

Determined to keep her personal business to herself, she pressed her lips tightly shut. She had gone to a lot of trouble to cover all physical evidence of the misery with makeup. Unfortunately, her emotions were another issue. Her feelings were barely in check, and she wanted to keep everything bottled inside until she got home.

Go away, Chris, she thought, pretending to be absorbed in the work on her desk. *I need time to get myself together before I deal with you. Go away. Give me a chance to get my brain unscrambled.*

But he didn't. Instead, he waited as she retrieved her messages. He followed her to the coffeemaker. After handing her coffee, he grabbed a mug and poured himself a cup. They accomplished everything in silence. His unnerving gaze constantly stayed focused on her.

Tia and Chris returned to her desk, and she

resumed her duties while Chris moved in and out of his office with questions and work for her. Most of their afternoon played out this way.

Around three o'clock, he returned to her desk. "I'm going to the store for a snack. Do you want anything?"

"No. I'm fine."

His eyes narrowed. "Are you sure? I haven't seen you eat anything today."

Tia opened her mouth, but the phone rang. *Saved by the bell,* she thought, reaching for the receiver. Maybe now she'd get a break from Chris's constant attention. "Legal Department, Tia speaking. How may I help you?"

"Talk to you later." Chris disappeared into the maze of workstations heading for the elevators.

Breathing a sigh of relief, Tia nodded and waved her hand in the air before returning to her call.

"Yes, you can," Jackie Edwards responded.

"Hi, Momma."

"Hey, Tia-Mia."

"What's going on?"

"That's what I'd like to know."

Frowning, Tia waited. What drama did her mother have going on? "What's on your mind?"

"I just talked with your *ex*-boyfriend."

There was a long silence as Tia's insides churned with nervousness. Sweat coated her palms, making it difficult to grip the telephone. This wasn't good. Tia had hoped for more time to gather her thoughts and come up with an appropriate excuse before telling her parents about Darnell. Tia struggled to keep her voice light. "What was Darnell talking about?"

"You know!" Her mother's voice flowed through the phone line.

Tia grimaced. *Oh man, she knows.*

"About us?"

"Yes," Jackie Edwards said.

"I'm sorry, Momma. I wanted to be the one to tell you."

"I would have preferred to hear about it from you. You've been with that man a long time. Are you sure you're doing the right thing?"

Darnell told her mother. That just made her brain hurt. Tia shook her head, dislodging the cobwebs clogging her tired brain. Okay, she knew she had had a restless night and felt sleep deprived, but this was way beyond anything she expected to hear. Had she stepped into the middle of a Twilight Zone episode? Maybe she'd slipped into some crazy alternate universe during the night.

Why would Darnell tell her mother anything about their personal business when he ended up looking like a fool? She pressed her lips together and tried to wrap her mind around her mother's conversation with her ex-boyfriend. How had that happened?

Jackie Edwards cleared her throat, bringing Tia back to the present with her next question. "So what happened?"

"Why did he tell you about us? When did you two meet up?" In awe of this whole concept, Tia tossed her free hand into the air.

Chris returned from the store with a bag of potato chips in his hand. He paused at Tia's desk, offering the open bag to her. She shook her head. With a casual shrug, Chris continued to his office.

"I called Darnell to ask him a question about our homeowner's insurance policy. While we were talking, I mentioned your graduation and that we were going to celebrate sometime in the future. He told me that you got mad at him because he mentioned how Adam always takes advantage of you, and things got out of hand. Darnell said you got upset with him and dumped him."

Cute fairy tale, Tia thought. He always played the victim. Would he ever be out of her life completely?

"Momma, that's not true."

"What is the truth?"

"Nia caught him at a club with another woman." Tia felt a fingernail tip snap off as her fingers curled tightly around the hard plastic of the telephone receiver. "Darnell came by my place so we could talk. I broke things off with him last night."

Jackie Edwards's voice dropped dangerously. She used the tone that stopped Tia and her siblings dead at whatever they were doing. "Another woman?"

"Mmm-hmm."

"That no-good bastard. He can't treat my child that way and get away with it. Wait until I get a minute with him. I've got a few special words for him." Mrs. Edwards stopped and then asked, "What in the world was he talking about? He told me you dumped him and that you wouldn't listen to reason. He asked me to plead his case."

"Don't bother. He doesn't have a case. We're done."

"Good!"

Adam's door opened. He strolled out of the room, scrolling through the messages on his cell phone.

"I've got to go, Momma. Adam just came out of his office." Tia's voice quivered. *Stop this right now,* she warned silently. *The hard part is over. You got rid of that lying idiot.* "I'll call you back later."

"No. Come home. I think you need a little TLC from your mother."

"Not tonight." Tia sighed. "I'm tired. I didn't sleep well last night. I'm going to go home and try to get some rest."

"Don't you dare," Jackie Edwards warned. "You need to come home. I'll expect you at six. Dinner will be on the table."

Tia chuckled sadly. No one refused Jackie Edwards. She was in protective parent mode, and she planned to take care of her youngest child. Refusing her wouldn't gain a thing. If she didn't agree, her mother might well pack up dinner and show up on Tia's doorstep. So she relented. "Okay. I'll see you after work."

She returned the phone to its cradle as Adam halted at her desk. "Tia, I'm on my way out of the building. I'm taking Mitchell Grimes and Ralph MacDonald to one of Jim Harrison's sports stores."

"Okay. I'll see you later." Keeping her face and voice passive, Tia nodded. This must have something to do with Wynn Evans's children.

"No, you won't. I'm out of the building for the

rest of the day. I'll talk to you tomorrow. Would you do me a favor?"

"Sure."

For the first time since leaving his office, Adam took a good look at Tia. He frowned. "You all right?"

"I'm good. I had a rough night."

"You sure? Is that all?"

Nodding, she answered, "Yes."

Adam patted her shoulder. "You take care of yourself. If you don't feel well, take the rest of the afternoon off. We don't have anything going on that can't wait."

"I'm fine. You have enough on your plate. Don't worry about me." She brought the conversation back to the business at hand. "What do you need?"

"Coordinate a meeting with Chris, myself, Jerr-Dann, and Vivian. I'd like to get them together one afternoon this week." He tucked his cell phone in his suit jacket pocket and picked up his briefcase. "You take care."

"Will do. Good luck," Tia called.

Adam smiled sadly. "Thanks. We need it. Wynn's ex has a head start on us." He strolled away from the workstation.

Tia didn't have the energy to deal with the Frenchman this afternoon, but she wanted to complete this task in case she decided to go home early. She printed a copy of Adam's schedule for the rest of the week and then headed to Chris's office. The sheets of paper were warm from the printer. She tapped on the door.

He quickly responded, inviting her into the office. *"Entrez."*

Tia poked her head inside the office. "Hi, Chris. Got a minute?"

Chris sat without his suit jacket and with the shirt sleeves rolled back, revealing arms lightly sprinkled with blond hair. He glanced up from the file on his desk and focused on her. He waved her into the room and said, "Please. Come in."

Tia crossed the floor and sank into a chair across from him. "Adam wants me to put together a meeting for you with a few of the legal department attorneys."

Chris turned to his computer and keyed in a code. "Let me check. Do you have a particular date in mind?"

"Thursday afternoon."

Using the mouse, Chris scrolled through a few items. "That day works. What time?"

Tia studied Adam's print calendar and said, "Three."

Nodding, he typed in the time. "Got it."

She offered a tiny little smile and rose. "Thanks. I'll talk to you later." Tia made the mistake of glancing at Chris. His eyes were filled with a mixture of accusation and concern. "Why didn't you tell me?" he asked.

Suddenly Tia's insides twisted. What was he talking about? *You know,* she thought. "Tell you about what? What do you mean?"

"I thought we were friends," Chris stated softly. His brilliant blue eyes blazed with sympathy and fire.

Frowning, she replied, "We are." Her heart hammered in her chest. Chris couldn't possibly know about Darnell, could he? No, of course not. There was no way he could have found out.

"Then why didn't you confide in me, let me know how things were going? I wouldn't tell anyone. But I could have helped you, listened to you and been there for you as a friend."

If she'd been anywhere else, Tia would have burst into tears. This wasn't about work. Chris did know. Tia refused to give up the truth until she had to. "What are you asking me?"

He rose, moved around the desk, and halted in front of her, blocking her escape. "Why didn't you tell me about your boyfriend?"

Even though she was unnerved by his intense stare, she forced herself to gaze directly at him. "How did you find out?"

Instantly, Chris's rosy cheeks turned scarlet. His lips pursed and an expression halfway between determination and guilt settled on his handsome face. He stood firm, explaining, "I heard you talking a bit earlier."

"Talking? When?" she asked slowly, digesting the words and what they meant. "Wait a minute. You eavesdropped on my call?"

Chris shrugged off her question in that French manner of his and answered, "Yes. I heard you when I passed your workstation."

Shaking her head, Tia raised a hand, putting an end to any further explanation on the topic. "That's terrible. That was a private conversation."

"I don't care. I needed to know," Chris replied in an arrogant tone. "What happens to you is important to me. You were different. Sad.

Wounded. Not my Tia Edwards. No smiles. Just pain. Your eyes were so unhappy. I needed to know. I couldn't stand it."

"I don't care." She shook with anger, and her voice quivered with suppressed emotions. "It's not an excuse."

"It's the one I have."

Chris dropped to his haunches at her side and reached out to cup her cheek. "You refused to talk to me. I knew something was wrong, but I didn't know what."

Trembling, Tia pushed his hand away and stood, gathering her paperwork. "Okay, you know. But I don't want to talk about it, and I don't expect to hear it all over the office."

He rose and pulled her into his arms, holding her firmly within his embrace. Tia found herself leaning into his arms, craving his warmth. She needed to feel like someone special cared about her and what she was going through. Chris continued to hold her close. "I'm your friend. You can always talk to me."

Could she? Were they playing a dangerous game that might possibly end with her getting hurt?

She stayed in his arms for several seconds before pulling away. Tia didn't need any more pain in her life. "Thank you. I appreciate everything."

Chris stroked her cheek with his fingertips. "Come to me at any time. Don't forget."

"I won't."

9

That motorcycle has been on my tail for three or four blocks, Tia thought as she parked her car in front of her parents' home. The biker slid into the vacant spot behind Tia's SUV and sat idling.

With a hand on the steering wheel and a nervous flutter in the pit of her belly, Tia waited an additional beat. She fumbled inside her purse for her cell phone, intent on calling her father to come out to the car and walk her into the house.

Eyes trained on the rearview mirror, Tia examined the biker. He switched off the engine, swung his leg over the machine, and climbed off the motorcycle. Her gaze focused on his feet as he planted them on the blacktop. *Wait a second. I've seen those boots before.*

Furious, Tia scrambled from the car, slamming the door. She marched right up to the biker. "Chris!" She lightly smacked his chest. "You scared the heck out of me. I thought I was being set up for a robbery."

He flipped the visor back and hastened to say, "I wouldn't let anything happen to you."

Ignoring Chris's declaration, Tia's hands clenched into fists at her sides, and her voice rose a notch. "What in the world are you doing here? Why are you following me?"

Chris pulled the helmet from his head and tucked it in the crook of his arm. He ran his fingers through his tresses. "I was worried. It's been a tough couple of days for you. I wanted to make sure you got home safely."

Amazed, Tia stared back at the man. She shook her head and softened her voice. "It's very sweet of you to be concerned. I'm okay. Don't worry about me."

He turned, taking a gander at the house. Curiosity was written all over his face. "Is this where you live?"

"No. I live downtown near work." Tia waved a hand to the house. "This is my parents' home."

He glanced around him, checking out the nearby properties, and asked, "Detroit has names for different parts of the city. What do people call this place?"

"Sherwood Forest," she replied.

Suddenly the front door opened, and Mr. Edwards stepped out of the house, bounced down the stairs, and rushed to his daughter's side. He pushed his way between the pair, eyeing the man at his daughter's side. "You all right, Tia?"

"Yeah," she replied.

Hands on his hips, Mr. Edwards frowned, tipping his head toward the younger man. "Who's this?"

Tia patted her father's arm reassuringly. "My coworker."

"Mmm." A note of suspicion lingered in his deep voice as he folded his arms across his chest. "What's he doing here?"

"He got concerned about me and wanted to make sure I made it home in one piece."

Chris added, "I wanted to make sure Tia was safe." Standing tall and straight, Chris returned the older man's gaze. He held out his hand and said, "I'm Chris Jensen."

Mr. Edwards grasped the younger man's hand and pumped it up and down. "Good to meet you. I'm Greg Edwards, Tia's father."

"It's a pleasure to meet you."

"I appreciate your concern for my baby girl."

"No problem." Chris turned to Tia. "I'll see you tomorrow."

Greg Edwards tapped the man's shoulder and asked, "Where are you headed?"

"My hotel," Chris answered.

"Hotel?" Tia's father grunted. "Are you living in a hotel?"

Chris nodded.

Tia sighed deeply and explained, "He's the attorney from France that I told you about. Gautier puts Chris up at the Detroit Marriott in the RenCen."

Mr. Edwards lifted his chin. "Mmm! I imagine you would enjoy a home-cooked meal or two."

"Very much so," Chris answered quickly.

Tia's father placed a hand on Chris's shoulder

and said, "Why don't you come in and have dinner with us?"

No! Tia cried silently. She didn't want Chris at her dinner table while her parents questioned her about her breakup with Darnell. "Pop," she began, "I'm sure Chris has other things to do."

"No. I don't. I'm free," Chris answered eagerly. "It would be an honor to share dinner with you."

"Well, come on in." Mr. Edwards led the way, strolling up the walkway with Chris behind him. Tia brought up the rear.

The trio climbed the stairs and entered the house.

"Tia-Mia, make the man feel at home." Mr. Edwards pointed at Chris. "Take his helmet. Put it away."

"Everything all right?" Mrs. Edwards called from the back of the house.

Mr. Edwards called back to his wife, "Yeah. We've got one more for dinner. Tia's work friend is staying."

"Friend?" Jackie Edwards exited the kitchen and made her way down the hall, wiping her hands on a towel. "Hi, baby." She kissed Tia on the cheek. She eyed Chris silently for a moment. "Who's your friend?"

"Momma, this is Chris Jensen. Chris, this is my mother, Jackie Edwards."

Chris took her hand, and with all the flourish of a true Frenchman, he kissed the back of her mother's hand. "It's a pleasure."

Momentarily flustered, Mrs. Edwards giggled like a teen caught in the middle of her first crush.

Tia rolled her eyes, thinking, *Chris is putting on a show.*

"Nice to meet you, Mr. Jensen," Tia's mother replied.

"Call me Chris. My papa is Mr. Jensen."

Mrs. Edwards collected herself. Her skills of ruling her family took over. "Let me set another plate. Tia, come help me. Greg, show Chris the family room. We'll call when dinner's on the table."

All the members of the Edwards family responded to Mrs. Edwards's bidding without question. Tia followed her mother into the kitchen, knowing that the older woman's brain was swirling with a zillion questions.

"Set a place for your friend, and then I need you to get the platter for the roast," Mrs. Edwards stated, moving to the range and opening the oven door. She slipped her hands into long oven mitts, removed a blue roaster, and placed it on the range.

Tia brought the white platter to her mother.

"Good. Thank you. Get me three serving bowls from the top shelf over there." Mrs. Edwards pointed to the cupboard.

Nodding, Tia obeyed her mother, waiting for her to start the inquisition.

"How long have you been working with Chris?" Mrs. Edwards asked.

Tia's hands shook and the bowls rattled together. Steadying herself, she returned to the range. This was a safe, easy question. If the rest were like this, Tia could handle them. "About a month."

Mrs. Edwards spooned green beans into a serving bowl. "Mmm. It makes sense. You were bound to have a few people from the home office show up here, since Gautier is a French company. Will this young man be in your office permanently?"

Tia shook her head. "No. I'm not sure how long he'll be with us. But I know he'll move on at some point. Maybe back to France or to another location."

"Interesting." She handed the bowls of green beans and carrots to Tia. "Put those on the table."

Tia completed her mother's orders. "What else are we having?"

"Potatoes. Pot roast. Apple pie with ice cream."

Impressed, Tia stated, "That's really nice for a weekday meal."

"It was for you. I wanted to give you a little TLC. But I see you've got someone else for that."

"Momma! Where did you get that idea?"

Mrs. Edwards waved away Tia's outburst. "No time for that now. Call your father and Chris to the dinner table."

Tia turned to the door, thinking, *We're going to straighten this out as soon as I get a chance.*

"Thank you for the lovely dinner," Chris said. "I don't get the opportunity to share a meal with such generous and welcoming people."

Tia's father drained his glass of Vernors ginger ale and said, "We enjoyed having you. Any time you want a little home cooking and company, come on by."

Smiling, Chris rose from the kitchen table and picked up his plate. "You're very gracious. I'll wash these before I go. Are you finished, Tia?"

Tia nodded.

Chris removed her plate, stacked the dishes, and started for the sink.

Mrs. Edwards pushed back her chair and headed for Chris. "Don't bother with those. You're a guest. I'll take care of them."

Dodging Mrs. Edwards's outstretched hands, Chris placed the dirty dishes on the counter next to the sink. "It's no bother at all."

"Why don't you and Greg go back to the family room and watch the game?" Mrs. Edwards suggested. "Tia and I will take care of the dishes and bring dessert in for everyone."

Greg pushed back his chair and rounded the table. He wrapped an arm around the Frenchman's shoulders and steered him from the room. "Come on, Chris. The baseball game should be heating up. Let's see how the Tigers are doing tonight."

Tia gathered the remaining dirty dishes and placed them in the sink. She returned to the table and removed the cutlery and glasses, wondering when her mother would resume her interrogation.

It didn't take long. Seconds after turning on the water, Mrs. Edwards asked, "What's going on with Chris Jensen?"

"What?" Tia faced her mother.

"You heard me," said Jackie Edwards as she

opened the dishwasher and began rinsing a plate under the water spray. "Who is he?"

"You already know that. I told you about him. He's the new attorney from France," Tia repeated while removing the salt and pepper shakers from the table and placing them on the countertop.

"Maybe I didn't ask the right question. Who is he to you?"

Tia marched across the kitchen floor and stood in front of her mother. "He's one of the attorneys I work with."

"No. That's not what I'm talking about. You and Darnell broke up less than twenty four hours ago. Today you turn up on my doorstep with a new man on your arm." Tia's mother rubbed her hands together. "A white man. What's going on?"

"Momma, you've got it all wrong. Chris is part of the deal I made with Adam."

Mrs. Edwards scoffed. "Adam's always in the middle of everything."

"You sound like Darnell, Momma."

Shrugging, Mrs. Edwards added, "If the shoe fits . . ."

"It's not my size. Darnell has always disliked Adam. I'm not sure why. But I suspect it involves jealousy. Adam shows him up for the lack of man he is. Darnell gets his kicks by stirring up messes. Don't listen to him."

"Okay. I'll put Darnell on the back burner for a few minutes, but I still want to know about Chris." She moved around the kitchen, removing dessert plates from the cupboard and forks and napkins from the drawer. "What's going on between the two of you? Are you dating? When did all of this start?"

"There is no 'all of this.' Chris and I are not dating. Where did you get that idea?"

"From Chris."

"What? I beg your pardon? Momma, there's been way too much Danielle Steel in your diet."

"Ha-ha. Cute. Real cute, Tia-Mia." Mrs. Edwards dropped her hands onto Tia's shoulders and said, "All I had to do was watch the two of you together. Chris barely kept his eyes off of you the whole time he sat at the dinner table. If I went into the family room right now and asked him how the fish tasted, I'd bet money he'd tell me it was perfect."

"You didn't serve fish. We had pot roast."

"My point exactly. His focus was exclusively on you." Tia's mother squeezed her shoulders before dropping her hands to her sides.

"What does that prove?" Tia asked.

"He stayed focused on you all through dinner. You were what he was interested in. Nothing else."

"I think you're wrong and that you're exaggerating the situation."

Mrs. Edwards laughed softly. "You are so naïve. Chris followed you home to make sure you were okay. Tia-Mia, he's slowly circling his prey like a fox before he pounces. You may be unaware of it, but that man has some serious plans for you, and I'm not sure I like it."

"I don't understand. Even if we were involved, dating each other, what's not to like?"

"Chris is here for a while! An unspecified amount of time. Am I right?"

Sensing a trap, Tia nodded slowly, trying to work out the details in her head. "Yes."

"At some point in the near future, he's going back to France," Jackie Edwards stated confidently.

"Possibly. So?"

"Baby, don't let him steal your heart. He's not for you. I know you and Darnell are finished, but don't make a second mistake. Give yourself a little breathing room before you venture into the realm of dating again. Don't test the water with any man before you've completely recovered from Darnell."

"I don't know any other way to tell you this. There's nothing between Chris and me. We're colleagues and friends. Period."

"Mmm-hmm." Mrs. Edwards laughed. "Tell your old mother anything. Come on. Let's dish up dessert."

"Momma, there's nothing for you to worry about. I'm fine. Darnell disappointed me and hurt my feelings, but I'm dealing with it."

Her mother studied her with that practiced ease that always made Tia squirm like a child caught in the middle of a lie. After a moment, Jackie Edwards nodded. "Be careful. Take your time."

Tia opened her mouth to deny the relationship again. Her mother lifted a hand, cutting off Tia's words.

"Think about what I'm saying. Don't rush into anything, especially not a new relationship with a man who could easily leave town as quickly as he showed up. I know you and Darnell were together for a long time, and sometimes relationships fall apart, just like yours did. You've got plenty of time to find the right man. He's out there for you. Give yourself the opportunity to heal before moving to the next man."

Her mother made perfect sense. Had she noticed something that Tia was deliberately ignoring?

Tia tried to offer her mother a reassuring smile, but her face felt unresponsive and unyielding. "Don't worry," she pushed from stiff lips. "I'm not looking for the next man. I've had enough, Momma. I want peace for a while."

"Okay. That's the last I'm going to say about it." Mrs. Edwards pointed at a cupboard. "Hand me that tray. I'm going to put the dessert on it."

10

Tia entered the executive wing of Gautier International Motors and headed for her workstation. Seconds after she locked her purse in her bottom drawer, Chris peeked out of his office. He spied Tia and hurried across the floor to her desk. Suppressed excitement oozed from him.

"I found it," he announced.

"Found what?" Tia asked, finding his excitement contagious.

They'd grown closer since the night Chris had followed her to her parents'. Chris had become a great friend as well as a colleague. Constantly at her side and tuned in to her every mood, he had been the kindest, most caring person Tia could want to help her through the first painful days of her breakup with Darnell. When she felt down, Chris found ways to make her laugh and keep her entertained. He never let her focus on the poor state of her love life for very long.

Maybe my mother is right. Is Chris interested in

getting involved with me? If I don't watch out, I'll fall for him, Tia thought. *No. You need to quit that line of thought. Our lives are heading down two very different and unique paths.*

"I found a house."

"House?" She frowned, gazing into his intense blue eyes. "I thought you wanted to find an apartment."

"No," he answered with an expressive shake of his head. "An apartment is no better than the hotel. The rooms are too close together. I can hear my neighbors making love."

That comment brought heat to Tia's cheeks. She sat quietly as Chris continued.

"I want privacy." Chris perched on the edge of the desk and folded his arms. "After we looked at those apartments, I thought about how they treated you, like you didn't exist." His handsome face turned to stone, and his voice resonated with fierce determination. "No one tells me who I can have as friends. I didn't like the way those people wanted to control our lives, so I decided on a house. As long as I pay the rent and keep things legal, I can do what I want."

"Makes sense. Where is this perfect place?"

A broad, happy smile quickly spread across Chris's face. His tone turned light. "Grosse Pointe Farms . . . the same community where we looked at that first apartment. I like it because it's not too far from here, yet it puts enough distance between Gautier and me. Believe me, there are days when I need it."

Smiling softly, Tia added, "I understand that.

Grosse Pointe Farms is a really nice community. I think you'll enjoy it."

Chris grinned. "It looks it. Since I found the house, I've driven through the neighborhood a couple of times. It seems calm and stable. There's a lot of families with children. I think I'm going to like the area."

"I'm glad. Living in the Marriott seems to have gotten old pretty quick." She sat for a moment and then asked, "What happens if you get reassigned back to France or someplace else? What do you do about your lease?"

"Ah! Good question. We negotiated a month-to-month lease."

"Did you?"

He nodded.

"I'm surprised the owner agreed to that."

"Me too. Reynolds suggested I use Gautier's name to help, and it did." He stood and cleared his throat. His full, sensual lips shifted into a somber line. "I know you have a busy schedule, but can I ask for your help one more time?"

Leaning closer, Tia answered promptly, "Certainly." Chris had been entirely too sweet to ignore his pleas for help. "What can I do for you?"

"Come see the house."

"What? Really?"

"Absolutely."

"Why?"

"I value your opinion. And I think you'll see things that I missed."

"Are you sure? Isn't there someone you respect that you'd like to take with you?"

"Yes." He jerked a finger in Tia's direction. "You."

Oh, man, she thought, *Chris knows what to say to make a woman feel cherished and important.* "I'm honored."

"I'd like you to come and take a look at the place before I sign my lease and hand over cash. You live in Detroit and know things about the surrounding areas. I don't want to make a huge mistake and find myself locked into something that doesn't work for me."

"When?"

"Today."

"Oh, I don't know." Tia glanced at her inbox, which was stuffed with work that Adam expected her to complete. She shook her head. "I've got lots to do." Adam wouldn't go for it. "Maybe after work."

Chris grabbed her hand and held it between both of his. That simple touch sent her blood pulsing in her veins. "I've already spoken with Adam. He suggested we do this at the end of the day. That way we're not leaving for hours and returning later. This way you won't have to return to Gautier."

Tia glared at him suspiciously. She leaned back in her chair, shook her hand free of his, and folded her arms across her chest.

Laughing, Chris added, "Really."

"I don't know."

"If you don't believe me, go ask Adam." Chris reached into his pocket and removed a single silver key, jiggling it in front of Tia's face. "Come on. Help me out."

"This is sounding better and better." She unfolded her arms and hit the switch to turn on her computer. "Okay."

Chris gave her a quick hug and then added, "Thank you. I'm glad that I convinced you."

Stunned, Tia stiffened. Blood pumped wildly through her veins. Every time he touched her, no matter how innocently, she found herself enjoying those gentle caresses while fighting the urge to respond.

What was Chris thinking? Was this part of his habit of always entering her personal space? Fighting back the desire to stay in his arms, she kicked the chair away and answered with a calm, reasonable tone, "What time do you want to leave?" She reached for the mouse and clicked on the Internet Explorer icon.

"I've got meetings until about three." Chris picked up a sticky-note pad and a pen from Tia's desk and scribbled a number on it. "I'll meet you at the house around four. Will that work for you?"

"Yes," Tia answered. Her nostrils were filled with Chris's scent. Her ears rang with the sound of his accented, sexy drawl. *Stop! Get yourself under control.*

He dropped the pad and pen on the desk. "Four o'clock."

Tia drove down Jefferson Avenue toward Grosse Pointe Farms. She glanced at the black street signs with white letters. Chris had chosen a wonderful area. He was right. Grosse Pointe Farms gave him the distance he needed from Gautier and the Detroit Marriott, yet allowed him the proximity he needed to avoid long commutes.

She turned onto a tree-lined street, moving slowly to check the addresses. Chris's Harley sat in the driveway. The ranch-style house was laid out on a half acre of land. Red and white striped awnings accented the redbrick structure. A large bay window covered one side of the front of the house.

Children played up and down the street. The distinct aroma of burning charcoal filled the air. This was a perfect place to live and raise a family.

Tia stepped onto the porch and rang the doorbell. Seconds later, the door opened and Chris grinned at her. He studied his watch for a second and then said, "It's fifteen after four. What happened? Did you get lost?"

She laughed. "No. I took my time. I wanted to check out your new neighborhood. After all, you said you wanted my opinion."

"Come on in," he said, holding the door open for her.

Tia stepped into the foyer. Windowed doors were located on both sides of the small space. Pale gray walls led into a hallway that branched into different rooms. Chris took her hand and hurried her down the hallway to the kitchen. "Let's start at the heart of the house, and then we'll move through the other rooms."

"You're my host." Tia moved around the kitchen, admiring the room. It was spacious. The walls were painted in a soft cream with a multicolored floral border. A granite-topped island sat in the center of the room with a built-in range and sink on one end. A black chair sat at the opposite end. In contrast, the appliances were stainless steel and black. The floor was covered in cream ceramic tile with charcoal-gray-colored geometric etchings.

Instantly, Tia fell in love with this room. Although she didn't make a habit of cooking, she preferred to prepare a meal in a room that had all of the accoutrements she needed. She turned to Chris and nodded approvingly. "I love your kitchen."

"Good. I'm glad you've given it a good report." He took her arm and led her out of the room. "Let's move on."

Chris steered her to the front of the house, and they passed through the cream and pale green living room. He stopped inside the empty dining room before leading her through the four bedrooms. The master bedroom included a skylight and a fireplace. All of the rooms were empty.

"Oh, Chris. This house is perfect, although I don't know what you're going to do with four bedrooms."

"One will be my office. And, of course, the large one will be my bedroom. The rest will be sorted out at a later date." He moved closer, into her personal space. The heat from his body reached out, drawing her closer as his unique scent swirled around her, intoxicating her like a love potion. *This is far too intimate. I need to get out of here,* she thought, taking a step away from his alluring presence.

Tia took a step toward the door. "What about a basement? Is there room for a washer and dryer? And, while I'm at it, are you going to hire a housekeeper?"

Chris nodded. "There's a finished basement with a laundry room. Yes, I believe I'll need a person to help me keep this place in order. What do you think?"

"You're the attorney. If you've reviewed the lease and it's fine, then I say go for it." She glanced at her watch and then started for the door. "I think it's time for me to get on my way."

He caught up with her in the hallway. "What's your hurry?"

"No hurry."

"Then let me show you the family room. We went by it on our way to the kitchen."

"Okay," Tia muttered, wondering why he just now decided to show her this particular room.

Waving a hand toward the rear of the house, Chris asked, "Are you hungry? Have you had any-thing since lunch?"

"No. I didn't have lunch. I wanted to make sure I had all of my work done before I left to come here."

"That was nice of you."

He led her into a room with dark wood paneling and cream carpeting. Three thick, lilac-colored candles on tall, narrow metal candleholders were lit, putting off a lavender bouquet fragrance. A brown blanket covered a section of the carpeting with a wicker picnic basket at its edge. White plates, wineglasses and cutlery were already set.

"Oh!" she moaned, impulsively turning to Chris and kissing his cheek. "How sweet. Thank you."

"You're welcome. Do you have time for a light meal and fine wine?" Chris cupped her elbow and urged her across the floor to the blanket. "I wanted to thank you for all of your help and support."

Giggling, she asked, "How fine is the wine?"

"Store-bought." He pointed toward the end of the block.

Tia decided to toss caution to the wind and enjoy some free and easy time with Chris. Besides, he'd gone to a lot of trouble to make this happen. She sank into the deep carpet on the edge of the blanket. He followed, scooting beside her.

"Here, you need to get comfortable." He reached for her foot, pulled off her pump, and then repeated the act on the other foot. Chris's hand caressed her feet and ankles and massaged her calves.

Tia's heart pounded erratically in her chest. His gentle caress touched off a spark that began in her toes and surged into a five-alarm fire in her belly. Sensing danger, she pulled her leg from his light grasp, tucked her legs under her, and pointed to the picnic basket. "What's for dinner?"

"We're having turkey and Swiss croissants, strawberry and poppy seed salad, with pinot noir."

Chris removed the items as he announced them, handing them to her.

Tia placed the sandwiches on the plates and split the salad between them. She held the glasses steady while Chris filled them with the wine. She leaned against the wall and crossed her bare feet at the ankle.

Chris settled in beside her and said, "Let's have a toast."

"To what?"

He waved his hand around the room and raised his glass. "Everything. You. The house. My job. Life. I want to salute you for being a good friend. Whenever I need you, you are there. I know Adam asked you to help me, but I think you've gone beyond the call of duty. And that makes you special to me. Here's to a wonderful friend who I've come to appreciate." Chris touched his glass to hers and then took a sip. Tia did the same. He leaned close and dropped a soft kiss on her lips. The meeting of lips felt as light and gentle as the touch of an infant's hand stroking her cheek.

Drawing back, he smiled at her. Unsure what to do next, she returned the smile and nervously placed her glass on the floor and reached for her plate.

Chris turned those beautiful blue eyes on her and asked, "So you are pleased with my new home?"

"Very pleased."

"Excellent!" Chris rested his hand on top of hers, stroking his thumb across the back of her hand. "I want you to feel as if this is your second home. Visit anytime."

Acutely aware of his touch, Tia's pulse quickened. Touched by his kindness, she patted his hand. "Chris, with time, you'll want to invite other friends to your new home. Don't feel obligated to have me with you every time you have company."

He smiled at her as if she'd said something really silly. "You'll always be welcome here whenever you like. Now, enough talk. Time to eat."

"That works." Tia reached for her sandwich and bit into it. Swiss cheese oozed from the sides. She licked the creamy cheese from her hands. It was heavenly. "Oh! This is wonderful."

Chris watched her movements like an alcoholic waiting for his next drink. When she gave him a quizzing look, he shrugged and said, "Eat up. There's plenty of food."

Although she maintained a composed, relaxed exterior, her insides felt like scrambled eggs. What was she doing here? Spending her free time with a man who would eventually leave her and return home? It was almost as if they were playing house, pretending to be friends when they knew they were much more. To hide her confusion, she took a bite out of her sandwich and slowly chewed.

Maybe her mother had been right. Did she feel more for Chris than she was willing to admit? All she knew for sure was that she wanted more from him. Chris's spicy scent filled her nostrils, and she craved the feel of his solid, strong chest against her. Or was she just replacing her feelings for Darnell for Chris? *I don't know,* she thought. What she did know was that she wanted more of those sweet kisses and soft caresses.

What did she plan to do? Should she pursue him? Did Chris have feelings beyond his friendship for her? There were dozens of reasons for them to stay away from the relationship thing and remain just friends, starting with the fact that he would be a temporary diversion, at best. Right now, all she could think about was the taste of his sweet kiss that made her crave another. She couldn't think logically while in his orbit. Home. That's where she needed to be. Once she got home, she'd go over everything and devise a plan of action.

11

Saturday evening, Tia pulled into the driveway of Chris's house and turned off the engine. Remorsefully, she shook her head, wondering how she ended up in this situation. Somehow, before the end of the workday Friday, she'd agreed to accompany Chris to the Dirty Dog Jazz Café.

Friday afternoon, Chris had sat on the edge of Tia's desk, waiting for her to finish a report for him. Jazz streamed from her computer speakers as they waited for the pages to print. A commercial for the café caught their attention, tempting them both. Before Tia realized it, Chris had picked up the phone, made a reservation for Saturday, and enticed her to go with him. So here she sat in front of Chris's house.

To be certain that she arrived on time, Tia checked her watch before leaving the SUV. She didn't want to get to his place too early, because she'd have to make small talk for a while. She climbed out of the vehicle and went up the steps. Standing on his cement porch, she glanced around her, noting the baskets of flowers hanging from the awnings and the iron lounger sitting on the porch. The exterior looked and felt like a home.

Chris opened the door with a broad smile on his face. *"Bonjour."* His happy mood reached out to her, and she found herself grinning back at him.

"Hi, yourself. Are you ready to go?"

"Yes." He took a quick glance at his watch. "We have a few minutes before it's time to go. Come in. Let me show you what I've done."

Tia entered the house, glancing around as she stepped into its interior. A small leather bench occupied a section of the foyer.

Chris took her hand and led her into the living room. A chocolate-brown leather sectional filled the room, accented with a square, dark wooden coffee table and smaller matching end tables.

"Very nice," Tia said.

"Thank you," he answered. "It wouldn't be possible without your help."

"Sure it would. You knew what you wanted. I just took you to the right stores." She strolled around the room, checking out the décor, touching the baby-soft leather fabric. "But it does look great in here."

As she talked, Chris's gaze took a leisurely skip down her body, pausing for a moment to admire her breasts, which fitted snuggly against silk fabric. The expression in his eyes made every inch of her skin burn.

Tonight Tia had chosen an outfit that would make her sister drool with envy. Lemon and hot scarlet splashed the black background of her silk off-the-shoulder top. Black silk trousers cupped her rear, and black leather sandals completed her outfit. The intensity of Chris's gaze made Tia's nipples harden in response. *Great*, she thought. *Now what do I do?* She folded her arms across her chest.

His smile broadened. "You look beautiful!"

The warmth of his gaze made her feel more attractive and desirable than she'd ever felt during her years with Darnell. She smiled to herself. It still amazed her that she'd spent years with a man who did nothing for her self-esteem or emotional state.

"You're looking pretty good tonight yourself. I'm going to have to watch you. Some cute honey is going to steal you away before the night is over."

"Never!" he declared with a passionate toss of his head.

Dressed in a cream V-necked cashmere sweater and tan trousers, Chris looked incredibly handsome. Tan leather loafers replaced his cowboy boots.

"Are you ready to go?" Tia asked.

Always the gentleman, Chris cupped her elbow and led her back to the front of the house. They stood in the hallway while he grabbed his keys and set the alarm. "Let's go."

Tia headed for her car and opened the driver's side door. She glanced up and found Chris strolling purposefully toward the garage. *Where is he going?* she wondered. "Chris?"

Turning to face her, he muttered, "Hmm?"

"Where are you going? The car is here."

"Oh!" At the garage, he punched in a code and the door rattled as it slowly rose. "I thought we'd take my bike tonight."

She closed her car door and moved toward him. "Bike? Are you sure?"

"Yes. *Oui.*"

"What about a helmet? Michigan law states that I must wear a helmet."

"Taken care of," he announced, walking toward the bike.

Tia followed his movements with her gaze. Chris strolled up to the bike and patted the top of two helmets.

"Voilà! You told me that you'd never ridden before. Tonight is the night. You're getting your premiere ride."

She backed away, shaking her head. "I don't know."

"There's nothing for you to consider. We're going on the bike." He removed a pink helmet from the seat and stepped in front of her. On the side of the helmet, she noted three silver glittery letters. On closer inspection, Tia realized that Chris had had her initials painted on the side of the helmet. "Why did you do this? It's not cheap."

Ignoring her question, Chris said, "Lean down." She did so and he popped the helmet over her head.

"Chris!" she exclaimed, opening her purse. "I'm serious. I'll pay for it. I can't accept this."

"Stop!" He placed his hand over hers. "I decide how I spend my money." He tapped her nose with his finger. "Not you."

"But, Chris," Tia began.

"No. Listen to me." His hands closed around the tender flesh of her upper arms as he forced her to look at him. "My home is paid for by Gautier. I have no bills. I can afford to purchase a helmet for the lady I spend much of my time with." He pulled Tia's strap tight. "Besides, I expect we'll be doing this again someday soon."

Tia opened her mouth to protest, but shut it instantly. What could she say? Chris could do what he wanted with his money. She had no right to tell him how to spend it. Sighing, she relented. "Okay. Let's go."

"Merveilleux. Très bien," Chris responded as he secured his helmet in place and climbed onto the bike. "Come here." The raspy quality of his voice sent shivers coursing through her body. He patted the spot behind him.

"Thank goodness I decided on pants tonight." She swung her leg over the seat and settled behind Chris.

"Hold on to me." He wrapped her arms around his middle. "Now lean into my back." Tia did what Chris asked of her. She locked her fingers together around his lean, muscular tummy. He squeezed her hand. "Perfect. Let's go."

"Do you know where you're going?"

"Absolutely. I drove by the café a few nights ago."

Alrighty, then, she thought, snuggling against the firm, round curve of his derriere. *I'll leave the driving to you, my friend.*

Chris hit the garage door remote after he roared out of the garage, interrupting the calmness of his quiet neighborhood. "You all right?"

"Good! I'm good!" Tia yelled back.

Arms wrapped tightly around his middle, Tia rested her cheek against his back, inhaling the subtle fragrance of his cologne and absorbing the warmth of his body. He cruised expertly and smoothly through the neighborhood to Kercheval. The ride exhilarated her. Being so close to Chris made her feel as if she were teetering between heaven and hell. The warmth of his body seeped into her every pore. She inhaled Chris's tangy scent, enjoying this precious time with him.

The ride ended all too soon. Chris pulled into the parking lot next to the café and halted the bike, allowing it to idle as he waited for the valet at the podium.

A young man hurried from the shack. "Good evening, sir."

Chris cut the engine and removed his helmet, tucking the gear under his arm. "Can you take it from here?"

"Yes, sir," the young man responded as he exchanged his ticket for Chris's keys.

Chris swung his right leg over the front of the bike and stood. He turned to Tia and offered her a hand. Gingerly, she took it and allowed him to help her from the bike. For a second, her legs wobbled. Chris's supportive hand at her elbow held her close and upright, giving her time to regain her bearings.

His hand caressed the skin of her bare arm. "Let's see what the Dirty Dog Jazz Café has to offer."

Nodding, she took his hand and they started for the door.

A hostess escorted them to a circular booth and placed menus in front of them. *"Merci,"* Chris stated, making the hostess giggle like a teenager high from hours of text messaging.

"Oh! You're welcome," she answered, and did a little dip before leaving the table.

Chris turned his amused gaze to Tia. She laughed. "That French accent captivated her."

"I guess that's good."

"Very." Tia took a look around the room. Highly polished hardwood floors and multicolored walls decorated the main room. Tables, booths, and the bar surrounded a small, intimate stage. "I think this is an interesting place."

"Ah, *oui,*" he agreed. "What would you like to drink? I assume you will have more than a glass of lemonade this evening."

"Yes, I will."

"Par excellence."

When their server arrived, Chris ordered wine and an appetizer of mixed vegetarian specials and shrimp cocktail. A combination of soft romantic jazz and blues surrounded them through the café's music system. They swayed to the beat, enjoying their treats as they waited for the live performance to begin.

Their anticipation increased when the lights lowered. Kimmie Horne filled the room with her sultry voice. A three-piece band played a selection of blues, classic, and contemporary jazz. Tia and Chris settled in and enjoyed the show. Chris's arm found its way around Tia's shoulders, pulling her against his side. For a moment, she held back, but then decided to relax.

Kimmie Horne concluded her set with a lively rendition of "Love Changes Everything." The lights came up and the band took a break. Tia did a little people watching as the waitstaff hurried from table to table to take food and drink orders.

Tia's gaze settled on a couple across the room hugged up together and kissing. She stared at the pair for a moment while her brain hurried to process what her eyes were seeing. She gasped. Instantly, Chris turned to her with a question in his eyes. "You okay?"

The foul taste of betrayal coated Tia's tongue. "No, I'm not," she answered in a shaken voice.

Chris scooted closer to her side, cocooned her within his embrace, and whispered, "What is it?"

Tia nodded toward the couple across the room. "That."

Frowning, Chris's gaze followed her movement and focused on the couple. "Who are they?"

"Darnell."

Chris's eyebrows lifted into his blond hairline. "Your ex-boyfriend?"

"Yes."

"Who is the woman?"

Tia shook her head, taking another look at the woman. She now sat contentedly at the table, viewing the goings-on of the café. Her long locks of amber hair feathered around her back and shoulders. She resembled the type of woman Darnell always wanted Tia to be. The woman's clothes flattered her ample frame, although Tia doubted Darnell's date had much room to breathe. Most of her cleavage hung outside her top instead of inside it. "I don't know. Probably the woman he's been seeing."

"What woman?"

I've told Chris this much, she thought. *I might as well admit the rest.* "My twin, Nia, bumped into Darnell and a date at a club. That's how I found out about what he was up to."

Chris took her hand and squeezed reassuringly. His voice was caring and soothing. "You can't allow him to control your life. He's the past. Don't give him more power than that."

"I know," she muttered softly. "This is the first time I've seen him since we split."

Chris smiled down at her and pulled her more firmly against his frame. "It's Darnell's loss. He should have treasured what he had."

She smiled gently at him and caressed his cheek. "I'm learning that you Frenchmen know how to make a lady feel good. Thank you."

Chris wrapped his arms around her and held her tightly. She felt so cared for. His tone dropped to a husky rasp. "No thanks needed. You are a beautiful, desirable woman who deserves to be appreciated and loved. Darnell had no idea what he had. It's his loss and not your concern."

Suddenly a shadow appeared over their table. Tia gazed up to find her ex-boyfriend standing in front of them.

"I thought I saw you." Darnell's gaze shifted away, and then he blew a kiss at the woman occupying his table. "What are you doing here?"

"Listening to music," Tia shot back. "What are you doing here?"

"Same." He gave Chris a quick, dismissive once-over before focusing on Tia. "I'm surprised to see you out and about. You tend to stay close to home."

"Unlike you," Tia replied, pointedly glancing across the room at Darnell's date.

"Hey, you were the one who said we were done," he accused.

"You were the one skipping around town with other women."

"What did you expect? I'm not sitting at home watching television while my life passes me by. Not for you. Not for anybody. You were always busy with your job." He spit the word *job* out of his mouth like it had a bad taste.

"Enough!" Chris declared, getting to his feet and easing out of the booth.

"Who's this?" Darnell jabbed his thumb at the Frenchman.

"Chris Jensen," Chris responded, studying the other man and dismissing him quickly.

Darnell blinked repeatedly as if he were working out a particularly difficult puzzle, and then a knowing light entered his eyes. He stared at Chris. "You work at Gautier, don't you?"

"*Oui.*"

Nodding, Darnell planted his feet apart and folded his arms across his chest. "Ohh! I know you."

"Oh?" Chris's voice conveyed how little he cared. "Should I know you?"

"Yeah. You're the one who kept my Tia too busy to be with me."

"'Your Tia'?" Chris chuckled unpleasantly. "I don't think so."

"Pfff!" Darnell scoffed. "You don't know anything about me."

"Actually, I know more than I care to."

"Like what?" Darnell challenged.

"Like the fact that you didn't appreciate a beautiful woman like Tia." Chris nodded toward Darnell's table and his date. "You prefer someone with a little more flash and less brain power."

"You don't know a damn thing about me." Darnell raised his voice a notch. "Who the hell are you to talk about me?"

"Just an observer of life." Chris turned his back on Darnell and slipped into the booth beside Tia. He slid an arm around her shoulders and pulled her close. The lights slowly lowered. "It looks as if the show is going to continue. You need to return to your table."

Dismissed, Darnell stood at the table like a child uncertain of what to do next. His arms flapped up and down like a bird whose wings were too heavy to get him off the ground. After a minute, he turned and, with a parting shot, crossed the café's floor. "Frigid bitch."

Chris stood. His hands balled into fists as he readied himself to confront the other man. Tia pulled on his arm, frantically begging, "Don't. Don't. Remember, he's not worth it."

"What an idiot!" Chris watched the other man head to his table and then turned to Tia. "Okay. I'll let it go this time. Your Darnell is not worth my time. Let's enjoy the show."

As Tia snuggled close to Chris, she wondered what all of this meant. Granted, it felt good to have Chris defend her. She couldn't let Darnell destroy their time together.

12

The words *frigid bitch* flashed on and off in Tia's head like a huge red neon sign and tied her belly into knots throughout the remainder of the evening. With just two words, Darnell had taken the joy from her outing. She tried to push those terrible words from her head and concentrate on the music, but she failed miserably. Why hadn't Darnell stayed on his side of the café and left her alone? *You know why,* a tiny voice whispered into her ear. *He hates that you kicked him to the curb and got the last word . . . until tonight.*

Determined to handle her business in a dignified manner, Tia sat quietly with her head held high during the second set. Regardless of how she felt, she didn't want to destroy Chris's night out. He had looked forward to it with such eagerness.

After the applause from the last performer faded and the lights came up, Chris turned to her, asking, "Would you like to cap off our evening with another glass of wine before we leave?"

Tia glanced toward Darnell's table and found him hugged up with his date. She squared her shoulders. She refused to let that lying cheater destroy every aspect of the evening. "Sure. One more to end our evening on the right note."

Grinning broadly, Chris signaled for their server and ordered a carafe of wine. They sat finishing the wine while talking quietly about everything from work to Chris's plans for his house. Once they emptied the carafe, Chris rose and helped Tia to her feet. They left the café and headed out the door to the valet.

Minutes later, Tia found herself tucked securely behind Chris as he steered the bike through the late-evening streets of Grosse Pointe Farms. *Frigid bitch.* That phrase still echoed in her head, sucking all the enjoyment from the ride back to Chris's place.

It wasn't all her fault. She wasn't completely responsible for the sad state of their physical relationship. There were two people in that relationship. She refused to take all the blame for their lack of a love life.

Maybe Darnell had been a poor lover. Was that what he'd always thought of her? And if she was cold, maybe he should have found a way to warm her up. They could have practiced ways to make lovemaking more exciting and thrilling.

Tia tightened her hold on Chris. *Now here's a man I believe will be a wonderful, giving lover.* Chris would be the type of lover who would get the job done thoroughly. There wouldn't be any doubt whether she was thoroughly loved and satisfied.

Stop it, she cautioned silently, giving herself a mental shake. *You don't have that kind of relationship with Chris. He is your friend and colleague.*

Once the idea started to roll around in Tia's brain, it refused to go away. What type of lover would Chris be? Would he be slow and thorough or fast and urgent? More ideas flashed through her head as she considered them together in the ultimate act of love.

As they neared his house, Chris slowed the bike to turn into the driveway. His garage door rumbled and rattled open. He drove in, cut the engine, and then carefully swung his leg over the seat and stood. Tia did the same with a helping hand from Chris. They stood quietly inside the garage with Chris's fingers intertwined with hers.

The darkened room practically crackled with tension as Chris gazed down at Tia. His lips pursed and his forehead wrinkled into a frown. Tia got the impression that he was weighing the pros and cons of a heavy decision.

What is he thinking? Tia wondered. *What's going on in his brain?*

"It's still early. Would you like to come in for a while?" His tone was light, but Tia detected a note of something more as he led her from the garage.

Tia shrugged. "Sure." She didn't have anywhere to be. The only things waiting for her were a quiet house and an empty bed.

They entered the house through the kitchen. Tia waited in the center of the room while Chris locked up.

"You haven't seen the family room since I moved

in. Let me show you what I've done." Chris steered her out of the kitchen with a hand at her elbow. They moved down the hallway to the family room.

The last time she'd been in this room, she and Chris had shared a lovely picnic on the floor. A comfortable-looking, dark chocolate leather sofa and matching cloth chair replaced the floor blanket. A huge flat-screen television sat mounted on the wall facing the sofa. A glass coffee table, end tables, and black Bose stereo system completed the room's furnishings.

"Go get comfortable." Chris grabbed the remote from the coffee table and hit a button. Soft romantic jazz filled the air. He headed for the doorway. "I'll be back in a minute. I'm going to put a little something together for us to taste."

Tia followed Chris's instructions and sank into the inviting sofa. The cool, smooth leather caressed her skin and held her gently. She kicked off her shoes and stretched her feet as her body swayed to the beat of the sexy piano tune.

Chris returned minutes later, balancing a small tray, dessert plates, a bottle of wine, and two wine goblets in his grasp. He slid the tray filled with sliced peaches, pineapple chunks, strawberries, Havarti cheese, and crackers onto the coffee table.

"Wow! You went all out." Tia popped a slice of cheese into her mouth.

Chuckling softly, Chris handed her a plate. "You're the only guest I've had so far. I have to impress you so you'll come back."

"That'll change." Tia took the plate, looking for a serving spoon or fork. "Once you're all settled in, you'll have plenty of company."

"I'm not concerned with that. You're great company." Chris watched her for a second and added, "Go ahead and use your fingers."

Frowning, she pressed her lips together. "You sure?"

"But of course. I know where your hands have been for the past few hours."

Laughing, Tia selected several pieces of fruit, a chunk of cheese, and a few crackers. She munched on a piece of Havarti cheese. The creamy dairy product melted in her mouth.

Chris poured white wine into a glass and handed it to her. He filled a second one for himself. "Enjoy."

"This is wonderful. It's a great way to end the evening."

"That's what I was thinking." Chris added fruit to a plate and scooted closer to Tia. He took a bite out of a strawberry, and juice spurted down his chin.

"What am I going to do with you?" Shaking her head, Tia put down her plate and glass and brushed away the juice with her fingers. Her hand caressed the long column of his neck, then moved lower and rested on his hairy chest.

"Keep me." Chris placed his hand over hers, holding it against his skin. His thumb stroked the back of her hand.

Tia's skin tingled and grew warm under his hand. She gazed into his eyes, and her heart nearly stopped in her chest. Barely checked naked desire burned back at her from his pale blue eyes. Something deep and primal stirred within her. Tia did something she'd never done before. She took the lead, leaning forward and lightly kissing his lips.

Surprise crossed Chris's face. The heat in his gaze warmed her cheeks. "Do you know what you're doing?"

"I think so," Tia answered honestly, leaning in for another kiss. This time Chris met her halfway. Somehow he returned the plate to the table and reached for her, bringing her against the hard contours of his body. His tongue slid across her lips, silently requesting admission. She complied, opening her mouth and sucking his tongue between her lips. He tasted of wine, fruit, and the unique essence of Chris Jensen.

Chris moaned softly, holding her tightly against him. His hands were everywhere, touching, learning the secrets of her body. Tia wrapped her arms around the strong column of his neck, giving herself up to the sweet taste of him. *This feels right,* she thought, snuggling closer and running her fingers through his silky hair.

He drew her over his lap, kissing her deeply. "Lovely," he muttered against her lips. His tongue explored further, tasting the recesses of her mouth.

Somehow they ended up sprawled across the carpeted floor with Tia straddling his legs. With slow deliberation, Chris popped each button on her silk top, feasting his eyes on her light brown flesh peeking through her lacy strapless bra.

Suddenly, the tempo of Chris's kisses changed. He slid the top down her arms and tossed it away. He then unhooked her bra and tossed it in the direction of her top. Tia leaned down for another kiss, rubbing her breasts against his hair-covered chest. He felt so good. She couldn't get enough.

Chris's tongue traced a path of fire down Tia's neck. His hands sought her breasts, kneading the soft flesh.

Her heart pounded. Hunger flamed within her. Chris captured a firm brown nipple between his lips and sucked for a moment.

Tia then unzipped his trousers and pulled them past his hips to his knees. Next came his silk briefs. Freed from the confining clothing, his male flesh stood tall and thick. Fascinated by the pink maleness, Tia took his shaft in her hand and began to move up and down, loving how he seemed to grow longer and thicker with each stroke of her hand.

Chris moaned, placing his hand over hers to show her how he enjoyed being touched. Tia followed his direction, becoming more daring with her movements. Pumping his shaft, she used her free hand to fondle his balls. Again Chris moaned. "God! That feels heavenly."

His lips covered hers as his hot tongue searched for Tia's. He stripped off her remaining clothing and blazed a heated path to the junction between her legs. She quivered, trying to hold herself still.

"Tia," Chris whispered close to her ear. "You are so beautiful." As he spoke, his hand parted the curly entrance and found her core. His fingers slipped between the folds and caressed her flesh. She gasped. The sensations were exquisite. Tia bit her lips to keep from screaming his name.

Chris flipped her onto her back and rained hot, openmouthed kisses on her face. His hand made the journey to her junction again and found the spot he'd caressed moments earlier. Leaning into his touch, Tia shut her eyes and swayed to the music in her head. Her interior walls began to shake, and she felt her orgasm drawing closer and closer. She didn't want Chris to stop. Tia tried to hold on, but the pleasure was too great and the sensations too intense. One more stroke of his fingers and she went over the edge, crying out as she shattered.

"Chris."

Grinning down at her, he asked, "Yes?"

Breathing hard and laughing softly, she lifted her head and kissed him. "Thank you."

"My pleasure, *chérie*." He kissed her again. She loved the smell and taste of him. It was unique and Chris's alone. "But we're not done." To prove the truth of his words, Chris slid his length into Tia's hot core.

For the second time, she gasped. Tia felt him deep within her. Chris lay still for a moment, allowing Tia to adjust to his size. Then he began to move, slowly at first, pushing deep within and then withdrawing several inches before sliding to the hilt.

Passion hot and intense flared between them. He thrust into her faster and faster. Tia wrapped her legs around his hips and met each movement with a downward push of her body. She moaned, feeling the light tremors that signaled the start of her orgasm. Tia's canal contracted, squeezing him tight.

Chris groaned, pushing further into her.

A powerful tremor hit her, followed by a series of sensations that caught her in its grip. Chris held her tightly against his body as the wet evidence of his release filled her canal. Tia gasped, riding out her climax while Chris continued to move inside her.

Damp and sated, Tia gently kissed his lips. "Oh, I liked that."

Brushing a lock of hair from her forehead, Chris grinned. "Me too." He wiggled his hips and asked, "Want to go again?"

"You can't possibly be ready to—" Tia hushed, feeling Chris's flesh swelled and stretched inside her. "Oh!"

His smile turned into a full grin. "I'll take that as a yes."

13

Consciousness slowly returned as Tia roused from the depths of sleep. She stretched, feeling more relaxed and rested than she could ever remember. Frowning, she glanced around the room. Her mouth went dry, and her heart began to pound in her chest. This wasn't her bedroom. She touched the gray comforter and wondered, *Where in the world am I?* Tia slowly turned to the right and gasped softly. Chris Jensen was sleeping soundly at her side.

Tia squeezed her eyes shut as images flashed through her mind. They had gone to the Dirty Dog Jazz Café and returned to Chris's place for a snack. Things had gotten hot and heavy. She ended up coming on to the Frenchman. She'd kissed Chris while straddling his hips and caressing his thick, pulsating shaft. Tia covered her eyes with her hand but couldn't destroy the images. *Oh, man!* She'd never live this down.

I've got to get out of here. She eased from the bed, making certain that she didn't disturb Chris.

Where are my clothes? She searched for her bra and panties. The carpeted floor offered no clues. They must have undressed in the family room. Tia blushed when she remembered how she had removed Chris's clothes and how he had helped her strip.

She tiptoed out of the bedroom and down the hall to the family room. Sure enough, their clothes were strewn all over the room, on the floor and on the furniture. Grimacing in mortification, she headed straight for her underwear and grabbed up her silk panties and lacy bra. A small sound from the hallway reached her ear, and she whirled around to find a naked Chris filling the doorway. She took a step back, holding the silk garment in front of her like a shield. "Oh!" she yelped, grabbing at anything that might help her regain her balance.

"Watch it!" He rushed across the floor and caught Tia before she fell. He held her arm, steadying her.

"Thank you." Tia pulled away from him.

"You're welcome. Good morning," he added in a husky drawl, leaning down to kiss her.

Embarrassed at being caught in this state of undress, she muttered a hasty hello and stepped away.

"I missed you. Why didn't you wake me?"

Because I'm not ready to face you, Tia thought, staring at the floor and hoping it would open up and swallow her. Her gaze landed on his chocolate silk shorts lying under the glass-top coffee table. *Oh, man!* She remembered how she had encouraged him to remove them so that she could see and touch him.

Standing in front of her, Chris took the undergarments from her hands, tossed them on the sofa, and took hold of her hands. "Clothes are the enemy. You don't need them right now."

"Stop!" Tia grabbed for her things. "Give them back."

"Come on. It's early. Let's go back to bed."

He gave her a little sexy smile and held out his hand to her. Tia's insides quivered, responding to the sexy drawl. She shook off his hand and dug her heels into the carpet. "I need to get home."

"Why?" Chris stroked his hand down her bare arm. "Tia, what's wrong?"

Her arms flapped up and down like a bird trying to fly. "This was a mistake. It shouldn't have happened."

"What? *Je ne entendre pas!*"

"You, me. Together." Tia twisted the bra's band around in her hand. "Things just got way out of hand. I don't know what I was thinking. I'm sorry."

"I'm not."

Now it was Tia's turn to ask, "What?" *I can't believe I'm having this conversation while I'm standing here butt naked.* Confused, Tia stared at the floor, trying to figure out where he planned to take this conversation.

"For months I've dreamed of being with you.

Making love with you. Finally, it happened. We were beautiful and *magnifique* together." His eyes drifted shut. Tia could tell that he was reliving their moments making love.

Unable to stand there another moment, Tia grabbed for her things and began dressing. Chris placed his hand over hers, halting her.

"Stop. I need my clothes."

"Why?"

"It's time for me to go."

"To where?"

She chuckled without humor. Where else would she go? "Home."

"You're going to leave without talking to me? Leave my home without waking me?" He put that lost-puppy-dog expression on his face that made her heart melt.

"I didn't want to wake you," Tia answered lamely.

His eyebrows lifted inquiringly. "Oh?"

She crossed her arms across her breasts. Her gaze landed on her clothes. Tia moved around the coffee table and reached for her top.

"Tia?"

She looked up at him. "Yes?"

"Talk to me."

"I don't . . . I don't know what to say," she stammered, running her fingers through her hair.

"How you feel would be a great beginning. Tell me what you're thinking, feeling. I need to know."

"I'm embarrassed."

Chris followed her around the room as she

gathered the rest of her clothes. "There's no reason to feel embarrassed."

"That's easy for you to say," she muttered.

"What?"

"Nothing." To avoid looking at him, Tia stared pointedly at the floor. "Would you put some clothes on, please?"

"No."

"Fine. I'll put on mine and get the heck out of here." Mustering all the dignity she could, yet shaking inside with embarrassment, Tia made a move to get past Chris. He stepped into her path and caught her upper arm in his hand. She felt the warmth of his touch clear down to the soles of her feet. Tia quivered, responding to his touch. *Stop this right now,* she thought. *That's how you got into this mess in the first place.*

"Don't leave. We need to talk."

"Not like this," she stated with dignity. "We've got to get dressed before I'll discuss anything with you."

"Only if you promise to stay put until I come back." He held her gaze with his own, willing her to agree.

They did need to come to an agreement and establish a few rules about how they would conduct business at work. She didn't want to walk into Gautier and find herself the subject of all the execs' gossip. Tia sighed, shutting her eyes for a moment. "Okay. I'll wait."

"I'll be right back." A grin spread across Chris's face. He headed for the door. After experiencing his full-frontal nudity, Tia was unprepared to see his firm, round cheeks as he strolled out of the family room. She practically drooled. The man was too perfect for words.

Not sure how long he planned to be away, she quickly dressed. She refused to have this conversation in the buff.

Minutes later, Chris entered the room dressed in a pair of jeans. His chest and feet were bare. "I've got on clothes. Come. Have breakfast with me."

Tia shook her head. "No. I should get home."

"Nonsense. It's barely seven o'clock. Let me get you a cup of coffee." Chris cupped her elbow and led her from the family room.

"But I . . . I . . . I . . . ," Tia stammered as she followed Chris. He directed her down the hall and into the kitchen. He patted a chair before heading to the counter. With economical movement, Chris set the coffee to brew and went to the refrigerator. "We can share a cheese omelet and then we can talk."

"Please, don't put yourself out."

"No bother."

Tia didn't know what to do. She had never dealt with the "morning after" following a one-night affair. Darnell had been her only lover, and their relationship had progressed at a slow but steady pace. What she had experienced with Chris was like an explosion from a gas leak that had burned unchecked.

"Coffee." Chris placed a mug in front of her and filled it. The strong aroma of coffee and hazelnuts permeated the air. He padded around the kitchen in his bare feet, preparing breakfast. Before Tia could come up with an excuse to leave, he slid a plate in front of her. A second smaller plate of buttered toast followed.

They ate their meal in silence. Chris seemed to anticipate her every need. Without uttering a word, he jumped to his feet to refill her coffee mug or add the apricot preserves to the table for her to spread on her toast.

When Chris slid the omelet in front of her, she didn't expect to be able to eat a thing. Yet, the meal he prepared tasted wonderful, and she ate every bite.

Chris pushed away his empty plate and leaned back in his chair, watching Tia as she nibbled on the last of her toast. The silence grew as he stayed focused on her. *What am I doing here?* she wondered. *I should have left when he went into the bedroom.*

"I'm sorry, Chris," Tia began.

He scratched the side of his face with a finger. "Sorry? Why? *Pouvez-vous expliquer cela?*"

"For coming on to you." She waved a hand around the room. "Putting you in this position and upsetting the balance between us."

"I'm not sorry." Tia went hot and tingly under Chris's intense gaze and husky voice. "Making love with you was wonderful, perfect."

Tia refused to admit it, but she truly enjoyed making love with him. Chris was a kind, considerate, and thorough lover. He performed just the way she had expected; he left her completely satisfied.

"I'm a man, not a child. I make my own decisions."

Frowning, she rubbed her forehead. "Maybe I should talk to Adam and suggest that you be re-assigned to another administrative assistant."

"Why would you do that? I like working with you."

"I like working with you, but can we get past what happened last night?"

"Work with you is fun. I don't want that to end." He smiled, making her heart jolt in her chest.

God, this man's smile does things to me. He is beautiful, Tia thought.

"I hope you feel the same way," Chris said.

"I do."

"Then what's the problem?"

She shrugged, uncertain how to explain her feelings.

"Tia, I like you." Chris reached across the table and caught her hand.

Okay, she knew he was interested in her. For the past few weeks, she'd ignored his feelings in favor of continuing her relationship with Darnell.

He smiled. "From the moment I met you, I wanted to be with you."

"Why didn't you say something?"

"You had someone."

"And now I'm single again."

"Darnell is a fool. Good riddance. He's gone and I'm here. We moved too fast. That's why you feel uncomfortable. But I'm not sad we made love. I've wanted to from the first touch."

"Where do we go from here? What do you want from me?" she asked. "How do we continue to work together?"

"Like we've always done," he answered promptly. "You like me. No?"

"Yes." Tia couldn't deny it. She found Chris incredibly attractive. But she'd just gotten out of a long-term relationship with Darnell. Was she ready to move on? "Yes."

"Then let's continue."

Think, Tia, think. Use your head, not your heart. Get everything out in the open and see what can happen. "There are a few things we need to discuss before we continue with anything."

"What's wrong?"

"I'm not sure this is the right thing for me right now," Tia muttered.

"I feel strong enough for both of us." He leaned closer. "Like what?"

"Color. I know love is blind, but other people aren't."

"Pfff!" Chris tossed his hand in the air. "I don't care what people think. We look gorgeous together."

"That sounds wonderful in theory, but you have to live it to understand. Sometimes it comes from people you don't know. Remember the lady at that apartment building? She wasn't pleased with us being together. She's not the only one. There are times when your family members will show dislike or prejudice."

"What do you mean?"

"My grandma Ruth doesn't trust white people. She's seen a lot of unpleasant things in her life. It might take a lot for her to warm up to you.

There's a possibility that she may never trust you or like you. Are you willing to deal with that?"

"Absolutely. You come first. I'll use all of my charm to sway your grandmama," Chris stated.

"That was just a sample of what you can expect. Not all of the time, but when you least expect it."

"I can't change what people think or feel, but I can promise you this—I'll protect you as best I can from anyone or anything that will hurt you. You will be my first consideration. Let's see where this thing takes us," Chris suggested.

"Do you mean at work?"

"No." He shook his head. "You and me together. I want to go out. Date. Spend time away from Gautier. Get to know you better."

Tia nibbled on her bottom lip. "I'm not ready for a sexual relationship."

Smiling, Chris replied, "You seemed more than ready to me."

She began to speak again. Only this time, Tia spoke a bit louder and firmer. "What we did last night, happened. It wasn't planned, but things got out of hand. I'm not ready for a repeat. Not yet. I need time."

"You can have it."

I can have it? Was I such a poor lover that he can wait because it didn't matter? she wondered, feeling a bit let down. "Are you sure?" she asked.

"Yes. I want you to feel comfortable with me. We have plenty of time." He lifted a finger and said, "Don't misunderstand me. I want to make love with you again. But the next time we are together, it will be because we both want it."

"Chris, what about your job? How can we have any kind of relationship? Reynolds could reassign you at any time. You're here today, but you can easily be gone tomorrow. I don't want my heart broken again. I've barely recovered from Darnell."

He dropped to his knees in front of her and took her hand between both of his. "That's true. And I don't have any answers or guarantees. Reynolds told me that I would be cross-training for months. If I have my way, I'll be here permanently. Just remember, I want to be here with you."

Tia reached out and touched his cheek. She wanted to believe him, to hold these feelings close and enjoy the feelings. *Maybe it could happen,* she thought, leaning down to kiss his lips. Chris rose to his feet and took her into his arms. He pulled her against his chest, and she went willingly.

Let it happen. Give him a chance, her inner thoughts whispered as she gave herself over for his kiss. *I think I will.*

14

Feeling pleased and happy with the world, Tia practically skipped down the hallway that led to her workstation. For the past few weeks, she had been living on a cloud of happiness. Miraculously, even after having the best hot, mind-blowing sex with Chris, they were successfully maintaining a professional image at work while spending their free time getting to know each other. When the workday ended, they went out to dinner or a movie or to sightsee around metro Detroit. It didn't matter what they did as long as they were enjoying each other.

Chris made it one of his missions to meet her one request. No matter what they did or how long they stayed out, he always ended the evening with a good-night kiss. She loved it. He got huge brownie points for being a great kisser, and she got the benefit of being kissed by an expert. This was exactly what she wanted: a great career, a post-undergraduate education, and a romance with someone special. Only, she didn't expect her romance to be with a white guy from France. Tia hurried to her workstation to see Chris.

Although she was having the best time of her life, she couldn't help but wonder how long her happiness would last. Reynolds had the power to destroy their blossoming relationship by transferring Chris to a different office. *I'm not going to worry about that,* she chastened herself. *I'm going to bask in the here and now and let the future take care of itself.*

Tia was eager to see Chris. Each morning, he greeted her with a cup of Starbucks coffee and a croissant. Her heart filled with happiness when she reached her workstation and found her morning treat. A small note sat under the white paper cup. *Meeting with Reynolds and Adam. Not sure how long. How about lunch?*

After stowing her purse in her desk drawer, Tia turned her attention to her morning coffee while working her way through her daily routine of e-mails and snail mail. Since both Adam and Chris were out of the office, she concentrated on completing a brief and deposition that needed to be finished before the legal department's next meeting.

As the morning sped by, Tia completed an array of work. When the telephone rang, she glanced at the clock and blinked in surprise at the time. It was nearly eleven. She picked up the telephone and recited, "Good morning. Legal Department. How may I help you?"

"Say hello to your old man," came the quick response.

"Hi, Daddy."

"How's my Tia-Mia?"

She frowned, asking, "Good. Is everything all right?" Greg Edwards seldom called the office.

"There's no trouble."

"So why the call at work?"

"I can't seem to reach you at home. You're out all the time, and I can't keep up with your cell phone number. So I decided to try you at the office," Mr. Edwards explained.

Guilt shot through Tia. *Oh, man! I've been so involved with Chris I haven't even checked on my parents. Get your priorities right, girl,* Tia chastised herself.

"You just said everything is okay. Is there more?"

"Not really." He cleared his voice. "There is something I want to ask you."

Her heart started to pound in her chest. Was there more wrong with her grandmother? "Okay. Go ahead."

"The family is meeting on Saturday for dinner. Do you think you can make it?"

Relieved, Tia clicked on her computer calendar. Oh, no! Chris had made her promise to keep the weekend free for him. He had plans for them. On the other hand, family gatherings were very important. Sickness and death were the only excuses accepted by Tia's parents. Unfortunately, she wanted to be with Chris. This thing between them was still new, and she enjoyed having him in her world. "Is this a special occasion?"

"No, but your grandmother wants to see everyone before her surgery."

Oh, yeah. Heart surgery! Pacemaker replacement. Her grandmother was not a spring chicken. Any surgery presented a boatload of potential problems. "I'll be there. Where's the party?"

"Someplace different. Your grandmother wanted it at her place, but your mother didn't want her to get too excited with preparation and cleanup."

Smiling, Tia remembered how her grandmother made a big deal of every holiday. At this point, Grandma Ruth didn't need the additional stress and strain. "It'll be at home, right?"

"Nope. We're going to rent a place and have the food catered."

"Oh, wow! Normally we cook," Tia replied.

"That's true. It's easier this way."

"Do you need me to do anything?" Tia asked.

"Be there."

Tia nibbled on her bottom lip. Should she ask her dad about Chris? Would it be the best place or situation to introduce him to her extended family? What about Chris? Was he ready to be involved in one of her family's major events?

"Tia?" Mr. Edwards queried.

"I'm here."

"What's on your mind?"

Cringing, she asked, "Can I bring someone?"

"A date?" He paused for a moment. "Not Darnell I hope."

Tia exhaled. "God no!"

"Mmm."

"What's that mean?"

"Nothing," Mr. Edwards said. "Who are you bringing?"

She couldn't get around this. Her family would learn she was dating Chris. She might as well make it sooner than later.

"Is there something you want to tell your daddy?"

"It's Chris. The guy we had to dinner a few weeks ago."

"Mmm."

"Stop that," she whined.

"Can't help it. You know your brothers aren't going to like this."

Yeah, she knew. She had some pretty vivid images of them threatening poor Chris. This would be his baptism into the Edwards clan.

"It's going to be interesting to see who acts the worst."

"Thanks, Daddy. You just make this sound better and better."

"I'm trying to help."

Concerned, Tia said, "It's probably not a wise decision to invite him. But it's something that will have to happen at some point."

Mr. Edwards sighed and then said, "Well, this will be an interesting event. I don't know what Grandma Ruth is going to say. One thing is for sure—she'll let you know exactly what she thinks so you'll know where you stand with her."

Tia cringed. Grandma Ruth could be incredibly candid. If Tia planned to continue with Chris, they had to come out in the open. "How do you feel about me and Chris, Daddy?"

"I want you to be happy. That's my first concern. And there's a lot to consider. But the true question is, how does he treat you?"

"Very well."

"Better than that idiot Darnell?" The disdain in her father's voice was clear.

"Much better."

"As long as he treats you well and doesn't hurt my baby, I can live with him."

The knot that had pulled tight in her chest began to unwind. Tia grinned. Her dad always said the right thing.

"Now, I can't speak for your brothers. You know how protective they are. But I'll be there to help you."

"Thank you, Daddy."

"You're welcome, baby."

"What time and where on Saturday?" she asked, twisting a pen between her fingers.

"Three o'clock at the Product Shop. It's in Livonia."

"Okay. I don't need to bring anything like soda, napkins, or paper plates?"

"No. Just you and your friend."

"I'll see you Saturday. And, Daddy?"

"Yeah."

"Thank you for understanding."

"It's my job. Bye, baby."

Tia returned the telephone to its cradle. Daddy was good. He tried to understand and give her support when needed. Her insides twisted because Momma was a different story. Jackie Edwards never liked Darnell, and it took months for her to accept his presence at their family outings. With Chris, she already made it clear that she suspected he had feelings for Tia, and she didn't seem very happy about it.

Tia sighed. The only thing she could do was let her mother get to know Chris, and hopefully he'd be able to charm her.

Chris waited as Tia scooted into the booth at Potbelly Sandwich Works in the GM Renaissance Center. She gazed at the menu scribbled across a blackboard and then watched Chris slide into the opposite side of the booth.

"How was your meeting this morning?" Tia asked.

"Long!" Chris sighed. "Lots of stuff going on."

Tia nodded. "Adam let me in on some of it the other day."

He ran his hands through his hair. "Let's not talk about work. I checked on tickets for the cruise last night."

Well, there it was. He just provided the opening she needed to tell him about their change in plans. She searched for the proper words to let Chris down easier. Although she planned to extend the invitation from her father, she didn't want to hold Chris to it. "Actually, I'm going to have to bow out of our date."

Frowning, his blue gaze pierced her. "What's going on?"

"My grandmother is having surgery soon, so she wants to see all of us before she goes into the hospital. My mother and father are planning a little get-together this Saturday." Tia reached across the table and covered his hand. "I'm sorry. I've got to be there."

"Is she going to be okay?" he asked.

"Mmm-hmm. But she's up there in age, so we're concerned."

"Then you must be there."

Tia nodded. "Yes."

"I do understand family. When does she have her surgery?"

"In two weeks."

"Do you want me to be there with you?"

Surprised, Tia stared at Chris. That was so nice of him to offer to be there. She wasn't sure if she wanted to drop him in the thorns of her family crisis. "You don't have to. It could be a long day."

"I don't mind. I want you to know that I'll be with you when you need me."

She linked her fingers with his. "You are so good."

Chris lifted their linked hands and kissed the back of Tia's hand. "You are very important to me. I know you have things to do on Saturday. What about later?"

"Maybe," Tia hedged.

"Which means what?"

"I have an invitation to extend."

"Invitation? From whom?" Chris asked.

"My father. He invited you to Saturday's get-together." She hurried to add, "Don't feel that you have to accept."

"I'd love to." He grinned. "That's nice."

"Are you sure? I mean, you had different plans for Saturday."

His eyes narrowed. "You don't want me to go, do you?"

"It's not that," Tia denied.

"Then what is it?"

"My family," she admitted. "They can be difficult."

"Because of me?" Chris asked.

"Yes and no. They don't like outsiders."

"That's fine. I'm not an outsider. I'll be there."

Tia opened her mouth and then shut it without uttering a word. Saturday would be an interesting day. Meeting the Edwards clan would put Chris in a difficult position, but he seemed up to the task.

15

"Tell me again," Chris said to Tia as he drove to dinner. "There's Junior; twins Andre and Andrew; plus your sister, Nia, who's your twin."

"Correct," Tia answered, slowly nodding.

Eyebrows lifting, Chris shook his head. "Wow! Two sets of twins! I'm sure your parents were surprised."

"Little bit," Tia replied, flipping down the visor to check her makeup. "After three boys, Momma and Daddy were determined to have a little girl. They just didn't expect two of them at the same time. They figured that since they had one set of twins, lightning wouldn't strike twice. Boy, were they wrong."

Chris chuckled, reaching for her hand and squeezing it. "Having two of you is perfect." Leaning over the steering wheel, he said, "We just crossed Inkster. Start looking for the building."

Tia squinted, trying to read the signs as the car

sped down the road. She pointed to a row of shops in a small strip mall ahead. "There it is."

Chris slowed the car and then made a left-hand turn. He pulled Tia's cherry-red Gautier Velocity SUV into a parking space. "Here we are," he announced, checking the parking lot. Chris pointed at an SUV in the next aisle. "That's your father's truck, isn't it?"

Tia glanced at the bronze Dodge Journey with a miniature box of Kellogg's Corn Flakes dangling from the rearview mirror. "Yeah." *Dad and his toys,* she thought. After more than two decades of working for Kellogg's, Gregory Edwards had remained as loyal to the company as the day he began working as a packaging engineer.

"This is the place. Let's see how the party's going." Chris hopped out of the car and hurried to the passenger door, helping her from the car. He held on to Tia's hand as they strolled up to the front door of the Product Shop.

Chris began swinging their clasped hands back and forth, saying cheerfully, "You can't hide forever."

With a sense of dread, Tia answered, "I know. I don't want to hide forever, just a little while longer."

Smiling, Chris pulled Tia against his side and kissed her forehead. "Things will be fine. Just relax. This relationship between you and me is new to everyone. We have to give your family a little time to adjust."

Tia pushed open the door, listening to the gentle tingle of the bell as the hearty aroma of ribs and baked beans filled her nostrils. She turned to Chris. "Mmm. I sure hope the food is as good as it smells."

"Me too. It smells heavenly."

"You're getting ready to eat some soul food," Tia explained.

Chris answered, "I'm ready for it."

A tall African American woman of medium build sat behind a glass showcase. "Welcome to the Product Shop," she greeted in a beautiful, soft tone. "Are you here for the Edwards party?"

Chris answered, "Yes."

Using the tip of her ink pen, the woman pointed them in the direction of the party. "They're in the Red Hatter rooms."

"Thanks."

As Tia and Chris made their way to the gathering, they passed through a room decorated in shades of red and purple with one-of-a-kind items lining the shelves. Above the Red Hatter room entrance hung a white banner with loud, colorful letters that practically shouted QUICK AND HAPPY RECOVERY!

Glancing in, Tia noticed a mix of family and Grandma Ruth's neighbors. Tia's oldest brother, Junior, entered from an opposite doorway with a sheet cake that he placed on a small table covered with a red tablecloth. Tia's mother followed with a tray in each hand. One held wing dings and crab cakes. The other was weighed down with spinach dip and chips. She placed both trays on the table next to the cake.

Junior waved Tia and Chris into the room.

"Come on in." Her brother's eyes narrowed as he got a good look at Tia's date. "Mmm."

Tia rushed over to her brother at the cake table and gave him a big hug. He returned the gesture, whispering in her ear, "Who's that?"

She motioned for Chris to come closer and grabbed his hand. "Greg Junior, this is my friend Chris Jensen. He's from France."

Eager to please, Chris held out his hand. Junior took a second or two to study the other man before taking his hand.

"So you're the new man in my sister's world," Junior said. His voice relayed a warning.

Chris seemed to understand with a minimum of words passing between the men. He nodded. "I think your sister is very special."

Junior gazed at Tia. "She is."

Her mother hurried over and hugged Tia. "Hey, Tia-Mia!"

"Hi, Momma." Again she reached for Chris's hand to bring him closer. Mrs. Edwards glanced behind her daughter, and her expression soured. She focused on Tia. "I see you brought your friend from work."

Chris moved forward and took Mrs. Edwards's hand. "Thank you for inviting me. I really enjoy being with Tia."

With narrowed eyes, Tia's mother replied in a soft but dangerous tone, "I'm sure you do." The older woman turned away and walked back to the food table to move things around. Junior followed his mother's lead, ignoring Chris.

Tia looked around, checking out the roomful

of guests. Her twin brothers, Andrew and Andre, sat with their current significant others and extended family. One of her uncles and two aunts from her father's family sat together at a table. Frowning a bit, Tia asked, "Where's Nia?"

Mrs. Edwards hissed through stiff lips, "At that shop of hers. Nia said she'd be here as soon as she got done with her last customer."

"Don't get mad, Momma." Tia stroked a soothing hand down her mother's arm. "Doing hair is Nia's livelihood. And she's good at it."

Sighing softly, a disappointed expression settled on Mrs. Edwards's face. "I know. But I still want so much more for her. Nia's so difficult. She can do better for herself. Doing hair should be her backup plan. Why can't that girl be more like you? Your sister needs to take control of her life and go back to school."

I've heard this song more than once. The battle lines had been drawn between their mother and Nia when her twin was a little girl. She refused to be dressed up like a little doll. She wanted to wear denims and wrestle with her older brothers. They clashed straight through high school and went into nuclear war when Nia refused to go to college. Instead, she enrolled in beauty school and opened her own business.

Tia squeezed her mother's hand. "We may be twins, but we have different goals and talents. Come on, Momma. Let it go. This is Grandma Ruth's party. Everyone should be enjoying it, including you. We can't settle things today." *If ever,* she thought, keeping that notion to herself.

"You're right." Her mother lifted her chin toward the opposite doorway. "Go speak to your grandmother."

Tia spun around in time to see her maternal grandmother amble through the door on the arm of Tia's father. Tia raced to her grandmother, hugging her tightly, keeping in mind that this frail little lady with the spicy personality required tender care. "Grandma Ruth. How are you?"

"Ain't no trouble," Grandma Ruth answered briskly. "I wanted to see everybody before I went into the hospital." She cupped the side of her mouth with her hand and whispered in a low, secretive tone, "Besides, your mother ordered the food from Famous Dave's. I love that place. Hospital food has nothing on Famous Dave's juicy ribs."

"What about your blood pressure?"

"Mind your own business. Don't worry about my blood pressure. I'll take care of it." Grandma Ruth poked a bony but manicured finger at Tia's chest. "You watch your own."

Tia laughed. "Yes, ma'am."

"Don't get sassy with me. I can still smack your butt."

"No, ma'am," Tia responded. "I'd never do that."

Grandma Ruth smiled. "But not today." She grabbed Tia's hands, took a step back, and ran a critical gaze over her. "Your momma told me that you have a new beau. Where is he?"

"Right here," Tia responded, wrapping an arm around Chris and pushing him forward. "Grandma, this is Chris Jensen. Chris, this is Mrs. Wilson, my grandmother."

Grandma Ruth dropped Tia's hand and took a step backward. She stared at Chris, frowning as she gave him a thorough once-over. "Where's the joke?"

"No joke," Tia answered, taking her grandmother's arm and leading her to a nearby table and offering her an empty chair.

Mrs. Wilson dropped into the chair, still continuing to stare at Chris. "When did you do this?"

Her grandmother's question made her a little angry. "What do you mean 'this'?"

"When did you start going out with white men? Look at him. He's got blond hair and blue eyes. Why does he have to have blue eyes?" She put a hand to her forehead and shook her head. "Lord, what is going on?"

"Grandma, Chris is a nice man. We work for the same company."

"That don't make any difference. Do you know what some of his blue-eyed friends did years ago? I don't trust white people and neither should you."

"Grandma, you've always been one of the most understanding people in my life. Why are you acting like this?"

"Don't trust them. You need to think about what you're doing." The old girl shook a finger at Tia. "The things that I've seen." Her face scrunched up like she smelled something foul. "They are tricky and sneaky people. I've seen them do some terrible things to us. They don't appreciate us or our skills. Let me tell you a thing or two. You can't trust 'em, and you certainly shouldn't allow them in your bed."

Trying to convince her grandmother, Tia took the chair next to her and said, "Grandma Ruth, Chris is a good man. He's good to me and treats me with respect. Besides, he's not from here. Chris is French. He respects me like an equal."

Shaking her head, Grandma Ruth continued. "I don't care. Get him away from me. I hope you figure out real soon that they can't be trusted."

Greg Edwards dropped a hand onto Grandma Ruth's shoulder. "Ruth," he stated in a stern voice, "that's enough. Remember, this is a party."

"I don't care. Tia needs to know."

"Tia-Mia is fine. You don't have to continue." Greg Edwards turned to Chris and offered his hand. "How are you? It's good to see you again."

"Thank you, sir. It's good to see you," Chris answered, studying Tia's grandmother.

"I'm going to get your grandmother something to drink," Mr. Edwards said.

"I'll do it," Chris offered. He turned to Tia's grandmother and asked, "What would you like to drink?"

"I don't want you to get me anything," Grandma Ruth answered stubbornly.

"She likes Coke," Tia replied, embarrassed by her grandmother's behavior.

Chris nodded and started for the refreshment table. "I'll be right back."

Pursing her lips, Grandma Ruth folded her arms across her chest and announced, "I'm not drinking anything he brings back if it isn't closed."

Tia's father turned and said, "Ruth, you shouldn't

act like this. That young man hasn't done a thing
to you."

"I don't care."

Shaking his head, Greg Edwards turned his attention to his daughter. "Tia-Mia, I'm glad you
brought your friend."

Relief flooded through her. "Thank you, Daddy.
I needed to hear that. Momma wasn't very nice
to Chris either."

He waved a dismissing hand. "Ah. Don't worry
about your mother. She's worried that you'll run
off with Chris and leave Michigan."

Laughing, she answered, "Hardly. I think Chris
is here for a good long while."

Chris returned with a Coke. He handed the
can to Tia's grandmother, along with a white
paper cup. "Here you are, Mrs. Wilson."

She took the can and looked it over, making
sure it hadn't been tampered with. After a
second, she popped the tab and poured the cola
into the cup.

"Where's Chris's thank-you?" Mr. Edwards asked.

Tia's grandmother narrowed her eyes at Greg
Edwards before turning away. "Thanks."

"Okay." Tia turned away, tapping a nervous
hand against her leg. *I need a breather before I wreck
Grandma's party.* As that thought concluded, she
felt the welcoming warmth of her oldest brother
as Junior looped an arm around her shoulders
and steered her away from their grandmother and
father. He held a can of Vernors ginger ale in his
hand. "So that's what's on the agenda these days.

When did this happen?" He gazed meaningfully at Chris, lifting an eyebrow.

Shaking her head, Tia laughed. "We just started dating. Once Chris found out that Darnell was out of the picture, he asked me out." *Made love to me and turned everything upside down,* she thought.

"You sure you're not holding out on your big brother?" Junior took a sip from his can.

"I'm positive. Why are you so concerned?"

Junior shrugged. "This guy is a surprise to the family. I don't want to see you get hurt. Remember, you just ended things with Darnell. Are you sure you're ready for another relationship so soon?"

"Yeah. I think I am." She shrugged. "Besides, we're taking things slowly. We know there are issues, so we don't want to rush anything."

"Good. Take your time," Junior suggested.

"Thank you," she said sarcastically.

Junior tapped the end of her nose with his finger. "Don't get smart with me, young lady. I'll sic your grandmother on you."

"Oh, no. Don't do that."

They both laughed.

"Be careful." Wrinkling his nose, Junior scowled. "I care about you, and I want to make sure you're happy."

A commotion at the door cut off Tia's reply. Like a movie star making a grand entrance on the red carpet, Nia Edwards burst into the room, capturing everyone's attention. Tia watched her twin sashay into the room, speaking into her

Bluetooth. Nia talked fast and loud while balancing a giant, gift-wrapped box in her one hand. "Nah! Not today. I'm closed. Call Tuesday for an appointment. Bye."

Andre reached Nia first and enfolded her in a bear hug. "Hey, little girl."

He released her and Nia was instantly engulfed in Andrew's embrace. "How you doing?"

Grinning at her brothers, she handed the box to Andrew. "Here, take this. Put it with the rest."

Tia studied her twin. They may have come from the same egg, but that's where all similarities stopped. Tia and Nia were completely different. Their personalities and philosophy about life were worlds apart. Tia took life very seriously. She planned every move and made decisions based on what she wanted to accomplish.

Nia let life happen. She didn't plan, nor did she intend to start.

They shared the same features and coloring, but Nia tamed her wild, curly mane into a slick bob that brushed her shoulders. Tia allowed the soft curls to flow freely. Tia preferred conservative business suits for work and tailored slacks and blouses for play. Nia wouldn't be caught dead or alive in the outfits Tia favored. Nia preferred her clothes so tight that the garments practically squeezed her to death. She wore loud, funky, colorful fabrics and outfits.

Today was a perfect example. Nia wore a pair of form-fitting, low-rise denims that revealed a large portion of her flat, pierced belly and tramp stamp. Her blue-green-yellow-pink strapless silk confection cut across the swell of her breasts, drawing attention to her curves.

"Hey, Tia, baby!" Nia's gaze swept over the guests, toward her sister. She raced across the room to her twin, throwing her arms around her. "Good to see you."

Laughing, Tia swayed back and forth within her sister's embrace.

Chris moved alongside Tia. "Hi, Nia."

Instantly, Nia turned to Chris. "Well, look at this." She turned to her sister. "When did you two start seeing each other?"

"Recently," Tia responded.

"Good. I couldn't stand Darnell anyway."

Tia laughed. It was a relief to have some positive feedback.

Junior joined the small group. "Hey, Nia."

"Hi, brother-man."

He laughed. "You know you're the only one I let call me that."

Grinning, Nia stated in a snappy tone, "As if you've got a choice."

"Maybe you should follow in your sister's footsteps," Mrs. Edwards suggested.

Rolling her eyes, Nia said, "Hi, Mother."

"Hello, Nia-Pia. I'm glad you pulled yourself away from that shop long enough to celebrate with your family."

"Yes, Mother. I made it."

"Oh!" Jackie Edwards shook her head sadly, examining her daughter from head to toe. "Why do you have on those god-awful jeans? Don't you have anything special to wear? Maybe we should take up a collection for you."

Nia rolled her eyes. "I have clothes, Mother."

"You don't act like it."

"Jacqueline!" Greg Edwards stated in a low, warning tone he reserved for moments just like this.

With round, surprised eyes, Jackie Edwards twirled around, facing her husband. "Yes?"

"Don't reveal all of our family secrets. Remember, this is a party."

Her husband's comment put Jackie Edwards in check, and she immediately changed her tune. "I'm sorry. You're right, honey."

Mr. Edwards opened his arms. "Nia, baby, come give your father a hug."

Saved by her father, Nia hurried into his embrace. "Good to see you, Daddy."

"You, too, baby." Mr. Edwards brushed a hand over Nia's soft, glossy hair. "You too."

Their mother's lips were pinched so tight they looked as if they'd been flattened by an iron. "You always spoil her, Greg."

"Why not? She's one of my girls. Come on, people. This is a party. Why don't we act like it? Nia, go get yourself something to eat and say hello to your grandmother. Tia"—he pointed a finger at a table across the room—"you've got presents to open for your grandmother. Junior, you get to make the announcement and help Tia open the gifts."

"Will do, Dad." Junior dropped his hands onto Tia's shoulders and steered her between the guests to the front of the room. He pushed her into a chair next to the gift table.

Greg Edwards wrapped an arm around his wife and pulled her along beside him. He helped her into a chair at the table with Grandma Ruth, grabbed a chair, and scooted it next to his wife, giving Tia a conspiring wink from across the room.

Grinning, Tia winked back. Her father always came through, putting an end to the family squabbles by taking charge and smoothing everyone's ruffled feathers.

Junior turned down the volume on the CD player and said, "Grandma, all of your grandchildren wanted to see you before your surgery. But we also wanted to give you something that would make the experience easier."

One of Tia's aunts said, "There's nothing that'll make it easier. That little woman is going to turn the hospital upside down."

"No, she won't," Tia replied.

Junior nodded. "Anyway, we've gotten you something that will help out." He handed the brightly wrapped package to Grandma Ruth. "Why don't you open it?"

She took the box from Junior and tore the paper off. Grandma Ruth pulled the gift from the box. "Cell phone?"

"Yeah. We thought you could call us whenever you need us. Take it with you wherever you go and call us."

"What am I supposed to do with this?" Grandma Ruth asked, leaning back in her chair while turning the cell phone over and over in her hands.

"Call us," Andrew stated firmly.

"How do I do that?" Grandma Ruth asked.

"I'm going to program everyone's number into your phone," Nia replied. "All you'll have to do is hit one button."

Andre piped up. "Yeah. When things aren't going right, punch in our number and we'll be there."

With a mischievous look on her face, Tia's grandmother dialed a number. Instantly, Jackie Edwards's cell phone went off. Laughing, Grandma put the phone to her ear and said, "I need your help."

Jackie Edwards replied, "I'm on my way. Be right there."

Chris put an arm around the back of Tia's chair and cupped her shoulder in his large hand. "I like your family."

Surprised, Tia stared at the man. "After the way they've treated you?"

He shrugged in that way of his and answered, "They are only protecting you. And I understand that."

"Do you? Then you understand better than I do. Junior started off coolly and the twins, I don't know what they think. Don't forget, Grandma Ruth has been downright mean." She touched his forehead. "Do you have a fever? Maybe you're delusional."

Smiling, Chris took her hand in his and kissed the palm. "Your family's words don't bother me. I would worry about my sister in the same way. But it doesn't change the way I feel about you."

Tia cupped his cheek and kissed Chris tenderly on the lips. "Thank you."

"No thanks needed," he answered, watching her family's antics.

Unable to resist, Tia glanced at Chris's handsome face. Her heart pounded in her chest as she remembered the things her family had said to him today. He'd been pleasant and taken everything they dished out without letting their words upset him.

She wondered where this relationship was headed. Would she be happy with Chris? Could her family accept this Frenchman with the nice disposition? Tia turned away, certain that wherever they were headed, it would not be a smooth ride. There would be some potholes and roadblocks that would make the drive uncomfortable and difficult at times, but she believed Chris was worth all of the aggravation.

She slipped her fingers between his, linking them together. Chris glanced at her and smiled. Tia felt her heart open and welcomed him. Yes, indeed, this was going to be one interesting adventure.

16

"I've bet everything on my wedding ring. I'm giving you the best that I've got," Tia harmonized with Anita Baker as she relaxed in the passenger seat of her SUV. Beside her, Chris hummed along while he navigated through the late Saturday afternoon traffic on Woodward Avenue in Detroit. He pulled into the driveway and stopped Tia's vehicle next to the valet shack at The Whitney restaurant.

Chris climbed out of the SUV and tossed the keys to the attendant before hurrying around the front to the passenger door. A huge grin of approval spread across his face as his warm and inviting gaze danced over her frame, which was covered in a low-cut peach sleeveless dress. The bodice curved into a hip-hugging pencil skirt. Chris took her hand and helped her from the car. Admiration filled his voice. "You look magnificent."

Delighted by Chris's compliment, Tia stood in

the circle of his embrace and caressed his cheek. She gazed at his charcoal suit, yellow shirt, and gray, green, and yellow striped tie. "Thank you. You look pretty good yourself."

Tia took a deep breath and let it out slowly, nervously clutching her handbag. This was their first appearance as a couple in front of the Gautier staff. Tia felt uncomfortable with the prospect of revealing this portion of her private life. Many of her coworkers knew about her relationship with Darnell, and she didn't feel up to the questioning looks and stares. She had always maintained a line that divided her personal and professional lives. She wanted to hold the new relationship close and not let anyone else in, but she knew she and Chris couldn't stay a secret forever. "Are you ready for this?"

"Absolutely. I want people to understand how important you are to me." Chris tucked her hand inside his elbow and led Tia up the stairs to the entrance of the restaurant. A woman directed them to an elevator secluded from the main portion of the first floor. The moment the doors shut, Chris wrapped his arms around her and pulled her against the length of him. "You are too beautiful to resist."

Anticipating his kiss, Tia lifted her head. From the first light touch of his lips against hers, her body responded, tingling and heating up. Chris nibbled the corners of her mouth. His tongue swept the interior of her mouth, exploring and tasting. She rubbed her breasts against the hard contours of his body as her tongue made contact

with his. He tasted so sweet. She never got
enough of him. Chris drank deeply from her. His
fingertips drew petite patterns on her back,
touching, stroking, and seeking. She responded
in kind, caressing his back and arms. The unexpected ding of the elevator bell brought them
back to earth. Slowly, Chris moved away, releasing her. Tia glanced into his eyes and her heart
galloped. Desire, hot and intense, blazed back
at her from the depths of his pale blue eyes.
Something primal spoke to her. But they were far
from home, and there would be embarrassing
questions if they tiptoed away from this event
before it began.

With a gentle finger, Chris pushed a lock of
Tia's hair behind her ear. "It's time to meet the
masses."

They turned to the door and exited the elevator into a large room. Helen, Wynn's assistant,
waited with a basket filled with programs. She
smiled at the couple and said, "Welcome."

"Hi, Helen." Tia gave the woman a quick hug.
"This is my friend Chris Jensen. Chris, Helen
Jenkins, Wynn's office manager. Helen, Chris is
from our office in France."

"Nice to meet you." Helen handed them programs and then waved her hand toward the left
section of the room. "The ceremony will begin in
a few minutes. You better hurry and find seats."

Cream-colored chairs were arranged in two
sections with an aisle down the center. A gold
arch sat at the front of the room, decorated with
white roses and lavender ribbons. Lilac fragrance

offered a gentle aroma while a gentle piano medley entertained the guests.

To the right, dinner tables were set up with white table linens. A crystal vase of white roses sat on each table. Lavender fabric covered each chair. Five servers dressed in uniforms of black and white moved around the floor, straightening tables and arranging cutlery.

A white frosted, five-layer wedding cake decorated with flowers of deep violet, purple, and lavender sat in a corner of the dining area. A huge lavender *C* topped the cake that shared space with serving plates, cutlery, and lavender napkins. In the opposite corner, brightly wrapped gifts and packages were piled high atop a long table. A glittery white birdcage hung from a hook, stuffed with envelopes.

A mahogany bar ran the length of one section of the room. The bar staff scurried back and forth, filling a fountain with bottles of champagne. There was an air of expectancy and excitement throughout the room.

Tia and Chris weren't the first to arrive. Family and friends were packed into the rows of chairs. Heads turned as they approached. Among the guests was JerrDan Hill, who sat alone. Krista and Brennan Thomas were accompanied by Liz and Steve Gillis. Tia and Chris waved to the couples as they searched for two empty seats. Members of the legal staff of Gautier International Motors and its affiliates were sprinkled among family and friends.

Tia hesitated, overwhelmed by the sight of so

many of their coworkers. Was she ready to go public with her relationship with Chris? As if he understood what was going through her head, Chris placed a reassuring hand at the base of her spine and urged Tia forward. She turned to him and met his warm and reassuring gaze.

Chris leaned close and whispered into her ear, "We can do this."

Reynolds and Michelle Gautier were seated in the center of a row near the arch. Their boss beckoned Tia and Chris to their row, pointing at the two chairs next to them.

With a hand on her back, Chris guided Tia to the two end chairs next to the Gautiers. They quickly dropped into the seats. "*Bonjour,* Michelle and Reynolds."

"*Bonjour,* Christophe and Tia," they replied. Reynolds leaned close to Tia and greeted her in English, "Hello. Good to see you."

"Hi, Reynolds, Michelle." Tia leaned forward to greet Reynolds's wife. "It's a beautiful day for a wedding."

"Yes, it is," Michelle responded, smiling warmly at Tia.

Reynolds glanced at his watch and said, "The wedding should start pretty soon. You know how Adam wants everything on time."

Tia nodded, remembering Adam's constant desire for promptness. The beat of the music changed. The guests turned in their seats to find Adam's father, Mr. Carlyle, escorting his wife down the aisle. The rose-colored gown and silver jacket made her look like a regal queen as she carried two roses in her hands, one white and one lavender. Mr. Carlyle looked equally handsome in a dove-gray tuxedo with a lavender rose in his lapel. Hands intertwined, they sat together in the front row on the right side of the room, smiling happily at each other.

Next came Wynn's mother and father. Peg Evans wore a teal-colored tea-length dress and matching shoes. Just like Mrs. Carlyle, Mrs. Evans carried two roses in white and lavender. Mr. Evans's tux matched Mr. Carlyle's suit with a lavender rose in the lapel pocket. Like the Carlyles, they took their places in the front row, but on the left side of the room.

Adam's sister, Sherry, appeared at the back of the room, dressed in a lavender tea-length dress. A wide cream-colored sash emphasized her waist and was tied into a large bow at the back. Jimmy Harrison, Wynn's eight-year-old son, escorted Sherry down the aisle and led her to a spot to the left of the arch. Jimmy discreetly disappeared. Minutes later, he returned with a second woman. This woman looked a great deal like Wynn, and Tia suspected this was Wynn's sister Kayla. Again, Jimmy led the woman to the left side of the arch where Sherry stood.

The flower girl started down the aisle. Dressed in a replicate of Sherry's and Kayla's dress, she stopped at every row and handed an item to each person. Whatever she was giving them made the adults grin and laugh. When she reached Tia and Chris, the child placed a silver item in her hand and closed her fingers around the woman's before moving down the aisle to the front of the room. She took her place next to Sherry.

"What is it?" Chris asked slowly. His lips grazed her ear, sending a current of delight surging through Tia as she opened her hand and revealed a Hershey's chocolate kiss. They laughed together at this surprising and wonderful treat. Chris wrapped an arm around Tia and hugged her close. "Absolutely magnificent. You are sweeter than any chocolate treat."

At the front of the room, the child's attempt to whisper reached the ear of the audience. "Can I eat a piece of candy, Momma?"

Sherry shook her head. "No. Save it for later."

As the ring bearer made his way down the aisle, Adam entered from a separate entrance. He stood tall and handsome.

The wedding march began. Everyone stood. At the back of the room, Wynn stood with her sons, Jimmy and Kevin. The boys flanked their mother and led her down the aisle. She made a radiant bride. Her cream strapless bodice was beaded. A large lavender sash fit tightly at the waist and tied into a large bow at her side. The fabric flared into a full skirt that reached her ankles.

Slowly and deliberately, mother and sons moved down the aisle. Wynn gazed directly at Adam. When he looked at her, a huge smile spread across his face. She returned the smile as she moved closer to him. The boys led their mother to Adam. When they reached the altar, Kevin offered his mother's hand to Adam and then stepped to the left of his mother where Jimmy stood.

Dressed in white robes, the minister waited at the opposite side of the arch. Wynn and Adam moved forward, facing the minister.

"Good afternoon, everyone. I'm Pastor Ford," the minister began. "This is a great day. It's the day Wynn and Adam have chosen to become a family." He talked about family and what it meant.

Chris reached over and took Tia's hand and brought it to his lips, kissing her palm. As usual, his touch sent her heart racing.

"Marriage is more than being in love," Pastor Ford stated. "It's a commitment to be with one person, to hold that partner's life as dearly as you hold your own . . . to be with them when they are ill or in the best of health. To listen." He paused and then repeated, "To truly listen to what that person has to say and answer honestly. There will be times when your partner won't agree with what you are saying or become upset with the answer you give. But that person will always be the one you turn to when you need advice, help, love, and support."

Chris squeezed Tia's hand. The feel of his hand cradling hers told her how much he understood the importance of the minister's words. He leaned close and said, "I feel that way about you. You're always the person I choose when I need advice or help."

"I want to be there for you," Tia admitted.

"And I want you there," Chris answered gently.

"So," the minister said, "who gives this woman?"

"I do," Jimmy answered.

"Me too," Kevin seconded.

The wedding guests laughed aloud. *How sweet*, Tia thought.

Adam grinned from one boy to the other and then said, "Thank you. I promise to take good care of your mother."

Nodding, Kevin seemed to consider Adam's declaration very seriously before answering, "Okay."

"You better," Jimmy warned instantly.

The rest of the ceremony went off perfectly. When the minister asked for the rings, Jimmy reached into his pocket, removed a round silver band sparkling with diamonds, and handed it to Adam.

Kevin reached in his pocket and handed his mother a plain silver band.

Wynn and Adam handed the rings to the minister. He held them in the air for the wedding guests to see. "These rings symbolize Adam and Wynn's commitment to this marriage. The rings offer a visible link to each other."

Adam and Wynn exchanged their vows.

"Ladies and gentlemen, I now present the Carlyle family: Wynn, Adam, Jimmy, and Kevin. Congratulations. Be good and kind to each other."

The family turned to face their guests. Tia had never seen Adam look so happy, and she realized at that moment that she wanted the same thing for her life. She offered a silent prayer that Wynn and Adam's life would be happy and drama free.

Adam turned to Wynn and took her face between his hands. He leaned down and lightly touched her lips with his. "I love you." Drawing away, he smiled down at his wife before leaning in for a second, more thorough kiss. Wynn wrapped her arms around Adam's waist and drew him against her. Her moans of pleasure were heard by their wedding guests. The guests clapped, whistled, and laughed.

Minutes later, Tia and Chris stepped up to the front of the receiving line to congratulate the new couple. Tia hugged Wynn. "Welcome to the Gautier family."

Wynn grinned broadly. "Thank you. It's good to see you."

Tia moved to Adam and hugged him tightly. "I wish you all the happiness the world has to offer."

"And you too," Adam replied, looking past her to Chris. "How long have you and Chris been going on?"

Embarrassed, Tia tugged a loose lock of hair behind her ear, taking a quick glance at her date as he conversed with Wynn. "A few weeks."

"No more Darnell?"

She shook her head. "No. Been there, done that. Don't want to do it again."

"Okay, then. I wish you and Chris all the best."

"Thank you."

Chris grabbed Adam's hand and pumped it enthusiastically. "Beautiful ceremony. I wish you and Wynn the best."

"Where are you headed for your honeymoon?" Tia asked.

Grinning, Wynn answered, wrapping her arms around Adam's waist, "Two weeks in Hawaii."

"Oh, man! That's great." Then Tia frowned. "Who's going to keep your sons?"

"My mom and dad." Wynn pointed toward the elder Evanses.

Tia hugged the couple. "Have a wonderful time."

Grinning at her new husband, Wynn winked and answered, "We will."

Adam wrapped an arm around his new bride and pulled her close. "Thank you. You guys are staying for dinner, aren't you?"

"Of course," Chris answered. "I understand The Whitney has excellent food."

Tia hugged Wynn and then Adam one final time before moving on. "We don't want to hold up the line. We'll talk to you guys later."

The reception went off without a hitch. As the evening progressed, Tia watched Adam and Wynn with awe. They were so happy together. The couple made time for all of their guests, stopping at each table to chat. Their first dance brought tears to Tia's eyes, because they looked so happy and in love. When Wynn fed Adam a piece of cake, he leaned close and whispered something in her ear that made her blush.

Perfect. That was the word that described them. Tia was genuinely pleased for them. She hoped for a bright future. She turned to Chris, gazing upon his handsome face and wondering what the future held for them. Would they have their own happily ever after?

There were so many issues to consider. Race was just one of the many things they needed to address. Any decision Reynolds made about Chris's future could destroy their future. What if Reynolds decided to send Chris to another office? What would happen to their budding relationship? Would or should she follow him to the next location?

What about Tia's family? From the beginning, her mother had questioned their relationship and had shown some resistance to it. How would her brothers react to this new man in her life? It had taken them years to accept Darnell.

How about Chris's family? How welcoming would they be to an African American woman?

Tia sighed. It was all too much to consider. *Let it go,* she decided. *Enjoy the party. Think about the future tomorrow.*

17

Offering up a silent prayer, Tia rode the elevator to the surgical suites of Harper University Hospital. Hospitals made her feel uncomfortable. Today was no exception. Tia scrunched up her nose against the odor of disinfectant and industrial cleaners as she rode the elevator.

She wished she were anywhere but here. Her family needed her, and she planned to be close by for Grandma Ruth. If Tia was lucky, she'd get a chance to see her before the doctors wheeled her into surgery.

Tia stepped off of the elevator and glanced each way. *Where was the waiting room?* she wondered, taking a tentative step to the nurses' station.

"Tia," called her mother from the opposite end of the hallway.

She turned. Mrs. Edwards stood in the center of the corridor, beckoning her. Tia changed direction. "Hi, Momma. Has Granny gone into surgery yet?"

"No. We got here about an hour ago. She's up and awake. She's being prepped now. Do you want to see her before they start?"

Tia nodded and then followed her mother. They stepped through a series of doors and entered a room filled with hospital gurneys separated by curtains used for privacy. Overwhelmed by worry, Tia swallowed hard and trailed her mother through the maze of curtains and medical equipment.

"Here we are," Mrs. Edwards announced, slipping between the split in the curtain. Tia did the same.

Grandma Ruth sat on a narrow bed with an IV stuck into her left hand and a blue blanket pulled to her neck. "Hey, Tia. Come give your grandma a kiss."

Love for this woman bubbled within Tia. Instantly, she went to her grandmother's side and hugged her. After a second, she asked, "Are you ready for this?"

The senior member of the family replied, "I might as well be. That doctor is ready to cut me open."

"Mother," Mrs. Edwards chastised. "You agreed to this. Don't talk that way."

"What choice did I have? I intend to stay alive long enough to see my grandbabies get married. Maybe I'll live long enough to see some great-grandkids. If this is the only way I can do it, then it will be done." She looked directly at Tia and added, "Although I'm not real impressed with your choice right now."

Embarrassed, Tia felt heat rise up the back of her neck. Yes, she knew her family was upset by her relationship with Chris, but like anything else in life, they'd get over it. All she needed to do was wait them out. "Let's not talk about that right now, Grandma. I'm here for you."

"Damn straight. This is my day." The old woman wagged a finger in Tia's direction and speared her with that look that made everyone squirm, including Tia's mother. "All right. But we're not done with this talk. When I get back on my feet, you and me are going to sit down together and work this out. Understand?"

"Yes, ma'am."

A woman in hospital scrubs poked her head between the curtains and said, "We're ready for you, Mrs. Wilson. I'm going to ask your company to return to the waiting area."

Nodding, Grandma Ruth opened her arms for one final hug. Tia and her mother rushed into her arms and hugged her close.

Tia kissed her cheek and rose. "I'm heading to the waiting area. You and Momma can have a moment."

"Okay. I'll see you later this evening," Grandma Ruth promised.

"That's a date," Tia answered.

"I'll be there in a minute," Mrs. Edwards replied.

Tia retraced her steps to the waiting room. Surprised, she stopped short of entering. "What are you doing here?"

Chris sat beside her father, talking softly. He

looked up and found Tia in the doorway. Smiling warmly at her, he dropped the magazine in the empty chair next to him and moved to her side. He laid a gentle, reassuring hand on her arm and then rubbed it up and down, making her tingle all over. "I wanted to be here for you. I thought you might need me."

Shaking her head, she asked, "How did you know which hospital?"

"I didn't want you to be alone, so I'm here."

"How?" Tia took a step back and gazed into Chris's eyes.

Chris shrugged. "You weren't ready to confide in me, but I knew you would need me. I called the hospitals until I found the right one. So here I am."

Call hospitals! Chris was a nut. "What about the office?" Her eyes narrowed as she pictured his calendar in her head. "Didn't you have a court date scheduled?" she asked.

"Rescheduled."

Tia wrapped her arms around his waist and hugged him close. "Thank you for coming, but I didn't want you to change everything for me."

"Of course I would. You're important to me." He led her to the empty chair next to his. "Today is for your grandmother."

"Thank you." Tia grabbed his hand and squeezed, trying to convey all of her fears and emotions in that one touch. "You didn't have to do this."

"Come. Sit. We've got plenty of time before things are complete."

Tia sat and stared at the television mounted on the wall. Chris sank into the seat next to her and wrapped an arm around her shoulders, drawing her against him. He kissed her forehead. "Relax. Everything is going to be perfect."

She laid her head on his shoulder. Being close to Chris soothed her worried nerves. Grandma Ruth was precious to them all. Although this was supposed to be an uncomplicated surgery, there were always risks, especially with an eighty-seven-year-old patient.

All was quiet for about five minutes until Junior and Nia strolled into the room together. "Hey, Dad." Junior waved at them. He glared hard at Chris's possessive arm around Tia, but he said nothing. Chris returned the glare with one of his own that said, "I'm here and you're not going to stop me."

Nia grinned at Chris and nodded approvingly. "Hi, Chris."

"Hello, Nia. *Comment allez-vous?*" *How are you?*

"Worried for Granny," Nia answered.

Tia stared at her sister. "Do you speak French?"

"Little bit."

Shocked, Tia continued to stare at her sister. "When?"

Nia placed her hand on her hip and stated indignantly, "Just because I didn't go to college doesn't mean I didn't learn anything in high school."

"Hey, sis." Junior squeezed Nia's shoulder to signal that she needed to calm down.

Standing on the opposite side of Tia, he asked. "You okay?"

Tia nodded.

"Is Granny Ruth in surgery?" Nia asked, sitting in a chair close to their father.

"Not yet," Mr. Edwards explained. "Your mother is still with her."

"Can we go see her?" Junior asked.

"I don't think so," Tia responded. "I was in the prep room with Momma when the nurse asked me to leave. They were going to give Granny Ruth her anesthesia."

Nia turned to Junior. "I think we're a little late."

Junior nodded as he leaned back in a chair and pulled a photography magazine from the back pocket of his denims. "Looks like it. I'll wait until after surgery."

"She's on her way," Mrs. Edwards announced as she entered the room.

Mr. Edwards met his wife in the center of the room and wrapped a reassuring arm around her. "Is everything okay?"

Eyes filled with tears, Mrs. Edwards nodded and pressed her lips together. She glanced at the members of her family until her eyes landed on Chris. Mrs. Edwards gripped her husband's arm, narrowed her eyes, and scowled at the couple, but she kept her thoughts to herself.

"Come on, hon. We've got a long time ahead of us. Rest a little bit." Mr. Edwards urged his wife toward a seat.

Andre and Andrew burst into the room. "Sorry we're late," Andre stated. "I couldn't find a parking space."

"How's Granny?" Andrew asked. He gazed at

Chris with a puzzled expression before dismissing the situation with a shake of his head and turning to his parents.

"Yes. Is she okay?" Andre queried.

"Just went into surgery," Mr. Edwards answered. He pointed at two available chairs. "Sit down. There's a long wait ahead."

The twins did their father's bidding and focused on the television mounted on the wall. A variety of talk shows filled their morning as they waited for news about their family matriarch. Junior finished reading his magazine and rummaged through the reading material in the waiting room. Nia played with her cell phone, texting people and answering messages. Her twin brothers stared blankly at the television.

Chris kissed Tia's forehead, stood, and started for the door. "I'll be back."

Surprised, Tia glanced up at him. "Okay," she muttered uncertainly. *Where in the heck is he going?*

As soon as Chris left the room, Mrs. Edwards demanded, "Why did you bring him here? He's not part of our family. He has no place here."

"I didn't," Tia said, feeling as if her mother was attacking her. Stunned by her mother's angry words, she felt small and insecure.

"If you didn't tell him, who did?" she asked as she rose from her seat and walked toward Tia. "Somebody had to let him know which hospital my mother would be at."

"Chris said he wanted to be here for me," Tia defended him.

"I don't want him here."

"Mother." Nia stuffed her cell phone into her purse. "This is Tia's friend. You've got Daddy to be with you. Don't take that comfort away from your daughter."

Mrs. Edwards's voice changed to an accusatory note. "It doesn't matter what the situation, you always take the opposite side."

"That's not what this is about. I'm not taking anyone's side." A flash of raw hurt spread across Nia's face before she hid it behind her standard cocky attitude. "Why shouldn't Tia have a friend who cares about her and wants to be at her side?"

Tia had had enough. She stood and demanded, "Stop talking about me as if I don't exist. I did not invite Chris here. He called around until he found the right hospital. It was his decision to come. You shouldn't get mad at him for caring."

"Enough!" Mr. Edwards stated in a firm but soft tone. Everyone in the room turned to the head of the Edwards clan as he rose from his seat. "Jackie, stop it. In case you've forgotten, we're here for your mother."

"I . . . I know that," Mrs. Edwards stammered.

"Then act like it. This is Tia's friend, and he's here for her, just like I'm here for you. This is not the time or place to voice any other concerns. Your mother is having surgery. Why don't you focus on that?"

Practically in tears, Jackie Edwards returned to her seat and tossed a dismissive hand in the air. "Fine. I won't say another word."

"That may be a good thing," Mr. Edwards

replied, taking the chair next to her. He took her hand between both of his. "Let's focus on Mom."

All was quiet in the waiting room when Chris returned. He carried several bags and a carton in his hands. He dropped to one knee in front of Tia's mother, removed a paper cup from the carton, and offered it to the older woman. "Mrs. Edwards, I thought a cup of coffee might help the time go by."

Mrs. Edwards's eyes widened in shock. She remained silent and folded her arms across her chest.

"That was nice of you, son. Thank you." Mr. Edwards took the cup from Chris. "You didn't have to do this."

"It's a long wait. I think everyone could use a little something." Chris offered the bag to Mr. Edwards. "There are *petit déjeuner* sandwiches and doughnuts. Enjoy."

He turned to Junior and offered Tia's eldest brother a cup of coffee. "There's a sausage sandwich and a cinnamon doughnut in this bag. *Bon appétit.*"

Junior took the bag. "Thanks, man."

"You're welcome."

"Nia, I brought you a cappuccino." Chris handed her a paper cup. "I didn't think you'd want anything more."

Tia's twin removed the top from the cup, and the aroma of coffee filled the air. "That was thoughtful of you. I appreciate it."

Chris handed another bag to Tia's twin brothers before returning to Tia. Surprised, Andrew took the bag, took out a sandwich, and then passed the bag to his brother. "Thank you," Andre replied.

Chris dropped into the chair next to Tia. "I know your nerves are stretched. Here is a cup of green tea. When you're ready, I have a croissant for you."

Her heart swelled with pride and something more. Chris always cared about the feelings of others. Although her mother had treated him shabbily, he still tried to help.

Like the sun coming out from behind rain clouds, Tia realized that she had fallen in love with Chris. His compassionate nature and concern for everyone around him was only one of the things that made him so dear and loving to her.

They concentrated on their meals. Chris's treat seemed to lighten the mood, although they were still worried about their matriarch. The anger had fizzled. Before long, Tia's brothers and sister were engaged in a discussion with Chris about the Detroit Tigers and the old Tiger Stadium. Time moved quicker and before they realized it, it was near noon.

Dr. Heuton stepped into the waiting room. The surgeon headed directly to Tia's parents. The room went silent. "Everything is done, Mr. and Mrs. Edwards. Mrs. Wilson came through the procedure perfectly."

"No complications at all?" asked Mrs. Edwards with her hands linked.

"She was perfect."

"So what's next?" Mr. Edwards piped in.

"Because of her age, we'll keep her for a few

days to make certain there's no infection. She might need a week or two of physical therapy. We'll see how things go."

Tia's father stood. "Can we see her?"

"Sure. Remember, she's under the influence of anesthesia. She may not make any sense."

Dr. Heuton shook hands first with Mrs. Edwards and then with Mr. Edwards before leaving the room. Everyone let out a collective sigh of relief.

"Thank God!" Nia got to her feet. "Let's go see her."

Tia followed her clan down the hall to the recovery room. Her mother and father swept into the room first. The rest of the family stood outside the open door, peeking in. Drugged, Grandma Ruth didn't display her usual sassy attitude. The drugs made her lethargic.

They waited for the go-ahead from their parents. Junior commented, "She looks pretty good for somebody right out of surgery."

Andrew nudged his brother and warned, "Don't say too much. She might hear you."

"Yeah." Andre nodded. "Remember that time she was babysitting and we thought she was asleep and she heard and saw everything we did? She told Mom and Dad on us."

"We were on punishment for a month," Nia added. "We couldn't watch television, we couldn't go outside, and we had to go to bed right after dinner."

"That's what we had coming to us. We shouldn't have had that kid in the basement," Tia reminded.

"Momma nearly lost her mind when she found out we had that runaway in the house for days while his parents were searching for him."

Junior whistled. "When Momma found out, I thought her head was going to turn around like in *The Exorcist*."

They all laughed.

"Hey, out there," Grandma Ruth called in a groggy, tired tone. "Come on in. Let me see you before I go back to sleep."

Everyone filed into the room, except Chris. He hung back, waiting in the hallway for them to finish their visit. Grandma Ruth looked past her grandchildren and directly at Chris. "You too."

Surprised, he glanced around before realizing that she was talking to him. He entered the crowded room but hung back.

"Well, it's good to see all of you," Grandma stated with a sloping smile. "Even you over there." She pointed at Chris.

Grandma Ruth let out a huge yawn and sank farther into the hospital bed. "I'm glad I saw all of you. I'm tired. I'll see you tomorrow."

18

Chris strolled up to Tia's workstation with his open laptop in one hand and his suit jacket in the other. "I just got a call from Reynolds's executive assistant. He needs to see me right now." He placed the computer on the corner of her desk and stuffed his arms into the jacket.

Tia grinned. The tip of her pink tongue was visible between her teeth.

For a moment, Chris stared, intrigued by the sight of her mouth. The urge to kiss her silly grin pulled at his heart. He ignored that impulse, instead concentrating on buttoning his jacket. They had agreed to keep things professional on the job. *Later*, he promised silently, wishing he could sneak a quick taste. Later, he planned to drink from her lips like a diabetic trying to quench his endless thirst.

Frowning, Tia touched his hand. Her soft, fleeting caress spread through him like molten lava. "You okay?"

I'm not going to let Tia know what I'm thinking. She'll tease me unmercifully if she knew I was focused completely on her mouth and how sweet she tastes. "Absolutely, my love. Why were you grinning?" Chris asked.

"Déjà vu."

"*Oui.* You're finally learning French," he teased, bowing from the waist.

"Ha-ha." She leaned forward and added, "You're so funny."

"I aim to please."

"And you do. In more than one way." Grinning back at Chris, Tia scribbled something on a small blue sticky note and stuck it to his monitor before he snapped it shut.

Chris felt his flesh lengthen in his trousers. *Great, just what I need to have happen before a meeting with the boss.* There were times when he found Ms. Tia Edwards far too enticing. Today was definitely one of those times.

"Adam ran off to Reynolds's office the day you started here. Do you think Reynolds has someone new in mind for your job?" she teased, grinning broadly.

"Oh! You're just full of good cheer." Chris tapped the edge of her nose with his finger. "Very cute." He picked up his laptop and started down the hall. He turned to face her and asked, "Lunch?"

"Sure. What time do you think you'll be back?"

He checked his watch. "I figure around one. This shouldn't take too long."

Tia waved. "See you."

I love that woman, he thought as he strolled down the corridor. Tia filled his life with such joy that he had a difficult time leaving her. One question remained in his head. Did she love him? They were cruising toward some very important aspects of their relationship. Maybe it was time for him to plan a special date at a special place to reveal his heart and learn how she felt about him.

Chris turned his attention to his boss and this impromptu meeting. *What did Reynolds want?* he wondered, doing a mental recap of his current projects as he strolled down the red-carpeted hallway to Reynolds Gautier's row of suites. No matter how hard he tried, he couldn't think of a single reason for this meeting. Normally, Reynolds, Adam, and Chris met on a weekly basis to discuss issues and problems that may have cropped up. This unscheduled meeting without Adam worried Chris.

Shaking his head, he chuckled softly. He felt like a kid being summoned to explain some misdeed to his papa. His projects were up-to-date. The real estate deal in Mexico had gone through as smooth as a fine glass of French Beaujolais wine, and the next phase of the acquisition of the Flint properties was moving ahead without a hitch.

Chris halted at a set of carved wooden doors. He straightened his tie before entering Reynolds's suite of offices. Whatever the problem, he'd find out in a few minutes.

He hoped Reynolds wasn't upset with something he'd done and planned to reprimand him. Everything in his life seemed to be going pretty well. A broad smile flashed across his face as he considered how his life had changed since moving to the United States.

Tia was at the heart of all of his good fortune. She was great, perfect. He'd never been this happy in any other relationship.

Although Mrs. Edwards hadn't warmed up to him yet, the rest of the family seemed to have accepted him. At the very least, Chris thought again, they tolerated his presence at their family functions. He could live with that, because he planned to be at Tia's side, whatever the situation.

Reynolds's executive assistant, Angela, greeted him from her desk when he arrived. Instantly, she rose and led Chris into Reynolds's empty office. Lips pressed together, Chris turned to Angela with a question in his eyes. Instantly, she began to explain. "Right after I called you, he had to step out of the office for a minute."

She waved a hand toward the empty chair on the opposite side of the desk and said, "Relax. Have a seat. Reynolds will be with you in a moment."

Chris nodded and then watched Angela leave the room.

Although he spent a great deal of time inside these walls, Reynolds's office always impressed him. Reynolds's office was larger than Chris's and Adam's offices combined. The massive desk, large leather executive chair, and accoutrements in the office declared Reynolds the leader.

Taking Angela's suggestion, Chris took a chair

facing Reynolds's desk, where he placed his laptop to turn it on. He scrolled through his current projects, preparing to offer Reynolds a quick update on his works in progress. His gaze fell on the note Tia had stuck on his monitor. *Don't forget, you owe me a kiss.*

Yes, I do. Chris's thoughts returned to that pink tongue he wanted to taste only minutes ago.

The door opened and the white-haired and portly Reynolds strolled into the office. "*Bonjour.* Sorry about the delay. I got caught by one of the design staff."

Chris stood, waiting until Reynolds stood behind his desk. The men shook hands.

Reynolds waved a hand at him and said in his native language, "Sit, sit." Once the older man sat, Chris did the same and they began an exchange in French. After speaking English so much, the attorney found it enjoyable and refreshing to speak in his native language.

"You've been with us about four months." Reynolds linked his hands and leaned forward. "You seem to have settled in and are getting on quite well."

"I like my job," Chris answered truthfully while silently trying to figure out where this conversation was heading.

"How about your home? Have you settled in?"

Nodding, Chris responded, *"Oui."*

Silence followed Chris's answer. He got the impression that Reynolds was debating his next move. Chris sat back in his chair to wait. No one rushed the head of Gautier International Motors. When Reynolds felt ready to explain, he would.

"I'm sorry. I didn't mean to cause you any additional stress. I should tell you that you're doing an excellent job. I'm pleased with how you've integrated yourself into the department and completed the work. Adam is pleased with how you've handled your assignments and so am I."

That sounded like good news. Why hadn't Reynolds put all of this in an e-mail or voice message? Why the face-to-face? "Thank you."

"There's more." Chuckling softly, Reynolds leaned deeper into his executive chair. He tented his fingertips. "I'm having some trouble in our home office."

"Oh?" Frowning, Chris leaned forward, anxious to hear what Reynolds had to say. After all, he trained in that office and knew most of the people in the legal department.

Nodding, Reynolds explained further, "I had to place the director on administrative leave last week."

"You're not talking about Pierce Joyce, are you?"

"*Oui.*"

Stunned, Chris sagged against the back of his chair and stroked his chin thoughtfully. He had trained under Pierce and found the man to be a wonderful mentor. This was quite a surprise. "You fired Pierce?"

"Not yet. It's coming."

"I'm sorry to hear that. I've always found Pierce to be extremely helpful."

"Pierce is very good at his work. I've always

given him high marks in that area. Unfortunately, he also considers himself quite the ladies' man." Reynolds pulled a legal document from his desk drawer and slid it across the desk.

Chris picked it up and studied it for a moment. It was a complaint filed in the French courts.

"It's come to my attention that Pierce has been far too free with his attitude, and hands, toward the females in the office. A case of sexual harassment has been filed against him and the company. Unfortunately, this is the first of several complaints. I had to take action fairly quickly."

Chris drew in a deep breath and let it out slowly. He knew the answer to his question, but he had to ask, "What does this have to do with me?"

"I need to move you," Reynolds stated firmly, folding his arms across his broad chest. "I want you to head up the home office for a while, at least until I decide what I want to do next. You've worked under Pierce, so you know his style, and his strengths and weaknesses. Chris, you're an obvious choice to replace him, even temporarily."

Pride, satisfaction, and exhilaration surged through Chris's veins. This was *the* opportunity of his career. Reynolds had just handed Chris a chance to direct the activities of the legal department in the home office. The French office was the biggest and oldest outside of the States. This was an honor.

His gaze fell to the sticky note Tia had placed on his laptop, and the excitement of a moment earlier evaporated. Conflicting emotions warred within him. He stroked the note, rereading Tia's sweet words. He couldn't do this. His relationship with Tia meant far too much to him to fly off and leave her.

Chris closed the laptop and sat quietly, searching for a path that would give him everything he desired. His heart lunged dangerously in his chest. His thoughts quickly shot into overdrive. Maybe there was a way to make this work. How long would he be needed? If it was a few weeks, he could handle it. Maybe Tia could visit. Or, he might suggest that she accompany him as his executive assistant.

Any decision Tia made regarding them had to include her family. His major concern involved Tia's mother. Mrs. Edwards would probably have a fit. The way she received this turn of events had the potential to destroy their future.

Adam would not be pleased with him taking his admin. The pair worked together like a well-oiled machine. That might cause a huge rift between the three of them. But Adam was a logical man; he'd understand. He may not like the idea at first, but he would come to accept it without malice.

Tia's mother would never relent. What about Tia? How would she handle this? What will she say? This was incredibly bad timing. Not now! Not when things were coming together so well.

The boss cleared his throat. "Did you hear me?"

Chris nodded.

"No comments?"

"How long?" Chris asked, swallowing a lump

the size of a glacier. He was fervently hoping the request was for a month or two.

"The move to France would be up to a year, maybe longer." He shrugged. "Perhaps a few months more."

Damn! Reynolds just trashed Chris's one hope. He had to ask the question, even if the answer wasn't what he wanted to hear. "Is there anyone else you can send?"

"There's no one with your expertise. I can't send Adam. He needs to be here to work on the United States issues." Reynolds pointed a finger at Chris. "You're it."

"Do I have a choice?" Chris ran his fingers through his hair.

"No. You're the best man for the job. You know the territory and the partners involved. I want you there."

Chris was afraid of that. The company was growing faster than anyone anticipated. "Can I have a little time to think things through and put my life in order?"

"Of course. Chris, I'm sorry. I know you've settled in and established a life here. I understand this request comes at a difficult time. But you knew the position was for a limited time."

"True. But I did expect to be here until next year."

"I expected to have you here that long. We both know that things change. This situation requires someone with your background and knowledge."

Lips pursed, Chris asked, "What is the absolute latest I can leave?"

"I want you there yesterday, but I'll give you up to a month." Reynolds raised a finger and added, "No longer."

Nodding, Chris rose, shook hands with Reynolds, and left the office. His mind was cluttered with thoughts.

The first thing he needed to do was talk with Tia and figure out a way for them to be together. If she was willing to come to France, that would make life easier. After that, he'd have to deal with her family. That was not going to be easy. Maybe he could find an ally in Tia's father. He seemed like a reasonable man. *Yes, until you start talking about taking his daughter to another country,* a little voice whispered.

Whatever the situation, Chris didn't plan to leave Tia behind. He would find a way to keep them together. Even if it meant pissing off Mrs. Edwards.

19

Tia sipped her morning cappuccino and nibbled on her strawberry croissant while scrolling through her computer calendar. After Chris delivered her breakfast treat with a reserved "good morning," he had retreated to his office and stayed there until later that morning when he and Adam headed out to an appointment.

They stopped at Tia's desk. "We're off to a deposition in Judge Archer's chambers," said Adam. "We should be back before lunchtime."

Waving good-bye, the two attorneys strolled away from the legal suite with their laptops tucked under their arms. Tia sighed. *What's going on with Chris?* Since his meeting with Reynolds three days ago, he had been more distant toward her. Something important was up that he decided not to share with her. This was not a good thing. They hadn't established a rule to reveal every detail of their lives to each other, but Tia could tell that something major was bothering him. Whenever she was near him, he made an excuse to leave. A new tension fueled his movements. When work brought Chris into her orbit, he made an excuse to hurry away at record speed. Being in the same room with Tia made him so tense that he'd cut short his conversations with others and left the room quickly.

Tia also noticed a subtle change in Chris's attitude and mood toward her since his meeting with Reynolds. There wasn't anything she could specifically identify as the cause of this new disposition. He never discussed what happened with the CEO. Not only was he more reserved and quiet, but they also hadn't spent any time alone together.

Tia's thoughts were suddenly interrupted by the giggles and thunder of feet racing toward her. Two young boys rushed up to her desk.

"Hi, Tia." Jimmy Harrison waved at her.

"Hey, Ms. Edwards." Kevin Harrison dropped his elbows onto her desktop and cradled his head in his hands, gazing adoringly at her.

"Hello to you, Jimmy." Tia turned to the younger boy. "Hi, Kevin. Where's your mother?"

Wynn Evans-Carlyle moved slowly and deliberately up to the desk. "Hi, Tia. How are you doing?"

Surprised, Tia's eyes widened. Wynn looked beautiful, radiant and happy. In addition, she sported a baby bump. Tia guessed the older woman must be five or six months pregnant. Oh, man! This was news. Wait until Adam returned; she'd have a few words for him for keeping this gem a secret. "Wynn, look at you!"

"Yes, I'm pregnant," Wynn confirmed with a long-suffering smile.

Tia shook her head. "Wow! You guys just got married and now you're adding to your family."

"Well, you probably figured it out that this wasn't a planned pregnancy. That doesn't change the fact that I'm going to have another baby."

Smiling approvingly at Adam's wife, Tia said, "Congratulations. Do you know what you're having?"

Wynn shook her head. "Hopefully one baby. Adam doesn't want to know ahead of time, so it'll be a surprise when he or she arrives."

Tia rose and moved around the desk to hug Wynn. "I wish you and Adam all the best. Although, I'm going to have to have a talk with my boss; he kept this little detail completely to himself."

"Don't get mad at him." She lightly tapped her chest. "I asked him not to tell. Honestly, I'm a bit embarrassed about this slipup."

"Why?"

Embarrassment flashed across Wynn's face and she looked away. "I'm too old for this kind of mistake. I should have handled my business much better than this. Slipups like this happen to teenagers, not grown women like me."

Tia reached for Wynn's hand and patted it reassuringly. "Don't get yourself all upset. These days, nobody cares about that. You're going to have a beautiful baby. By the way, when is the baby due?"

"Toward the end of the summer. August twentieth is my due date."

"Thanks. I have to keep that in mind." Tia returned to her chair, swiveled it to the computer, and clicked on the calendar. She keyed the date into her tickler file and then turned to the boys. "So what brings you guys here today?"

"Baseball!" Jimmy cheered, waving his hands above his head.

Kevin nodded, adding, "We're going to see the Tigers play."

"Cool." Laughing softly, Tia rubbed the top of Kevin's head. "Who's playing?"

"Blue Jays," Wynn answered, moving slowly to the visitor's chair. Sighing heavily, she dropped into the chair, stretched her legs in front of her, and flexed her sandal-clad toes. "It's good to be off my feet."

"Hmm." Troubled, Tia studied Wynn's sandals. "My dear, that's going to be a lot of moving about for you."

Smiling, Wynn leaned closer to Tia, cupped her hand to her mouth, and whispered, "A whole lot of bathroom going, too. I'm hoping we're in one of the company suites. That will make the visit a whole lot easier."

"Yes, it will."

Wynn glanced toward Adam's office. "Where is that man I married?"

"Deposition," Tia answered. "They should be back pretty soon. What time does the game start?"

"Two." Wynn wiggled around, searching for a comfortable spot.

"You going to be all right?" Tia asked.

Wynn nodded, rubbing her baby bump. "This

baby means business. My boys never kept me up at night the way this one does."

"Maybe it's a girl."

She shivered and wrapped her arms around her body. "I don't want to consider it. Anyway, Adam promised Kevin and Jimmy burgers at Fuddruckers."

Tia shut her eyes, dreaming of a Fuddruckers meal. "Oh, man! Take me along. I love their food."

"So do I," Wynn confessed. "The best part is that I don't have to cook. That's the main reason I'm here."

Chris strolled up to Tia and Wynn. "Hi, Wynn." He leaned down and kissed Adam's wife on the cheek. His gaze landed on her belly. "Look at you!"

Nodding, Wynn rubbed her hand across her swollen belly. "I know. I know. I just heard that from your friend here."

His gaze skipped past Tia and landed on a spot beyond her shoulder. "Hi, Tia."

She felt a bit let down by his inability to look directly at her. She couldn't say anything with Adam's family in the suite. Instead, she responded with a pleasurable and professional, "Hi, Chris."

"I definitely wasn't expecting this." Laughing, Wynn confessed, "It sort of snuck up on us."

Grinning down at Wynn, Chris took her hand and squeezed it. "Congratulations."

"Thank you. Don't be surprised when you receive an invitation for Adam's baby shower. He's been talking about it since we all went to Krista and Brennan's."

Chuckling softly, Chris promised, "I'll keep that in mind."

Frowning, Wynn asked, "You're back. Where's my husband?"

"Right here." Adam strolled up to the workstation, placed a hand on Wynn's shoulder, and leaned down to kiss her on the cheek. "Hey, sweetheart."

Wynn turned in the chair to face her husband. Happiness spread across her face. "Hi, hon. How did the deposition go?"

"Good." Adam loosened the knot at his throat and turned to the boys. "You guys ready to go to lunch?"

"Adam!" they yelled in unison, rushing into his arms and nearly knocking him to the floor. He laughed out loud, scooping a boy in each arm and cradling them like footballs. Effortlessly, he swung them from side to side. Their screams of delight and laughter were heard throughout the suite.

When Adam put them on their feet, Kevin asked, "Are we still going?"

"Hmm. Let me think." Concentrating, Adam tapped a finger against his chin, pretending to consider their question, and finally answered, "Of course. I'm going to change, and then we'll be on our way." He started for his office and stopped. "Sweetheart, you want to come and help me?"

A blush colored Wynn's cheeks. "Sure."

"Tia, will you keep an eye on the kids for a few minutes?" Adam asked. "Maybe take them to the store for a treat."

"Will do."

"Thanks, Tia." Wynn rose and followed her husband into his office, shutting the door after her.

Tia turned to Kevin and Jimmy. "Come on. Let's go to the store and get something to drink."

"Yeah," Kevin answered.

Jimmy glanced toward Adam's door and shrugged. "Sure."

Amazed at how different married life had made Adam, Tia shook her head. She reached inside her desk drawer and grabbed her wallet. "This way." She pointed to the elevator and turned a hopeful gaze on her boyfriend. "Chris, would you like to come with us?"

"No." He shook his head, sank into her chair, and waved them away. "Thanks anyway. I'll hold down the fort while you're away."

Nodding, Tia turned toward the elevators. She had hoped he would have shown some sign of interest. Obviously, he didn't care. She swallowed her disappointment and ushered Jimmy and Kevin onto the elevator. "We'll be back in a few."

Chris sank into Tia's chair and switched on her voice mail as he watched the trio disappear behind the elevator doors. The minute they were out of sight, he ran his fingers through his hair and let out a sigh of relief. *I feel like such an ass, rat, and cheat,* he thought. Each and every minute he kept the truth from Tia made him feel like the lowest subspecies of life.

The throbbing behind his temples shifted to the frontal lobe and went from a constant beat to an almost deafening pounding. He shut one eye and massaged his temples, hoping to calm the raging storm in his head. Everything he'd sacrificed and worked for sat out of his reach until he talked to Tia.

The elevator chime rang. Chris glanced at the doors and was relieved that it wasn't Tia and the boys returning so soon. He needed time to figure out a way to approach this problem and find a resolution. He swiveled from side to side as he considered ways to get out of his predicament. How did he plan to make his relationship with Tia work out when he moved back to France?

Chris had seen the hopeful glint in her gaze when she asked him to join them on their trip to the lobby store. He couldn't. Not yet. Not until they finally talked and worked through this situation. Chris didn't want to play nice or give her false hope and then hit her with one of the most difficult situations. She didn't deserve that.

For the past three days, he had avoided any private moments with her while he debated how to tell her his news. But each time he approached her to talk about his meeting with Reynolds, something interfered. On one instance, Adam had work to discuss with Tia. Another time, Tia's mother had telephoned. It was almost impossible to have a private conversation at the office. Chris didn't feel right hitting her with Reynolds's request at her home. Since the office and her home were out, they needed a neutral place to talk. A restaurant might provide the perfect atmosphere to discuss their future without interruption.

Twenty minutes later, Tia returned with Jimmy and Kevin. The boys rushed out of the elevator and across the suite. At that moment, Adam's door opened and Wynn's giggles echoed through the area. The newlyweds left Adam's office and started for Tia's workstation.

Since marrying Wynn, Adam acted and looked like a new man. He teased and laughed with everyone. There was a different spirit about him that radiated outward and touched his coworkers with the intensity of his emotions. Chris studied the woman at his side. There was no doubt that Adam loved this woman. It was clear to everyone.

As usual, Tia looked beautiful, but there was something fragile about her that he hadn't noticed before. That wasn't true. It had been there all along. He'd ignored it while concentrating on his own issues. Seeing the sadness in Tia's eyes felt like a knife had been plunged into his heart. The strength of Tia's pain gripped him and made him feel one shade worse. This couldn't continue.

What did he truly want? The answer came swiftly and without hesitation. Chris wanted what Adam had found, the peace and happiness that came with loving and being loved. He wanted Tia to be happy and to share that radiant smile that shimmered over him and made him feel wonderful. He couldn't have it until he took the first step.

What was he waiting on? There was a simple way to make this work out.

Tia eased toward her desk cautiously. "Hey," he greeted, vacating her chair.

She smiled, but the light didn't reach her eyes as she slid into her chair.

"You guys ready to go?" Adam asked. He'd changed from a business suit to a polo shirt, denims, and sneakers. His arm rested against the doorjamb.

"Yeah!" they yelled back in unison.

Wynn peeked from under his arm and pointed a finger at Tia. "You're not going anywhere until you thank Ms. Edwards for taking you to the store and watching over you while I helped Adam."

"Thank you," Jimmy answered promptly.

Kevin ran up to Tia's side and wrapped his arms around her. "Thank you, Ms. Edwards. When are you coming to our house?"

"Yeah. That's a good question. Why don't you and Chris come over for dinner before I give up cooking?"

Adam hugged his wife close and added, "Yes, you should. We'll schedule something next week."

"It's a date," Chris replied, not wanting Tia to reject the invitation before he had a chance to talk to her.

Instantly, Tia turned in her chair and stared at Chris. Her forehead crinkled into a frown. He ignored her expression.

"Tia, Chris, it was good to see you both." Wynn halted and thoughtfully considered. "I don't think we've seen you since the wedding."

"I do believe you're correct," Chris agreed.

"Okay. We're out of here. Tia, Chris, I'll see you guys on Monday." Adam took his wife's hand

and pointed toward the elevators. "Kevin, Jimmy, hit the button."

The boys raced to the elevator, but a split second before they reached it, the doors opened. Jimmy and Kevin hurried inside. "Come on."

"We're coming."

Chris waited until after the doors closed behind the family before approaching Tia. "It was good to see them."

"Mmm-hmm," Tia responded, scooting her chair to the desk and clicking on her Word icon. She reached for a manila folder, opened it, and began scanning the pages for the task she would work on next.

Chris hovered near her desk, searching for a comment that would bring her attention back to him. Tia ignored him, spreading the work across her desk and picking up her pen to edit a document. Seconds later, she began typing furiously. After the way he had been treating her, he understood her reluctance to open herself up to him.

"What do you have planned for this evening?" Chris asked.

Tia's fingers hovered above the keyboard for a moment and then returned to her work. "Nothing much."

"Have dinner with me."

Again her hands halted. She swallowed loudly and flexed her fingers above the keyboard long enough for Chris to notice it. Hope exploded like a firecracker in his veins. Tia wasn't as indifferent as she wanted to appear. He hadn't killed their relationship or done irreparable damage.

"I don't know," she responded, focusing on her keyboard.

Chris moved closer and lowered his voice, "Please, have dinner with me. There are things we need to discuss. This is not the place to do it."

"Oh?" Tia quit typing and focused on Chris. "Really?" she offered in an offhand tone. "There hasn't been much communication from your end for the last few days. What do we need to talk about now?"

Okay, she's got you. Think it through and don't mess up, Chris warned himself silently. He wiped his sweaty palms against his trouser legs and said, "I need to talk to you about my meeting with Reynolds. Please give me the chance to explain."

Tia's expression remained impassive, but her fingers fluttered nervously over the keyboard. The tight knot of worry loosened. Things might work out. Talking meant a great deal to her. Such a long moment passed that Chris wondered if he'd misread her body language.

"Okay." She gazed at him with hope gleaming from her beautiful eyes. She wanted to believe. "I want to know. I'm not going to deny it."

"And you will. I promise. But not here."

"Where? When?"

"Tonight. I'll pick you up from your place at six and we'll have dinner."

20

At 10:00 p.m., Tia turned the key in the lock and opened her town house door. She fished around the wall for the light switch and pushed the button. Instantly, soft lighting illuminated the room. She entered the small hallway with Chris trailing after her.

"May I sit?" Chris asked.

Tia gave her consent with a wave of her hand toward the living room.

"Thanks." He eased past her.

Annoyed, Tia made an ugly face at his back. After a moment, she shook her head and shrugged. It didn't matter. Everything she did lately had little or no effect on him.

The conversation Chris promised to have at dinner never materialized. He had taken her to Sindbad's on the Detroit River and encouraged her to order the whole lobster. Throughout the evening, her dinner companion kept a steady stream of dialogue going about every topic except the one he promised. Each time she brought up Reynolds's name or the company, Chris cleverly and quickly changed the subject. They dined, drank wine, ate dessert of key lime pie, and then headed to her place.

Tia folded her arms across her chest and tapped her foot against the floor. They would not continue this way. If Chris didn't start explaining real soon, she'd tell him to leave her home and never come back. Their so-called relationship would be over. Granted, losing Chris would be devastating, but she'd survive. She'd get on with her life.

During her breakup with Darnell, Tia learned a valuable lesson—take charge and stop waiting for life to come to you. She didn't plan to repeat any of her previous mistakes.

Since all of her previous efforts to talk to Chris had been ignored, Tia had decided that the best course of action was to let Chris maintain his silence until he felt ready to talk. For three days, she had held to this resolution until today, when Chris asked her out.

As Tia neared the living room, the theme music from the ten o'clock news wafted through the air. She found Chris sitting on her sofa channel-surfing with the remote. Deliberately putting some distance between them, Tia sank into the leather recliner located across from the television. She waited for several minutes for Chris to open the conversation. The silence in the room grew louder and more pronounced.

Angry and frustrated, Tia opened her mouth

to demand an explanation when Chris switched off the television, put the remote on the table, and turned to her. An impassive mask covered his face, but his eyes burned with an intense flame.

"I didn't want to talk about this at Sindbad's," Chris explained.

Caught off guard by this turn of conversation, Tia snapped her lips shut and glared at Chris, waiting for him to continue.

He leaned forward, laced his fingers together, and let them hang between his spread legs. "When I stepped through the door of Reynolds's office, I thought he was planning to fire me."

"But he didn't," Tia responded.

Chris shook his head. "No."

"What did he want?" she asked cautiously, drawing her bottom lip between her teeth. Now that the time had come, she felt conflicted about what she would hear. Did she really want to know what went on in Reynolds's office that fateful day? Of course she did. Unfortunately, this added to Tia's insecurities. She didn't feel confident enough in their relationship to ask all of the questions that troubled her.

"Reynolds asked me about how I was settling in. He wanted to know if I felt comfortable with everything going on around me."

"And then?" Tia asked quietly, leaning closer to hear each word of Chris's story. Her insides churned. Somehow, she knew their world was on the brink of a major life-changing moment.

"He put a stop to a lot of things," Chris answered so softly Tia almost didn't hear him. The words were far too important to ignore.

"What did he want?"

Tia gazed at Chris's face and saw pain and frustration looking back at her.

"There's been some trouble at the home office." Chris took a deep breath and let it out slowly. Up to this point, he'd focused on the floor. Now he captured and held her gaze as he continued. "Reynolds had to put the chief attorney on administrative leave pending an investigation."

Tia's heart pounded erratically against her rib cage. She had an unpleasant idea where this tale might be headed. "What's that got to do with you?"

"With Pierce on administrative leave, there are some legal issues that need to be resolved. I can't explain further. Let's just say the office is in an uproar."

Stunned, she leaned back in her chair and muttered, "Oh, man!" Now she understood part of the reason he'd kept this discussion to himself. Reynolds would not want this information hitting the office rumor mill nor reaching the media. Besides, if it were leaked, Reynolds would know from whom.

Her mouth went dry. The stiff set of Chris's shoulders and the taut expression on his face revealed that he hadn't reached the end of the story. There was still something more he needed to tell her. Her erratically beating heart kicked into a full gallop while her palms turned sweaty as she anxiously awaited an unpleasant end.

The room felt hot. Tia tried to draw fresh air into her lungs, but it didn't happen. Instead, all she could muster were short, shallow breaths. That didn't stop her from encouraging him. "Go on. Tell me the rest."

"Because I trained under Pierce, Reynolds felt I would be the best person to replace him. He wants me to take over the home office's legal department." His pale blue eyes begged her to understand.

Tia did. She understood what a huge leap in his career this offer meant. But an important question loomed: Where did that leave her and their new romance?

Wait, maybe this isn't all bad. Don't jump to any conclusions, she cautioned silently. *Give Chris time to explain the whole situation. This is a wonderful chance for him. If he makes the right moves, he could wind up as a senior vice president like Adam. He could be gone for a few weeks and back before I really miss him.*

"For how long?" Tia questioned in a small, emotionless tone. She held her breath, waiting for his answer.

"A year to eighteen months."

Tia gasped and fell back in her chair. She shivered, feeling the heat seep from her body as the cold chill of reality took possession. That meant the end of their relationship. They couldn't survive an extended period like eighteen months. "What did you tell Reynolds?"

Chris rose from the sofa and crossed the room, crouching next to her chair. He reached for her hand and held it tightly between both of his, massaging the cold limb. "What could I tell him? Tia, I don't have a choice. Reynolds made it clear that I'm needed and must leave within the month."

She looked everywhere but at him. "What about us? Where does that leave you and me?"

"Scrambling."

Confused, she frowned back at him. "What?"

"We're searching for a way to be together, to not let this situation destroy us. Believe me, this is not how I wanted to do things, *chérie*. We agreed to take our relationship slow and easy, to get to know each other before taking things to the serious level. *Malheureusement,* the world of business and Gautier International Motors has no interest in our plans. So, I've had to make adjustments for our future."

Tia didn't like the sound of his conversation. It almost sounded as if he'd already made a decision for the both of them and merely came here to tell her of his intentions. She braced for the worst.

"Look at me, Tia."

Doing as he asked, she studied the man she'd opened her heart to and learned to love. "Yes."

"I love you. *Je t'aime,*" he whispered in his native tongue.

That got Tia's attention. Those were the words she longed to hear from him, but she didn't expect to hear them, at least not so soon. Should she respond in kind? The feelings were there. After all, Chris planned to leave her. Was it the right thing to do, to expose her feelings this way?

He drew in a shaky breath and forged ahead, "This is where you say something appropriately similar. Even in English, I'd understand."

Tia opened her mouth, but words failed her. Doubt filled her. Should she admit the truth and accept the consequences, or should she guard her heart and shield her feelings? Her first instinct was to protect herself, but nothing good ever happened when she hid from life. One thing she knew for certain: If she didn't try, she'd end up alone, regretting her decision. Ending up alone was still a possibility, but at least she would have given the relationship her best.

She'd spent years with Darnell, and it had gotten her nothing but a lot of wasted time. Since Chris entered her life, she felt loved, cared for, and treated like something precious. He sought her opinion and listened to her questions on many topics.

Tia drew air into her lungs and took the plunge. A lump the size of a football made it difficult to speak. She pushed past it and said, "I love you, too." There, the words were out, lingering in the tense air.

A smile of pure joy spread across Chris's face. He dropped her hand and took her face between his large hands. He gazed into her eyes. "Tia, *je t'aime,*" he announced a second time. Chris switched to English and repeated, "I love you. I have from the moment I met you in Adam's office."

A light brush against her lips reminded her of Chris's first kiss. It left Tia quivering and craving more. His warm, moist lips moved over hers in an intimate caress. Eager, Tia parted her lips. Instantly, Chris tenderly sucked her lower lip into his mouth, nibbling gently.

His scent filled her nostrils, making her head swim. Tia wrapped her arms around him. Her hands crept up his arms and slid around his neck, tugging him closer. Moaning softly, Chris dropped his arms to her waist and pulled her hard against him.

Chris's tongue stroked hers, seeking, tasting, and teasing. Her hands ran through his blond hair, enjoying the feel of the fine tresses between her fingers.

He ended the kiss and stood. He took Tia's hand and led her from the room. They strolled down the hallway, up the stairs, and into her bedroom. Stopping next to the bed, Tia sank onto the mattress. Chris sat next to her. He leaned down and kissed her. Anticipation made her heart pump faster and harder as she returned the kiss. She grew warm with excitement as the taste of him flowed through her, and the idea of making love with Chris for the second time was becoming a reality. Everything she remembered about that ultimate act had been wonderful and satisfying. She really wanted to share it with him again.

As the kiss deepened and lingered, Chris's fingers lightly glided across the curve of her neck, gently settling on her shoulder. His nearness made her senses spin out of control, creating a sense of wonder and longing.

While he kissed her, she slipped her hand under

his sweater and caressed the hot skin and tight muscles. Her hands stroked his nipples. She rolled the hard buds between her fingers and tweaked them. Chris moaned tenderly into her mouth.

He worked her top from her shoulders before ending the kiss. He removed the rest of her clothes and then turned his attention to his own. Once they were both completely naked, his appreciative gaze slid over her body. "You are magnificent."

Tia examined the differences between their skin tones, running her hand against his chest. It amazed her to think that although they come from such different cultures, it didn't matter. They belonged together.

Chris took Tia's erect nipple between his lips and sucked. She arched her back, encouraging him to continue with a hand to the back of his head. He trailed a single finger down the middle of her throat, where he lingered against her Adam's apple before continuing its path to her breast. Her skin quivered every place that he touched. His thumb halted at her breast, stroking back and forth across the sensitive nipple. Not satisfied, he took her breast into his mouth and sucked on the bud, sending heat flowing through her and settling between her legs.

Tia cradled his head, pushing her breast farther into his mouth. "That feels so good," she encouraged.

Releasing her, Chris answered, "It tastes good, too."

She planted her feet on the mattress and

scooted up until she reached the center of the bed. She lay back and opened her arms, beckoning Chris to her. He followed her down and spread himself over her, taking her lips in a series of loving kisses.

As Chris kissed her, his hand made a journey lower, finding her hot female core with his fingers. He combed through the curls shielding her slit, moving between the folds and stroking her most sensitive parts. He stroked back and forth, establishing a rhythm that she found herself moving to. They danced. With each pass of his thumb, Tia's insides grew warmer as the first involuntary tremor hit her and continued in waves until she could no longer control herself. She flew into orbit. Her hips flew up off the bed as she called out his name. "Chris!" Wave after wave of pleasure made her blood surge through her as she slowly returned to earth.

"Yes?" he rose from the bed, left the room, and returned minutes later with a foil-wrapped item. He tore open the packet and quickly rolled the latex over his thick flesh. Chris settled next to her and took her into his arms. Wanting to give him a measure of the ecstasy she'd just felt, Tia moved her hand between their bodies, searching for his rigid length. She found the engorged shaft and toyed with it, stroking up and down, learning its size, shape, and texture. Chris caught his breath and placed his hand over hers, demonstrating how he liked to be touched.

He removed her hand and in one quick thrust joined their bodies. Panting, he slowly began to move inside her, sliding deep within her canal and then almost withdrawing, learning how she enjoyed being loved. He buried his face against the soft column of her neck. Again and again, Chris's thrusts pumped inside of her, stroking her female walls with his shaft. Tia clenched her interior muscles and wrapped her legs around his waist. She met each downward thrust of his body with an upward lift of her hips, holding him tightly within her hot, liquid walls.

He moaned, "You feel perfect, *chérie*."

Smiling, Tia had to admit that he did, too.

They climbed the stairs to heaven together, giving and taking love, moving together, soaring together as one until Tia couldn't hold back any longer. Her legs began to tremble and her heart sped up. She held on to her composure until he reached between their bodies and stroked his finger along her slit. She exploded, crying out his name a second time.

He followed her lead, climbing a step or two higher and then crashing. They floated to earth together. Chris took her face between his hands and kissed her deeply. "I love you, *chérie*. Thank you for letting me love you."

Caressing his cheek with her fingertips, Tia answered, "You're welcome. It was everything I expected and more."

Chris settled down next to her, pulling her into his arms. She felt the warmth of perspiration on his chest against her breasts. *"Je t'aime."*

Tia threw an arm around his middle and snuggled close to his side. She inhaled the aroma of pure male and sex. "I'm going to take a nap, and then I want to do that again," she told him.

Chuckling, he hugged her against his side. "We will, *chérie*. We will," he promised.

Sighing, Tia shut her eyes and relaxed. "Good."

21

The insistent ringing of the telephone pulled Tia from her wonderful cocoon of sleep. Partially awake, she fumbled for the receiver. What she encountered was warm, male flesh.

Tia opened her eyes in time to see Chris roll away and reach for the phone. She moaned in protest at losing the connection of warm, naked flesh against naked flesh.

"*Bonjour? Bonjour?*" His brows bunched together as he waited for a response and then returned the phone to its cradle.

"Wrong number?" she asked.

Chris shook his head. "No. They hung up. They didn't like the accent."

"Oh, well. I like the accent and everything else about you." Tia shrugged, craving contact with his warm, solid frame and scooting closer to his side.

"Good morning, *chérie*. In case you've forgotten, I love you," he whispered with a smile on his lips. Eyes twinkling, he leaned down to kiss her and caress her lips while stroking her face with the tips of his fingers.

Tia's smile turned into a full grin as she felt her body leap to life from his innocent touch. "Good morning to you, too. And in case you've forgotten, I love you, too."

"Never!" he promised with another mind-altering kiss.

Stroking the long, lean line of his back with her fingertips, Tia returned his kiss. Her body quivered as his hand slid up her inner thigh, stopping inches from her hair-covered mound.

As he leaned down for another kiss, the phone rang again. Chris picked up the receiver. This time he switched to English. "'Ello?" He paused, listening to the person on the other end. "Just a moment." Chris handed the receiver to Tia. "It's for you."

Naturally, Tia thought, rolling her eyes toward the ceiling. *After all, it is my town house.* She put the phone to her ear and said, "Hello?"

"Well, I didn't expect that."

Tia's heart almost stopped. Heat burned her cheeks and raced up the back of her neck. She reached for the sheet and draped it over her body, turning a little away from Chris. Great! Of all the people to call her . . . Tia fought the urge to duck under the sheet. "Hello, Momma."

Oh, man! This is so embarrassing. No! Stop this! I have nothing to be ashamed of. I'm an adult. This is my house, she chastened. *I pay the cost to be the boss. Yeah, but she's still my mother. Momma knows I'm grown, and what I do in my bedroom isn't her business.*

Frowning with concern, Chris settled on his elbows, stroking her cheek with his finger. "Something wrong?"

Tia shook off his hand and placed a quieting hand to her lips.

"It sounds like you have company. Did I catch you at a bad time?" Mrs. Edwards stated with a touch of sarcasm in her voice.

"No. Chris came over for breakfast. But I've got the stove on. Let me call you back a little later," Tia improvised, crossing her fingers in a childhood gesture she used whenever she spun a tale.

"No can do," her mother stated. "This will only take a minute. I won't be home for a good while. Your father and I are driving to Chicago for a couple of days, and we won't be back until late Sunday evening. So I'm going to say what I have to say and let you get back to your breakfast."

"Okay. Go ahead." All Tia wanted was to get off the phone and end this embarrassing moment.

"Yours and Nia's birthday is coming up. I'd like to have a birthday dinner for you at home with your brothers. Put it on your calendar."

"Sure. When?"

Chris flipped onto his stomach next to her. He watched her with a sensual glimmer in his eyes. Suddenly, his expression changed from sated to mischievous. He grinned at her, lifted the sheet, and ducked under it.

Tia stared, lips pressed together. *What is he up to?* she silently wondered. His naked derriere sat exposed in the air. Suddenly, she understood what Chris had in mind. Tiny kisses began at her knees and moved closer and closer to her center. He palmed one of her breasts in one hand, toying with her nipple with his fingers. She gasped softly.

"You all right?" her mother asked.

"Yeah. The bacon grease popped on my hand," Tia lied as an inferno caught fire in a different location. She grabbed Chris's wrist with her free hand and tried to pry it away from her body. He refused to budge.

"Be careful," Mrs. Edwards warned. "You've got delicate skin. I don't want you hurting yourself."

"I won't."

She rolled onto her side in an attempt to dislodge his hand. Chris compensated by rolling toward her. He moved up her body, returning his attention to her breast. He stroked the other nipple with his tongue, licking it as if it were a sucker, starting under the sensitive flesh and slowly moving up and over until he'd tasted the complete bud. He circled it with his tongue, causing Tia to move restlessly as a flicker of heat burst into a flame. After a moment, he took the brown button into his mouth and sucked strongly on it. Instantly, her body responded and rose off the bed. Moaning, Tia cupped her hand over the mouthpiece as she twisted back and forth on the bed. She was so involved with what Chris was doing to her that she almost missed her mother's next comment.

"I've got to check with your twin," Mrs. Edwards explained. "Dinner will probably be next weekend after she closes her shop for the night. You know, there's another way to do this. How does Sunday afternoon work for you? That way, we don't have to worry about that damn shop, and your brothers are always available on Sunday. I like that idea much better. How about you?"

She panted softly. This man was driving her crazy. No matter how she turned, he followed. The pleasure was excruciating. She wanted it to stop, and yet she didn't. She wanted to scream, but she couldn't. "That'll work. Sounds good."

"Good. We have a plan."

Not sure if she could hold on any longer, she waited. *Please, Momma, hang up*, she begged silently. She couldn't take much more of Chris's taunting.

Without a word, Chris's physical assault ended. With a swift kiss to her belly button, he scooted from under the sheet, hopped off the bed, and started for the door. At the entrance, he turned, winked, and then disappeared down the hall.

With a sigh of relief, Tia fell back on the pillows. Thankful, but unfulfilled, she lay there with the phone to her ear. He had stopped. She was happy, right? Or was she?

"I'll get back with you once I've talked to your sister and brothers."

"Okay."

"And, young lady?"

Tia hated that tone. Throughout her childhood, nothing good ever followed that phrase. "Yes?"

"We'll talk about Mr. Frenchman real soon. It's time for a reality check," Mrs. Edwards warned.

Dreading this conversation, Tia shut her eyes. "Yeah, we do need to talk. Give me a call when you get back. Have fun in Chicago. We haven't done lunch or gone shopping in a while."

"We used to do something every weekend. I wonder what happened. Oh, I remember. Mr. Frenchman came along."

"Bye, Momma. You and Daddy have a safe and fun trip."

Breathing a sigh of relief, Tia disconnected the call and returned the phone to the cradle. She really didn't want to talk with her mother about Chris. Life didn't always present a person with choices. Chris was part of her life now, and Momma needed to accept him. Hopefully, her dislike of Chris would change and she would accept him into the family.

The object of her thoughts strolled into the bedroom and scooped Tia into his arms.

"Hey!" she exclaimed. "Where are you taking me?"

"You'll see."

He headed out of the bedroom and down the hall to the bathroom. As he pushed open the door with his foot, steam from the shower met their naked bodies.

"Oh!" she exclaimed as Chris strolled into the room, pushed back the shower curtain, and deposited her in the bathtub. The warm water sprinkled over her. He followed her into the shower and pulled the curtain closed, cocooning them in their own private little world.

Without uttering a word, he reached for her, pulling her against his body. His head dipped and he took her lips in an overwhelming kiss. Their tongues dueled as the water cascaded over them.

Chris moved away and grabbed the shower puff. He squeezed out a generous portion of shower gel and rubbed the puff to a frothy head. He stretched out her arm and ran the soapy puff up and down her wet skin, repeating the gesture with her other arm. Before long, he'd washed her entire body, paying close attention to the curly hair at the junction between her legs. With an encouraging hand, he moved her forward as the sprays of water rinsed away the soap.

Chris smiled, running an admiring gaze over her body. Tia grew warm as his eyes stopped at her breasts and lingered. He moved close and took her face between his hands, and then he nibbled along her jawline until he reached her mouth. He parted her lips with his tongue and took another kiss. His tongue swept across hers, tasting and touching. Tia couldn't get enough. She moved closer, rubbing her body against his. After a moment, Chris smiled and said, "You know what I really want to do?"

Panting, she answered, "No. What?"

"I want to taste you."

Tia's eyes grew large. All the air rushed out of her. This had never happened to her before. Worried, she studied Chris. *Was he serious?* she wondered. Tia had her doubts, but Chris had been such a wonderful, sensual lover that she couldn't refuse him.

"Trust me," he said, nipping at the sensitive cord of

her neck. He made a trail of damp, openmouthed kisses down her shoulder to her breast. Like earlier, he licked her nipple, circling the brown nub with his tongue before taking it into his mouth.

His hand moved lower, cupping her warmth and slipping a finger between the lips. Chris took the bud between his fingers and rubbed. Tia almost lifted off the ground.

"Hold on," he warned. Chris wrapped his arms around her waist, keeping her on her feet.

Tia sighed as her legs quivered. She became seriously concerned that her legs wouldn't support her.

His tongue was doing wonderful things: caressing, kissing, and sucking her breast. He let her nipple slip from his lips before dropping to his knees. The spray from the shower head flattened his blond locks against his skull.

Focused on his goal, Chris ignored the water and circled her navel with his tongue. He hovered near her feminine core. His hand stroked her rear cheeks, cupping the flesh as he urged her forward. Tia tensed, feeling the heat, considering what Chris was about to do. He gently parted her legs and moved between them. Chris drew in a deep breath. "You smell wonderful."

Ever so lightly, he flicked his tongue across her bud.

Tia trembled against his tongue. *Oh, man!* Her hands curled into his hair. She wasn't sure she could handle this type of intimacy.

Chris gazed up at her and smiled. "Excellent. You taste so sweet. But I want more," he said.

"Much more." He proceeded to latch on to her nub and drink from her essence. He held her firmly as the onslaught from his tongue began, making it almost impossible for Tia to stand. She leaned against the tile wall, resting her head as the sensations overtook her.

Tia's hips rose to meet Chris's lips. The sensations were so intense that she found it difficult to concentrate on anything but the feel of his tongue as it swept across her clit and then surrounded the bud. He sucked long and hard on her flesh, making Tia wish for a sweet release but loving every minute as it continued.

Fighting against the coming orgasm, her legs shook uncontrollably as her fingers dug into his shoulders. She moaned appreciatively at his non-stop assault on her body. "Chris!" she cried, certain she wouldn't be able to stand much longer. Tia felt his smile against her thighs, and she took great pleasure in knowing that Chris was enjoying touching her this way as much as she was loving being touched.

Chris took her higher and higher as his tongue did its magic, making this one of the most unforgettable experiences of her life. Her interior walls quivered, about to shatter. Chris was making her feel so good. She didn't know how long she could hold out.

Unable to hold back, she cried out his name, "Chris!" Drained, sated, and completely limp, Tia fell into Chris's arms.

Getting to his feet, Chris caught her. "Wrap your legs around me, *chérie*," he directed.

Tia did as she was told and was rewarded with the joining of their bodies. They moaned together. The hot length of his flesh filled her. She clenched her canal muscles around his shaft. A fierce growl escaped Chris's mouth.

With an arm wrapped around her, he pressed her against the cool walls of the shower tiles and pumped into her with renewed energy. They came together in a fierce, loving dance that Tia didn't want to end.

Tia folded her legs at the ankle around his waist and greeted each downward thrust with an upward lift of her body. Chris was wonderful. She loved the feel of him moving in and out of her. She felt like a part of him.

Rotating his hip as he thrust inside her, Chris moved faster, harder, creating a new wave of sensations within her. Suddenly, it was all too much; she couldn't hold back anymore. Her interior walls shook with the force of his movements. The tempo of his loving changed. Chris stroked her with his flesh. Her blood pounded. Tia exploded. Seconds later, Chris moaned out her name and she felt the warm, wet release of his orgasm.

Tia's legs released him and slid downward. Her feet touched the bathtub and Chris slipped his arms under her legs and lifted her off her feet. He strolled out of the bathroom with Tia in his arms. After placing Tia in the center of the bed, he kissed her and said, "I'll be right back. I'm going to turn off the water."

Minutes later, Chris returned with a huge towel in his hand. He dried her skin and then dropped the towel on the floor. Chris snuggled against her.

Tia shut her eyes and relaxed in the shelter of his arms. The last thing she remembered was Chris whispering into her damp hair, "I love you, *chérie.*"

22

Chris carried an exhausted, sated, and naked Tia back to the bedroom and placed her among the bedding. She turned on her side and snuggled into the pillow.

He sat on the edge of the bed and ran a caressing hand from her neck down to her spine, settling over her rear. He kneaded the warm flesh and leaned close to nibble along her neck and shoulder. Chris whispered close to her ear, "Come on, sleepyhead. It's time to get up. We've got things to do today. I'm going to make breakfast."

Food! Tia's eyes popped open and landed on Chris's derriere as he moved across the floor and picked up his trousers. She enjoyed the flash of flesh as he stepped into the pants and pulled the zipper into place.

"As much as I'd like to spend the day in bed with you, there are other things that need our attention. I'll see you downstairs in a few minutes."

Nodding, Tia moaned. She didn't want to get

up. Turning on her side, she shoved her face into the pillow as the pungent odor of sex rose from the sheet, permeating the room. She shut her eyes, and the image of Chris on his knees in front of her became vividly real. Water cascaded over his blond head and down his broad shoulders. It had been some of the best sex of her life, and she couldn't wait to have more.

She inhaled. Images of their time in the shower flashed before her. Heat rushed up her neck and settled into her cheeks when she thought of the things she had allowed Chris to do to her. Under the warm spray of the showerhead, she'd learned new and very enjoyable variations of lovemaking.

Chris was thorough and loving, which made Tia feel very special to him. He had created the most powerful sensations she had ever experienced. Maybe this was what it meant to love somebody completely. Or, perhaps it had been such a long time since she had made love that everything seemed new and different.

Whatever the reason, she enjoyed every moment with him and felt connected to him in a way that she had never felt with Darnell. She scoffed. Darnell had never taken her to the places Chris so effortessly had. She felt as if their bodies and their souls were connected when they made love. There were times during their intimate moments that she felt as if Chris anticipated her every need, giving to her unselfishly.

Once he left the room, Tia rolled off the bed to get dressed. She removed underwear, a pair of navy sweatpants, and a matching long-sleeve sweatshirt from her dresser drawers and slipped into them. With a hand on the side of the bed for support, she dropped to her knees to search for a pair of running shoes. Tia pulled pair after pair of work and play shoes from under the bed. "I've got to clean this up real soon," she muttered, pushing aside several pairs of work pumps. Finally, she found her Nikes. Tia rose and put them on.

There were still a lot of questions that needed answers. Where were they headed next? Tia placed her right ankle on her left knee to tie her shoe. She reversed the procedure and did up the left shoe. Although they had admitted their true feelings for each other, nothing else had been settled. Did Chris expect her to wait until he returned from his assignment in France? That would be more than a year of waiting. She grunted. That idea didn't appeal to her. Was she supposed to visit him once he returned home? Maybe after breakfast they could sit down and hash out the particulars of their relationship so that she didn't feel as if her life would be in limbo.

Tia took a moment to tidy her bedroom. A flush of red heat colored her cheeks when she picked up their clothes and folded them. She laid the garments on a chair and left the room, bouncing down the stairs. On the first floor, the aroma of frying bacon and brewing coffee filled her nostrils.

Elton John's "Bennie and the Jets" was playing from the radio. Chris sang along to the tune, except his rendition was a little different.

Tia giggled. It was really cute to hear the lyrics sung in a sexy French drawl.

Chris rounded the corner and took her into his arms, giving her another one of those kisses that sent her senses into space. "Good morning."

Brushing her hands through his hair, she replied, "Hey."

Chris asked, "What were you laughing at?"

"You. B-B-B-Bennie and the Jets," she imitated his French accent.

"Keep it up and I'll get you."

Grinning, Tia added, "As long as you get me like you did this morning, I'm all for it."

He ran his tongue across her lips, savoring the taste of her like she was a precious chocolate. "My pleasure."

His reference to their interlude in the shower made Tia feel incredibly embarrassed and shy. Lowering her head, she brushed a lock of hair from her forehead. She stepped around him, entered the tiny dining area, and took a seat at the table. Chris followed behind her, stopped next to her, and brushed a caressing hand from her warm cheek to her neck before continuing to the kitchen.

Bare-chested and shoeless, Chris moved around her kitchen as if he'd cooked meals in her house for years. He smiled at Tia as he started another song in French. He watched her over the counter.

"Did you find everything you needed?" she asked, moving the cutlery from the left to the right and back again.

"*Oui.* Your kitchen is wonderfully stocked." He

picked up a pot holder and removed a pan from the range. "Breakfast is almost ready."

Tia rose, intent on helping Chris in the kitchen.

Chris waved her back. "Sit, sit. I can handle this meal."

Following his instructions, Tia sank back into her chair. The table was set for two, excluding plates. She picked up the pitcher of orange juice and filled his glass with vitamin C. She sipped the chilled beverage.

"We're having cheese and mushroom omelets, bacon, and English muffins," he announced from the range. "I found strawberry jam in the fridge."

"Sounds good."

"Do you cook often?"

She shook her head. "No. Only when necessary."

Frowning, Chris asked, "How do you eat?"

"Takeout."

Grunting, Chris said, "That's not healthy." He wagged a finger in Tia's direction. "We'll have to do something about that."

Tia grinned and then added, "If you plan on cooking, I'm all for it. But it's not something I do on a regular basis."

"Maybe we'll share the duties."

She pretended to consider the issue, tapping a finger against her chin. "I can work with that."

Chris strolled back and forth between the dining room and kitchen, placing plates of hot food on the table. Finally, he returned with two empty plates. He placed one on his place mat and the other in front of Tia.

She glanced down and frowned. Something small and glittering sat in the center of the plate. A ring. A huge pear-shaped diamond. Two smaller square diamonds flanked the larger one, and small diamonds surrounded the silver band.

Chris moved to her side, dropped to one knee, and grabbed her numb hand within both of his. "We got very busy and carried away last night. I didn't have a chance to ask you the question on my mind."

The huskiness in his voice shook her to her core. She found her insides quivering in response to his voice.

"Tia Edwards, I love you. I know that we've got a lot of stuff to sort out, but I do believe that we can do it. Will you marry me and come to France?"

Tears pooled in Tia's eyes. She knew they needed to talk and work out details. Today wasn't the day for all of that. She dragged her tongue across her dry lips and cupped Chris's cheek. "I love you, too."

His eyes glittered with hope and love. "Is that a yes? *Oui*? No?"

Tia nodded.

A spark of sheer joy ignited and spread across his face. Chris took the ring from the plate and slid it onto the ring finger of Tia's left hand and kissed it. "I promise to love you even when you're groggy."

"I'll love you when you get up and act entirely

too chipper and happy in the morning." She giggled and leaned down for a quick kiss.

Helping Tia rise from her chair, Chris drew her into his arms and held her close against him. "Thank you for loving me."

"No, thank you."

Overcome with emotion, Chris's voice shook when he waved a hand at the table and said, "Come. Sit, sit. We need to eat before the food grows cold."

Sitting down, Chris reached for her hand. "I have one more thing to say to you. No matter what happens between us or how angry you make me, I promise to end our evenings with a kiss."

"Good, because you're a great kisser." Grinning, Tia took his hand and kissed the palm. "I look forward to that."

Nervously, Tia twisted her brand-new engagement ring back and forth on her finger as she glanced at the computer clock for the fifth time. Today was D-day. They had decided to make their engagement and future plans public.

Chris ambled out of his office and stopped at her desk, whispering in her ear, "Wish me luck."

As usual, the sound of that husky, accented voice made her quiver inside. She touched his hand and squeezed it. "Good luck."

He drew in a deep breath and let it out, showing her a not-so-steady hand. "Can you believe it? I'm nervous."

"Not you," Tia teased with a note of fake surprise

in her tone. "Not my big, handsome Frenchman." She grinned and stroked his cheek. "Poor baby. He's never nervous."

"That's true." Chris pulled on the tie knot. "Except for today. What about you? Do you want to wait until I get back and then we'll talk to Adam together?"

Shaking her head, she answered, "No. This is between him and me. I want to tell him by myself."

"So certain?" His eyebrows rose. "Should I be jealous?"

"No. I love you. But Adam's been good to me, and he deserves to hear about our engagement from me. This is sort of like you with Reynolds. He's been your friend and a mentor for years. Reynolds deserves to get the news from you."

"You're right."

Tia tilted her head toward the hallway. "Now go."

"Man. You are one bossy woman."

"Am I? Well, at least you know it now. It gives you all the time in the world to renege on your proposal."

"Never. See you later." Chuckling, he squeezed her hand and started through the maze of cubicles, heading to the executive offices.

A part of her felt like a rat. Since coming to work for Adam, she'd learned so much. Plus, he always pushed her to do and be more. Without Adam's urging, she would never have finished her bachelor's degree. After all, she had a good job. Why bother wasting her time on furthering her education?

There wasn't anything else she could do until Adam returned from his breakfast meeting with Judge Archer. Tia focused on her routine duties for the time being.

Deep into her work, Tia didn't hear Adam when he returned. She looked up and there he stood with his cell phone attached to his ear.

He stopped at her desk and picked up his messages. Talking softly into the phone, he took several steps toward his office, halted, and returned to Tia's workstation with a puzzled expression on his face.

"I'll call you back." He disconnected the call and slipped the phone into the breast pocket of his suit jacket.

"Hi," Tia greeted. *What was he staring at?* she wondered.

"What's that on your finger?" Adam pointed at her left hand.

Oh, man! The time has come. There wouldn't be any small talk before she hit him with the engagement stuff. "A ring."

"Does it mean what I think it does?" he asked dubiously.

"Yes."

"To whom?" he asked in a soft tone.

Adam's question surprised Tia.

He added cautiously, "It's not Darnell, is it?"

Grimacing with distaste, Tia received a second shock. "God, no! Why would you ask that?"

He let out a hiss of disgust. "Sometimes things happen. People make up regardless of who they're seeing. I didn't want it to be Darnell, but I had to ask. It's Chris, correct?"

Nodding with a smile on her face, Tia twisted the ring around her finger. "Yes."

Adam ran a hand over his face and then added, "That also means you'll be leaving Gautier and me within the month."

"Yes."

He circled the desk and came up behind her, lifting her from the chair. Adam took her into his arms and hugged her close. "I'm going to miss you. You've become an integral part of my day." Grinning, Adam let her go and returned to his place on the other side of the workstation. "Well, I guess I should have expected it. That boy has been one step behind you since the day he arrived."

Fighting back tears, Tia admitted, "I'll miss you, too."

"Hey, what's going on here?" Chris asked, strolling up to Tia's workstation.

Adam turned to Chris and stuck out his hand. "I understand congratulations are in order."

Grinning, Chris took Adam's hand and pumped it up and down. "Yes, they are."

Adam pinched his chin with his forefinger and thumb. "I assume that you've just come from Reynolds's office."

Chris nodded.

"When are you leaving and taking my favorite executive assistant with you?"

"Couple of weeks. A month at the latest," Chris answered.

Adam nodded. "That's what I figured. Tia, I need your recommendations on who you think would make an adequate replacement, although no one can replace you."

"Thank you." Tears pooled in Tia's eyes. Telling Adam hadn't been as difficult as she had expected. Her boss always put the needs of his staff ahead of the company. She would miss him and the position. Adam gave her challenging work that allowed her to grow as an employee of Gautier.

Pulling herself together, Tia gazed at Chris and smiled. She moved to his side and slipped her fingers through his. Her future belonged with him. Although she felt nervous and a wee bit worried about what the future held for them, she belonged at his side.

23

    With expert driving skills, Chris zipped into a space behind Junior's truck and cut the bike's engine. Panic and dread made Tia's heart pound as she glanced at her parents' home. She never considered her parents' home a place to fear. It had always been a haven. Although it was her birthday celebration, she felt certain things were not going to be jovial for very long. Today's party would be filled with drama and would end very differently from other family gatherings.

    Chris removed his helmet, grabbed the strap, and slipped it over the metal handlebars. He then tossed his leg over the handlebars and stood, holding out a hand for Tia.

    They stood on the street in front of her parents' home. Tia handed her helmet to Chris, and he placed it next to his. She finger-combed her wavy locks as he waited next to the bike. Offering Tia a reassuring smile, Chris placed a possessive hand at the small of her back and guided her up the walk. At the stairs, he turned to her and asked, "This is your last chance. Are you fine with the way we've planned things? Do you want to change anything?"

"No." Her insides twisted into one big knot. Grimacing, Tia admitted, "To tell you the truth, I really wish I could run away and not deal with this."

Chuckling softly, Chris stroked her cheek with the back of his hand. "Sorry, *chérie*. We've got to talk to your family today. We're out of time. Reynolds is pushing for a date when we'll be flying home. He wants it to be sooner rather than later."

"I know," she whined. "But I can wish, can't I?"

He leaned down and tasted her lips. "Always. There will be days that I plan to make your wishes come true. Unfortunately, today isn't one of them. We have to talk to your folks, and whether you like it or not, they need to know about our future together."

Nodding, Tia twisted her new engagement ring around her finger. With a regretful sigh, she removed it and slipped the silver band into her capri pants' pocket. "I'm going to act like we're still dating."

"Correct."

"You're going to take my parents aside and ask for my hand in marriage."

"Mmm-hmm."

"And then all hell is going to break loose, and I'm going to sneak out the back door," she added with an edge of sarcasm.

Laughing, he hugged her. "No, it's not. Your parents are reasonable people. They'll understand."

Dream on. You don't know my mother, Tia thought, patting her pocket to make sure her ring was safe.

The front door to the house opened, and Junior stepped onto the porch. "Hey, you two. Come on in. How are we going to have a party when one of the birthday girls is hanging outside?"

"Good question." Chris took Tia's hand and climbed the steps. "How are you doing, Greg?"

"Perfect." He slapped his hand into Chris's palm and pumped it up and down before letting go and turning to his sister. Junior wrapped Tia in a huge bear hug. "Happy birthday, little girl."

Tia returned the hug. "Thanks, but I'm not a little girl."

"You'll always be to me," Junior replied.

"What's Momma cooking?" she asked.

Her oldest brother rolled his eyes. "Everything."

The trio laughed.

"Come on." Junior steered Tia toward the front door. Chris followed. "Let's get inside." Junior grabbed Tia's arm and led her inside the house with Chris bringing up the rear. "We're all in the family room."

As they closed in on the family room, Junior stopped. His face was scrunched into a mask of embarrassment. "Uh . . . Uh . . . ," Junior began.

"What?" she asked.

"There's something you need to know before you go in there."

Lips pursed, she waited.

Junior scrubbed a hand over his face. "Look, I don't know how he figured this out." As he spoke, a man stepped into the hallway from the restroom.

Shocked, Tia gasped. Darnell! Who invited him? Whipping around to face Junior, she poked a finger at his gut. "You should have warned us."

"I'm sorry. I didn't know what to say," Greg Junior admitted.

Grinning, Tia's ex-boyfriend strolled up to the trio and stepped between Tia and Chris, taking her into his arms for a hug. "Happy birthday, sweetheart."

Stunned by Darnell's reappearance in her life, she stood like a statue as he pulled her into his embrace. For half a second, she allowed the embrace to continue and then she tore herself from his arms. "What in the heck are you doing?"

Darnell tried to hold her again, but this time Chris stepped between them. He wrapped an arm around Tia and gave Darnell a look that dared the other man to try anything. Wisely, Darnell put a few feet of space between them.

Shaking her head, Tia asked a second time, "What are you doing here?"

Smiling persuasively, Darnell answered, "I couldn't let my Tia's birthday go by without a shout-out."

"Actually, you could. I find that very interesting. If I remember things correctly, last year you couldn't be at my party because you had a game to play."

He did have the good sense to look embarrassed. It was probably all an act, but Tia didn't care. She didn't have much to say to him. Tia wanted Darnell to know that she hadn't forgotten and that there was no place in her life or her family for him.

"Ah, girl. Why you keep bringing up that stuff? This is a new day."

Tia smiled at Chris. "It certainly is. How did you know my family was getting together today?"

Darnell tossed a hand in the air. "Please. Y'all always do something for birthdays. I knew something was up when I drove by and saw all the cars."

"Hmm," Tia grunted, reaching for Chris's hand. "Come on. Let's go see the rest of the family."

Darnell glared hard at Chris's and Tia's linked hands. "So that's how it is?"

"Yes, it is."

All of the ruckus had alerted Mrs. Edwards. She poked her head out of the kitchen and frowned. "Is that Darnell?"

Always the salesman, he opened his arms and strolled down the hallway to Tia's mother. "Hey, Mom. How you doing?"

Folding her arms in front of her, Mrs. Edwards sidestepped Tia's former boyfriend. "First of all, I'm not your mother. Second, what are you doing here? You weren't invited."

"Don't be like that." His thousand-watt smile

dimmed as his arms dropped to his sides. With a nervousness that Tia had never seen, his hands fluttered aimlessly and then settled inside his trouser pockets.

"That's exactly how I'm going to be. You're not welcome here. You and Tia are not a couple, so go away. Leave my house."

"But . . . but . . ."

"Let me explain it to you. You can't treat my child any old way and think you're welcomed here. You're not." Mrs. Edwards placed a hand on Darnell's arm and steered him back down the hall to the front door. "No buts. Good-bye." She helped him onto the porch and shut the door in his face. Leaning against the door, she first studied Junior and Tia, and then her eyes narrowed when they settled on Chris. There was a definite chill in her gaze and a shift in her body language.

Before her mother could start in on Chris, Tia grabbed his arm and steered him toward the back of the house. "Come on." Tia and Chris entered the family room. Andre and Andrew were already perched in front of the fifty-inch high-definition television. The twins were watching a movie. Andrew glanced around and waved. "Hey, little sister. Happy birthday. How you doin', Chris?"

Chris gave the pair a two-finger salute. "Good. What about you?"

"Ditto," came Andre's response.

"Thank you," Tia responded.

Tia inched her way across the room to the patio door. Her father was outside turning ribs and chicken on the grill. She stepped onto the wooden porch. Chris followed. "Hi, Daddy."

With a smile on his face, he turned and waved the barbecue tongs in Tia and Chris's direction. "Hey, Tia-Mia. Hi, Chris. Come give your daddy a hug."

She crossed the patio and rose on tiptoes and kissed her father's cheek.

Patting her shoulder with his free hand, he said, "That's more like it."

"How you doing, Chris?"

"Hello, Mr. Edwards. Do you need some help?" Chris asked.

"No. I'm fine. Give me a minute. I'll be in."

"When you're done, I'd like to talk to you and Mrs. Edwards for a moment."

In the middle of turning a piece of chicken, Mr. Edwards halted and then gazed at Chris, trying to read his thoughts. "Okay. I'll be done in a few minutes."

Smiling gently, Chris nodded at the older man. "Thanks."

"I'm going to find my mother. I'll be back."

"Okay."

There were only a couple of places her mother would be: in her bedroom or in the kitchen. Tia chose the kitchen and found the elder Edwards checking a variety of dishes. "Hello, Momma."

Mrs. Edwards glanced up and focused on Tia, studying her youngest child. She moved from one pot to the other, stirring and checking the dishes. "You all right?"

Nodding, Tia answered, "Yeah. Thanks for

getting rid of that jerk. I don't know where his brain is."

"No problem. Like I said, he can't treat my baby any old way and think I'll let him dance in here like one of the family. Darnell is not part of my family."

Mr. Edwards led Chris into the kitchen and headed to the sink while Chris moved to Tia's side. The older man washed his hands, dried them on a paper towel, and dropped it into the garbage bin. Always the supportive partner, Tia's father moved across the room and placed himself at his wife's side.

They stood like adversaries across the kitchen. Her parents leaned against the kitchen island, their gazes sharp and assessing as they waited. Mrs. Edwards examined her daughter's belly and then skipped to her bare ring finger. With a sense of satisfaction, a petite smile touched the older woman's lips. Her smile screamed volumes. It said, "Good! There's still time. Things between my child and this man haven't gone that far yet." Tia grunted far too softly for anyone to hear. *That's what you think*, she thought.

Tia glanced from her mother to her father. Although Mr. Edwards appeared calm and unconcerned, a layer of tension filled the room. Her father's shoulders were bunched, and his stance remained guarded. Chris's pleasant demeanor didn't do much for the atmosphere. Her parents knew something was up, but they weren't sure what it was.

With an expectant look on his face, Mr. Edwards opened the conversation. "What is this about?"

Chris placed an arm around Tia and tugged her close. "I want you to know that I love Tia and that I'd like your permission to marry her."

"NO!" shouted Mrs. Edwards.

Startled, Greg Edwards nearly jumped. "Honey?" He reached for her. Jackie Edwards jerked away from his touch. Shaking her head, she shouted, "NO! NO! I knew something like this was in the works. I hoped we could end things before you got too involved with him."

Stunned, Tia gazed back at her mother. "Momma, this isn't a bad thing."

Mrs. Edwards took a step closer to her daughter and grabbed her hands. "You can't marry him."

"Momma, stop."

"Where do you plan on living?" Mrs. Edwards pressed.

"We're not sure," Tia hedged.

"France?" She surmised.

Tia stared at her mother. How would Momma know that? "Maybe. For part of each year."

Mrs. Edwards faced Chris and shook her head. "You can say anything you want. I don't care. I've thought about this since you brought him home. You are not taking my child across the world to France." Tia's mother turned to her daughter. "Have you thought about what you're doing and how far France is from here? What if something goes wrong? Where will you go? We wouldn't be able to get to you right away. It's at least a ten-hour flight from here to France. I won't have it."

Mrs. Edwards dropped Tia's hand and moved to the stove to lift the lid from a simmering pot. "You need to think about what you're doing."

Chris marched across the kitchen floor and took Mrs. Edwards's hand. "Please give us a chance. I promise that I'll be the best husband that I can be for your daughter. I love her."

"Jackie," her father began in a soft but firm voice. Normally that tone worked to calm everyone down. Not today.

"I'm not listening to anyone else," she stated. "These are my final words. I won't have it. You are not marrying this man."

"Nothing's going to happen to me, Momma. I'm grown. I can take care of myself."

Snorting, Mrs. Edwards folded her arms across her chest. "Famous last words. You couldn't get your situation with Darnell under control." She glanced Chris's way. "How do you expect to handle this man? He's nothing like Darnell or any boy you've brought home. This man could be anything from physically abusive to a mass murderer. I won't allow you to leave the country with him. The answer is still no."

Mr. Edwards must have decided it was time to intervene. He placed a hand on his wife's shoulder. "Jackie. Listen to me."

Mrs. Edwards shook it off. "No, Greg. I mean what I'm saying. Tia is far too trusting. Think about it. France! Not Ohio. We couldn't help her if something happened. By the time we reached her, she could be dead."

"Tia is a grown woman, Jackie." Mr. Edwards

kept a calm, reasonable tone. "You can't make her decisions for her. If she loves Chris and he loves her, then she's going to do what she wants. It's our job to support and help her in any way possible."

"No." She turned her back on her husband. "Tia-Mia, I want you to think some more. We haven't even touched on the race thing. Have you considered how his family will react to you? Will they accept you? Welcome you into their family? I don't think so."

"My family already knows about Tia," Chris chimed in. "I talk about her all the time. They can't wait to meet her. They've already seen pictures of us, and they know who she is to me. We're not like the people here."

Ignoring Chris, Mrs. Edwards continued. "What about children? I know you want them. Have you considered the cultural difference? Can you bring your children up the way you want? Will the Jensen family have certain expectations about how your children will be raised?"

"Momma, stop. You're upsetting yourself. This is a good thing. I've found somebody who loves me and I love him. Whatever Chris and I have to do, we'll do it. Everything is going to be fine. We'll work it out. Really, we will."

"I'm sorry. I can't accept this." The older woman paced the floor. Tia's father tried to stop his wife and hold her. She pushed past him without a backward look.

This time when Mrs. Edwards turned to Tia, there was a glint in her eyes that worried her daughter. Tia had expected a bit of resistance, but not this complete denial.

"What about your dreams? You've been talking about going to law school for the past few months. Are you going to just let that go because of him?"

"I want Tia to be happy with me. If law school is what she wants to do, law school it will be with my full approval and support. I'm here to help her in any way that I can, not be a hindrance."

"Pfff." Jackie Edwards waved a hand through the air. "I don't care what you say. What you're talking about doesn't mean a thing to me. I don't believe anything that comes out of your mouth."

A tap on the door halted the next explosion of words. With a look of apprehension on his face, Andre stuck his head in the kitchen. "Excuse me."

"Not now, Andre," Mr. Edwards said. "We're in the middle of something."

"I know. This can't wait."

Tia's mother banged the silver pot lid onto the countertop and snapped, "What is it?"

"It's Nia. She says that she's at Grandma Ruth's house and something's wrong with her. Nia said that she called EMS, and they are taking Granny to the hospital. She said we need to meet her at Harper Hospital."

"Oh my God!" Mrs. Edwards said, dropping the spoon in her hand and moving toward the door.

"Jackie." Greg Edwards hurried after his wife

and grabbed her by the shoulders. He turned her to face him. "Stop! I'll drive you."

The couple left the room. Minutes later, Tia opened the garage door for her parents, and a minute later their car moved down the driveway.

Chris took her hand and pulled her along behind him. "Let's get to the hospital."

Tia nodded and they headed for Chris's bike. The rest of the family hurried out of the house for their cars.

24

The Edwards family assembled at the hospital, waiting for some good news about Grandma Ruth's condition. The only difference from their previous visit was that the emergency room was now the backdrop instead of the surgical suite.

Tension filled the space as Tia's family gathered together. Some sat in hard red plastic chairs, and some paced the beige tile floor. The words coming from the television that was suspended from the ceiling were merely background noise. Everyone was too anxious about Grandma Ruth's condition. All they could do was wait to hear some word from a doctor.

From Tia's spot across the room, she watched her mother. She noticed signs of worry spread across her face and her body stiffening. Her wrinkled brow and tight posture revealed how upset and tense she was.

Tia wanted to go and be with her mother, but the harsh words Jackie had said earlier kept her from making the first move toward reconciliation. Mr. Edwards placed a supportive arm around his wife and drew her against his side.

Chris studied Tia as he drew her against his side. "You all right, *chérie?*"

"Yeah. Scared, worried. I want my granny to be all right."

He kissed her forehead. "It'll be okay. I believe it. You have to as well."

Tia bit down on her bottom lip to stop the quivering. "I know you're right, but things don't seem real good right now."

He captured her face between his large hands. "Listen to me, sweetheart. Your grandmother is still alive. There's always hope as long as she's still with us. Mrs. Wilson is a tough bird. I don't believe she is ready to leave here or us."

Tia nodded and leaned against Chris, soaking up his strength. After a few minutes, Chris excused himself and disappeared down a hallway.

This was her chance to try and mend things between her and her mother. Tia rose and walked across the floor to her mother. "Momma?"

Mrs. Edwards gazed up at her daughter. The pain and worry in her mother's eyes tugged at Tia's heart, and she rushed into her mother's arms. They sat huddled together for several minutes, wrapped in their own world.

"Granny is going to be fine. Everything is going to be okay." Drawing away, Tia patted her mother's shoulder. "It'll be okay. If Grandma Ruth puts her mind to getting better, she will."

"I don't know," Mrs. Edwards admitted. Her

voice quivered with each word. "My mother isn't young anymore."

"Momma, Grandma Ruth is strong. She has a mind of her own."

"True," Tia's mother agreed.

Chris returned to the waiting room, loaded with snacks and coffee for the family. He distributed the cups of coffee and chips and doughnuts to everyone. A round of "thanks, man" from Tia's family followed as he handed over the brew. Chris cautiously approached Mr. and Mrs. Edwards. He handed one cup to Mr. Edwards. Tia's mother shook her head when he showed her the pastries and coffee.

"No, thank you," she stated, holding Tia at her side.

Mr. Edwards leaned close to Chris and whispered something in his ear. Chris nodded and moved away, sitting across from mother and daughter.

As the minutes ticked by, Chris watched the pair. He never said a word, but he studied Tia and her mother with a critical gaze. Tia wondered what he was thinking.

An hour passed by, but it seemed more like an eternity. A doctor strolled from the triage area with a chart in his hands and stood in the center of the waiting room. "Jackie Edwards," he called.

She stood and grabbed Tia's hand, dragging her along with her. "I'm Jackie Edwards." Greg Edwards stood next to his wife.

Junior rose and drew close to the doctor and his parents. The twins and Nia joined him, waiting for some news about their beloved grand-mother.

"Mrs. Ruth Wilson is your family member?"

Jackie Edwards nodded. "She's my mother."

"Are you her next of kin?"

"Yes."

"I'm going to take you back to my office so we can talk."

"Wait a moment." Mrs. Edwards turned to her husband. "Greg."

"I'm here." He moved closer to his wife. Mr. Edwards turned to his kids and said, "You guys wait here. As soon as we know something, we'll come out and give you the news."

Tia made a move to return to Chris's side. Mrs. Edwards snatched her hand and pulled her along beside her. "I want you with me."

Tia glanced at Chris. He nodded.

He smiled encouragingly and leaned back in his chair. He looked as if he were willing to wait all night for her to return.

After talking with the doctor, the trio returned to the waiting room. For the second time, Tia's siblings stood and surrounded their parents. Chris hung back and remained on the fringes of the small group.

"What's going on?" Junior asked.

Andrew stepped closer to his parents and questioned, "How's Grandma Ruth doing?"

Nia asked the next question. "Is she coming home tonight?"

Greg Edwards raised his hands and quieted the

group. "Hold on. First of all, your grandmother had a stroke."

"Stroke," Nia muttered. Tears filled her eyes and slowly slid down her cheeks. Conflicting emotions drew a mask on her face. She wiped away her tears and said remorsefully, "This is all my fault." Nia wrapped her arms around her waist. "I should have known what to do to help her more."

"No. It's not." Her father wrapped her into his arms and said, "How could you have known? Apparently, the old girl hasn't been taking her medicine. You did what you could. First of all, you got her to the hospital as quickly as possible. That probably saved her life."

Silent until this moment, Andre asked, "So what happens now?"

"Mother will be staying at the hospital for a few days," Mrs. Edwards explained. "It's going to take a few days of testing to determine the effects of her stroke."

"Will there be permanent paralysis?" Chris asked.

Mrs. Edwards frowned. She looked at Chris as if she'd forgotten he was there. "The doctor doesn't know. They're going to wait until tomorrow to start running some tests. Mother is tired and needs to rest."

"Do we need to stay here?" Junior asked.

Andre nodded. "Yeah. That makes sense. Grandma Ruth is here alone. One of us should be with her."

"I'm sorry. I hadn't even thought that far."

Jackie Edwards rubbed her forehead as if it hurt. She glanced in Chris's direction. Her expression was thoughtful. "Tia, would you mind staying tonight?"

Surprised, Tia studied her mother. She would have expected her mother to want to stay at the hospital for the first few hours with her mother. It wasn't what she expected to do tonight, but she didn't have a problem with it. "Sure."

"No," Nia stated. "You go home. You have to go to work. I'll stay."

Greg Edwards asked, "Are you sure?"

Nia nodded. "Yeah. I'd like to. Go home. Come back tomorrow and take over. I'll call if you're needed. My being here tonight will give everyone a chance to relax and sleep and come up with a game plan for the rest of her stay."

Chris stretched out among the bedding, waiting for Tia to join him. He drew in a deep breath and let it out. Today had been beyond anything he'd ever encountered. Tia climbed into bed beside him and scooted close, tossing an arm around his waist and hugging him.

None of the evening had gone according to plan. From Mrs. Edwards's outburst at the birthday party to spending the evening in the hospital's emergency room waiting for news about Tia's grandmother, it had been an action-packed and emotional time for everyone.

"I'm sorry things got out of hand." Tia kissed his cheek.

"None of it was your fault. Besides, you tried to warn me that your mother wouldn't take our engagement very well." He held Tia against his shoulders. "I expected some resistance to the idea, but not as much as we received."

She blew out a puff of air. "Told you."

"Has your mother always been so possessive of you?" he asked cautiously. Chris didn't want to alarm her. Today had been difficult enough, but he needed to know what he was up against.

"Yes. I'm not sure why."

"It's sort of unusual." Chris caressed her arm, stroking the sensitive skin up and down. "I guess I would understand it more if you were an only child or even the only girl. But you have an identical twin."

"My mom and Nia have never been close. Their relationship has always been strained and difficult. I think my mother was disappointed that Nia refused to be the girly-girl she envisioned her to be."

He smiled and kissed her softly. "Yet, you are."

Tia shrugged. "Sort of. I think part of it comes down to convenience. Normally, I don't work on the weekends. I had time to shop with Momma, do different stuff with her. I made time to be with her."

"Mmm."

"What does that mean?" She lifted her head from Chris's shoulder.

"It's going to very lonely and unpleasant for your mother when we move to France. I'd hate to see that."

"Me too. But we've made our plans."

"How can we make this easier for your mother?" Chris asked. "I hate the fact that she's upset."

"I don't know. She really scared me tonight. I've never seen her act this way. She had this wild expression in her eyes that I've never seen before. I knew telling her about us was going to be bad, but"—Tia eased closer to Chris—"things turned out a lot worse than I thought."

"Your grandmother getting sick didn't help."

"Nope, it didn't."

They rested quietly for a few minutes. Chris lay in the bed thinking about how Jackie Edwards had tried to sabotage their engagement when she came up with so many scenarios of why Tia shouldn't be with him. Obviously, the older woman had spent a lot of time thinking about their relationship . . . and ways to put a halt to it.

"Is there anything I can do for your grandmother?" Chris asked. "Is there some way that I can help you?"

"I don't think so. Junior, Nia, and Andre are going to be with Granny for the next few days and then I'll take my turn."

"I'll be with you," Chris stated, pulling her closer to his side. "You won't be alone."

Tia balanced herself on her elbow, leaned over Chris, and softly kissed his lips. "Thank you. You are so sweet. I appreciate everything you've done."

"It's only because I love you so much." He brushed her hair away from her face and stroked her cheek. "What concerns you concerns me."

"Can we hold off for a few days on our plans while I try and work things out with my mother?"

Chris had half expected this request, but it still felt as if she might be wavering on the subject of marriage. He swallowed the protest on his lips and uttered the correct words. "Sure. That will be fine. This will give your mother a little time to get used to the idea."

"Thank you for understanding. I know we have a lot going on right now."

"I'll talk to Reynolds on Monday, and then we'll know what we have to do."

25

Three days later, Tia's nose twitched from the ever-present odor of alcohol and disinfectant as she searched the halls of the hospital for the ICU. She stepped into a room with a single bed and beeping, clicking, and hissing machines. She found her sister flipping through a magazine next to the empty bed.

Nia stood. Her slick, shiny bob and large hoop earrings jingled when she moved. Dressed in a pair of tight pink denims, a strapless lemon top splashed with a rainbow of colors, and cream stiletto heels, Nia looked as if she were on her way to go clubbing. "Oh. Hi, Tia. I thought you were transportation bringing Granny back."

"Nope. Just me. I'm here to take over."

"Good."

Tia moved to the whiteboard on the wall and studied the instructions scribbled in green erasable Magic Marker. "Where did they take Grandma Ruth?"

"MRI."

Nodding, Tia took the chair next to the bed and picked up a *People* magazine. "You know you can call me. You don't have to do things alone. I can put in a little more time with our grandmother and give you a break."

With a wave of her hand, Nia dismissed her twin's suggestion. A teasing light entered her brown eyes. "Nah, I'm fine. My schedule is more flexible than yours. Besides, I heard that you got yourself engaged. That's where your focus should be. Keep that man happy," she said with a little twist of her shoulders. "Let me see the ring."

Grinning sheepishly, Tia extended her left hand, showing off her engagement ring. "Yes. I sort of did."

Whistling, Nia got up and took her hand. "That is some rock that Frenchman put on your finger. You better be careful when you're out and about. I don't want anybody to snatch it."

A little embarrassed, Tia tugged her hand away and placed it in her lap. "Hush. Stop talking trash."

"Nothing silly or trashy about what I'm saying," Nia denied. "That ring is beautiful. You be careful."

Extending her hand, Tia admired her ring. "Yeah. Chris did a great job of picking this out."

Nia returned to her seat and crossed her legs, leaning back in her chair. "How did Mother take the news?"

Tia ran her fingers through her hair. Her steady heartbeat kicked into overdrive. She dropped her head and answered, "Not very well."

"That's what I heard."

"From who?" Tia demanded.

Nia stared at her sister, giving her a "don't be ridiculous" expression. "Oh, come on. Everybody heard."

Hanging her head in shame, Tia admitted, "Yeah. They did. It was terrible. The things Momma said and the way she cut Chris to pieces. I've never seen her act that way."

"Yes, you have," Nia contradicted.

Frowning, Tia stared at her sister. "You're wrong. No, I haven't."

With an exaggerated sigh, Nia fell back in her chair. "How quickly we forget."

"Say what you've got to say."

"When you bought your town house, I thought Mother was going to die. You may choose to forget, but I remember how she acted for days after you moved—the hysterics and the tears. The only thing she didn't do was take to her sickbed. I think Daddy made her get herself together and start moving ahead."

Tia opened her mouth to respond, but her twin continued to talk.

"Let's face it, you are her favorite child. She wants you with her and nothing else will do."

Nia placed her purse on their grandmother's bed and recrossed her legs, swinging her top leg back and forth. "Whenever our mother goes into mother-hen mode, she acts just like that. You are her baby. The four of us understand that. The big difference with this situation is that she's trying to force you to choose between her and someone you love. Mother doesn't want you to leave, and she'll use every trick or weapon she has to get her way."

Snorting, Tia folded her arms across her chest. "Well, she sure did on Sunday. Daddy couldn't get her to calm down. Normally he can use that tone and she backs down, but not Sunday. Momma fought him as hard as she fought Chris. I didn't recognize our own mother."

"So what are you going to do about it?"

Frowning, Tia gazed at her sister. "What do you mean?"

"You told Daddy and he told me that you planned to leave real soon. Chris got this huge promotion and you need to get to France. When are you leaving?"

Tia looked away. Her life felt so unsettled right now.

"I don't know. With Momma's reaction and now Grandma Ruth, I can't leave Momma when so much is up in the air."

"Sure you can. Pack your bags and go." Nia waved her hands away.

"Nia! How can you be so heartless?"

"Don't 'Nia' me." She tossed her head defiantly. "This is a no-brainer. You've found a wonderful, sexy, well-educated man who wants to spend the rest of his life with you."

"That's enough."

"No, it isn't. Get real."

"I am getting real."

"If you don't want him, give him to me."

"NO!"

Nia smirked. "Not willing to give up Chris, are you?"

"I can't leave with Momma so upset. Plus, we're sharing the responsibility right now. What will happen if I leave?"

Nia laughed. It was a harsh, unpleasant sound that grated on Tia's nerves. "Things will go on as they always do. Junior, the twins, and I will divide up the responsibility and take care of whatever we need to do. If you're not here, we'll make up the difference."

"Gee, thanks."

Her twin's voice softened. "I don't mean to hurt your feelings. What I'm trying to say, and not very well, is that we'll get by. That's what family does. When one can't make it, the others step up and do the rest."

"What about Momma?"

"What about her?" Nia snorted and then added, "It's time for you to leave Mother. I've said it to you before and I'll say it again. Mother has a man. Why shouldn't you have one of your own?"

"You don't understand. Momma and you have never been close."

"No, we haven't." A flash of pain crossed Nia's face. For a moment, Tia questioned whether she had seen the expression. "And that's not really your concern. I do know this: It's time for Momma to cut the cord and let you get on with your life."

"She's concerned that I'll be in another country

and if something goes wrong, she won't be able to get to me quick enough."

"So." Nia shrugged. "You're grown and you know how to handle your business. I'm pretty sure that you know how to leave a bad situation if Chris turns out to be a piece of crap, although I doubt that will happen." A self-satisfied smile curled her lips. "I mean, you kicked Darnell to the curb pretty quick. You know what to do."

"I don't know about this."

"You better figure it out. I don't think that hunk of love you've got yourself is going to wait very long. He shouldn't have to. Chris has told you what he needs and has been honest about what's going on with him. Maybe it's time for you to return the favor and give him a little respect along with a lot of love."

Tia shut her eyes, seeing her mother's upset and lost face.

"Momma is so distraught. There's so much on her right now."

Nia speared her sister with a stern look. "Do you love Chris?"

"Completely."

"What would you do if he told you that he's tired of waiting and packed up and left? How would you handle that?"

She felt as if Nia had punched her in the chest. Grimacing, Tia could barely stand the idea of Chris leaving her. No. She didn't want to experience that. "He can't leave me. I love him."

"That's what I wanted to hear. You've always been Mother's pet. I think it's time for the pet to find her own way in the world." She glanced out of the glass wall that faced the nurses' station. "Here's my last word on the subject. Love that man and let him love you. That's the only way to go."

Nia stood as two men in blue uniforms wheeled a gurney into the room. A nurse followed, carrying a chart. Startled, she stared at the two women and then said to Nia, "I didn't know you had a twin."

"That I do." Chuckling, Nia answered, "How's my grandmother?"

"Dr. Ernst had a series of tests done to determine the extent of the damage caused by the stroke." She glanced at the chart. "I think this is the last of the tests. Once the doctor reviews the results, I'm sure he'll have a consultation with you and your family to recommend a treatment plan."

"Thank you," Tia answered for the both of them. She looked down at her grandmother. The senior member of the Edwards family appeared worn and tired. One side of her face looked slightly distorted.

She touched her grandmother's arm reassuringly. That simple touch got her attention. Grandma Ruth focused on Tia. She tried to smile, but the muscles in her face didn't respond.

"That's okay," Tia whispered.

Tia wanted to cry. Poor dear. She had suffered so much lately. *I can't leave like this*, Tia thought. *My conscience won't let me. When Grandma Ruth is better, Chris and I will head to France.*

* * *

Chris glanced at the clock on Tia's screen and straightened his tie. "It's time." He watched Tia's eyes widen in alarm as her hand fluttered nervously over the keyboard. She had every reason to be nervous. Hell, he felt nervous. Above all else, Reynolds was a businessman who ran a multi-billion-dollar company. He didn't know how the president of Gautier International Motors would react.

After discussing Mrs. Wilson's stroke, they had decided to talk with Reynolds about delaying their departure to France. Although Chris hadn't said anything to Tia, he really didn't expect Reynolds to agree to their request. Delays cost money, and Reynolds ran his company in the black. For his purposes, Chris hoped Reynolds would show some compassion and give them a break.

"Good luck," Tia said.

Smiling reassuringly, he reached for her hand and squeezed. "Thanks. I hope I won't need it."

"Me too," she muttered as he strolled away. He quickly disappeared between a maze of cubicles as he headed down the hall toward the executive row.

Chris took a deep breath and turned the knob before stepping through two carved wooden doors. He headed directly for Reynolds's executive assistant.

"How are you, Chris?" she asked.

"Good. I'm here to see Reynolds."

"Oh, yes. Mr. Gautier is expecting you." She waved a hand at a frosted-glass entrance. "Go right in."

"Thanks." He stepped around the desk. He tapped lightly on the door and waited for a reply.

A gruff accented voice replied, "Come in."

Reynolds sat behind a huge desk. He dropped the report in his hands, rose, and stretched out a hand to the young attorney.

Chris shook the older man's hand, instantly switching to rapid French. "Thanks for seeing me. I know how busy you are."

The older man followed suit. "Sit. Sit." He waved a hand at an empty seat across from his wide expanse of a desk.

Complying, Chris sat, taking a minute to organize his thoughts.

"What can I do for you?" Reynolds asked, linking his fingers and placing them on the desk. His calm demeanor immediately put Chris at ease.

Chris cleared his throat and pulled on the end of his tie. "We've got a problem. Tia and I planned to fly to France at the end of the month. Everything was in order, but Tia's grandmother has suffered a stroke."

Frowning, Reynolds said, "I'm sorry to hear that. But how does that affect our plans for you to take over the France office?"

"I don't think I can leave town when we planned. I need additional time. We want to stay until Mrs. Wilson is on safer ground."

Pursing his lips, Reynolds leaned back in his chair and tapped the tips of his fingers together. "This is an unexpected development."

Unexpected? What does that mean? Reynolds presented the perfect poker face. Chris wasn't sure what to think, but he decided to forge ahead. "Yes, it is. We were hoping for a little more time before we have to leave."

"Mmm," he said. "How long?"

"A few weeks would be useful."

"Fine. I'll give you two additional weeks. That should give you enough time to determine Tia's grandmother's condition."

Two weeks! That's not enough! Chris silently yelled. He swallowed that thought and said, "Great. We appreciate it."

Reynolds stood to indicate that the appointment had ended. He offered his hand, which Chris shook before he returned to his office.

26

After more than a week, all of Grandma Ruth's tests were finished. The Edwardses invited their children to the consultation with Dr. Ernst to hear his evaluation.

On Friday morning, the entire Edwards family crammed into Dr. Ernst's tiny office. Tia and Chris arrived to find the rest of her family already there. Mr. and Mrs. Edwards, Junior, Andre, Andrew, and Nia waited nervously for additional information about their precious Ruth Wilson. Tia stopped, scanning the room for an empty seat. Tia's mother waved her over, pointing at the spot next to her. One empty chair remained. Tia turned to Chris with a question on her lips.

"Don't worry about me," he said. "Go. Sit." He stood against the wall next to her chair.

Tia took a quick glance at the people in the room. As usual, her father sat calmly next to her mother. One hand rested on his wife's hand; the other sat still on his knee.

In contrast, Tia's mother looked like she would pop at any moment. With one arm stretched across her middle, she rocked slightly back and forth. This situation was almost more than she could handle.

From her father to her twin, everyone appeared on edge. Nia worried her rose-colored lipstick away as she chewed the corner of her mouth and picked at her nails, working the polish from one finger. After a moment, she jumped to her feet and restlessly moved around the office. She paused here and there, reading the certificates, degrees, and diplomas that littered the office walls. She returned to her chair, flopped down, and started sorting through her purse, pulling items out and then returning everything before zipping it up.

Her brothers fumbled with their cell phones as if the electronic devices presented a lifeline to the world. Andre kept turning the item over and over in his hands as the moments ticked away, while Andrew flipped open the letter pad, tapped on the mini-keyboard, and snapped it shut. Junior kept moving around the room. His hands were shoved into his trouser pockets, and his gaze kept darting to the door.

Tia's belly churned with nervousness. She didn't have a good feeling about the outcome for the day. She believed that whatever the doctor told them would change and upset everyone in the family.

Frowning, Mrs. Edwards touched her husband's hand and asked, "Didn't we agree to nine o'clock?"

Mr. Edwards nodded, patted his wife's hand, and said in a reassuring tone, "Nine it was. Remember, Dr. Ernst has other patients. We have to wait our turn."

She sighed, toying with the strap of her handbag. "I know. Waiting is making me nervous."

He smiled at his wife and said, "It'll be fine. Whatever happens, we'll figure things out and work it out together."

They exchanged a look that communicated something special between them. Mrs. Edwards laid her head on her husband's shoulder. "You're a good husband. You've always been with me, no matter what."

"That's my job." Tia's father kissed Mrs. Edwards's forehead and smiled gently at his wife. "I try. To me, that's what marriage is about."

Dr. Ernst entered the room with a thick manila folder in his hand. "Good morning. How is everyone?"

An assortment of "hellos" and "good mornings" followed.

Mrs. Edwards sat stiffly in her chair. Mr. Edwards patted her hand and whispered, "Don't forget, it's going to be just fine."

Tia let out a shaky breath. That little sound must have reached Chris's ears. He linked their fingers, stroking the sensitive skin near her thumb. Her insides were quivering with worry. Finally, they were going to get information that would make it possible for them to start planning Granny's recovery.

Tia focused on Dr. Ernst. He didn't look much

different from the first time they entered his office as children. Over the years, Mrs. Edwards had called upon Dr. Ernst to get their school shots when their pediatrician was booked. During one long summer, he put a cast on Andrew when he fell off his bike and broke his arm.

Standing at five feet eleven, Dr. Ernst had a booming voice that commanded attention, but he could also be soft and soothing when necessary. A thick, bushy mustache graced his upper lip and was in contrast to the thinning dark hair on his head. His narrow face and sharp, all-seeing dark eyes reminded Tia of a hawk ready to pounce.

He took his chair behind the desk and opened the file. He lifted the frame of his narrow glasses and readjusted them on his nose. "The neurologist and I discussed Mrs. Wilson's case. She did have a stroke last week. We've done a battery of tests and have found that her motor skills have been affected by her illness."

"What does that mean?" Mrs. Edwards asked.

"Your mother is having trouble walking. Speech is a problem. Each of you has been in her hospital room at one time or another. When you ask her a question, she uses every form of communication except verbal. When she speaks, it's a slow and difficult process. Plus, it's almost impossible to understand her."

"Which side of her body is affected, Dr. Ernst?" Mr. Edwards asked.

He tapped the right side of his head. "The stroke hit the right side of her brain. Her sight is slightly hindered. From the MRI, I'm happy to say that she doesn't have any residual blood clots or tumors. I think she'll be just fine once we stabilize her medicine and get her into a regimen that will help her."

"What caused the stroke?" Andrew questioned.

Nia held her belongings tightly. Tia understood how badly her sister felt about Grandma Ruth. She blamed herself for what happened.

"Well"—he paused and then continued—"your grandmother has admitted to peppering her diet with too many bad foods like potato chips, pork skins, and ham sandwiches. I believe she'll be fine once all of her vitals return to normal and she stops eating unhealthy snacks."

Leaning against the wall, Junior asked, "How do we get her back on her feet?"

"First thing we're going to do is put her in rehab," Dr. Ernst replied.

Mrs. Edwards raised a hand to interrupt the physician. "Wait. Have you said anything to my mother about this?"

"No. I thought your mother would handle the situation better if her whole family visited when I bring up the topic."

"Are you sure this conversation wouldn't go better with just you and her?" Tia's mother inquired.

"No." The doctor continued. "Your mother will go to rehab for a few months. Physical therapy will help her regain her strength and ability to walk. The facility also has speech therapists on site. That'll provide some support for her communication problems."

"Where do we come in? What should we do?" Andre asked.

"Your grandmother is going to need your support, encouragement, and help. This is not going to be easy for her. She's going to be living away from home for a good part of the year without the benefit of everything she's used to. You're going to have to make it comfortable. I want to see you visit the site often. She'll need you."

"That's not a problem," Nia stated. "We'll be right there for her."

Dr. Ernst closed the file. "I don't doubt it. I'll see you and your siblings at Mrs. Wilson's bedside." He took a deep breath and let it out slowly. "I know this is difficult and you're not going to like the next part, but I have to recommend it. Allow her to vent when she's frustrated, but don't do things for her. Let her accomplish them on her own. Don't coddle her. She needs to learn how to function on her own again."

Surprise lit up Mrs. Edwards's face. "Are you saying we should ignore her needs? Not help her when she needs us?"

Dr. Ernst lifted his glasses from his nose and then returned them to the exact same spot. "I'm suggesting you should let her help herself. You're not doing your mother any good if you do all the work for her. While in rehab, she'll learn how to function independently. Let her do that without interference."

Shaking her head, Mrs. Edwards said, "I don't know. I can't do that. That's my mother. What kind of daughter would I be if I ignore her when she needs me?"

The doctor lifted a hand. "Let me explain further. I'm not saying ignore her. Think of her as a baby who needs encouragement when she's learning to walk. You don't pick up your child each and every time she falls. There are times when you let her fall and wait until she picks herself up. That's the attitude you need for Mrs. Wilson."

The Edwards family talked among themselves as they considered what Dr. Ernst had suggested.

"This might be the hardest thing you've ever done for your mother," the doctor stated. "In the long run, you'll hinder her recovery if you supply all of her needs."

"I don't know," Mrs. Edwards said.

Tia touched her mother's hand. "It makes sense, Momma. We're so used to helping that it doesn't seem right to let her struggle. But it is."

Mrs. Edwards latched on to her daughter's hand. "Will you help?"

"Of course."

Clutching her hand, Tia's mother demanded, "Promise me!"

"Momma!" Tia replied.

"Make a promise," Jackie Edwards insisted.

Shrugging, Tia said, "Okay. I promise. I'll be here for you and Granny."

Mrs. Edwards sighed. "Thank you. I'll need your help to get through this."

Tia squeezed her mother's hand. "I'll always be here to help you."

She stroked Tia's cheek. "You're the best, Tia-Mia."

Tia glanced Chris's way. He stood stiff and unyielding. His face looked as if it were carved in granite. *What's going on with him?* she wondered.

Chris spoke up in his French-accented voice. "Dr. Ernst, will Mrs. Wilson get better? Will she be all right?"

The doctor's sharp gaze moved over to the Frenchman. "I have all the faith in modern medicine and her strong personality that she will recover completely." He lifted a finger and waved it in the air. "Remember, all the work is hers. She must make up in her mind that she wants to get back on her feet."

"And now? Is she in danger?" Chris asked.

"No. She's stable. The treatment team wouldn't move her or release her to the rehab if there was any danger of her having another stroke."

"Excellent." Nodding, Chris gave the doctor a vague, unfocused smile and leaned back against the wall.

"When will my mother-in-law be transferred?" Tia's father asked.

"The day after we talk to her," the doctor responded. "I want the family to be at her bedside when I talk to her. I don't want her to feel like she's going to a facility to be abandoned by her family."

"We'd never do that." Junior pushed away from the wall and moved closer to the doctor's desk. "She's our family. We work together."

"Perfect," the physician said. "Let's talk to her tomorrow morning, say about ten?"

"Sure."

"Yeah."

"Works for me."

Dr. Ernst rose and so did Tia's parents. He extended his hand, first to Mrs. Edwards and then to Mr. Edwards.

"I'll see everyone tomorrow morning at the hospital at ten." He edged his way to the door and opened it. He held it open as the Edwards family filed out of the office.

Silently, Chris followed Tia out of the office and to the car. She felt an undercurrent of something. Tia couldn't put a name to the emotion sizzling below the surface. Chris held open the elevator door for her, and they descended to the first floor in silence.

Something's off, she thought as a chill iced her skin. Tia rubbed her hands up and down her bare arms as they exited the building.

27

Tia and Chris stepped into the sunshine. She turned to him and asked, "Do you want to stop for something to eat before we head back?"

He shook his head, moving through the rows of parked cars toward her Velocity. "No. Let's get on home."

Surprised, Tia paused outside the medical building and stared after her fiancé before hurrying to catch up with him. He always enjoyed discovering new cuisine when they were out. She climbed into the passenger seat and snapped her seat belt into place. Chris did the same, then started the engine and headed toward the freeway.

They made the entire drive home in silence. Cars whizzed by them as they cruised along I-75 on their way to downtown Detroit. Tia kept snatching quick glances at Chris as they traveled, trying to gauge his mood and his reaction to the meeting. Unfortunately, his poker face gave nothing away. *With that expression,* she thought, *he might be able to work his way through the Detroit casinos.*

All too soon and without a word being spoken, Chris turned into the court where she lived, stopped outside her town house, and hit the remote on the visor. The garage door rattled and groaned as it opened. Chris pulled the SUV into the empty space, switched off the engine, and shifted in the driver's seat to face her. Hands tightly clenching the steering wheel, Chris asked quietly, "Can we talk?"

Tia ran a gaze over the man next to her. His unyielding posture made her heart skip a beat. Butterflies hatched and flitted inside her belly. Darnell had been the last person to say those words, and look what happened to their relationship. Tia wrapped her hand around the door handle. *No, I don't want to talk,* she thought. *But I need to know what's rolling around in your head.* "Sure. Come on in."

"Thanks." Chris handed the car keys to Tia. Always the gentleman, he exited the vehicle, hurried around the front to open the passenger door, and helped Tia out. Together, they entered the town house and headed for the living room.

Tia tossed her purse on the sofa and stood uneasily in the center of the living room. She shoved a shaky hand inside her pant pocket, wondering what she should do next. *Turn on the television? Make a snack?* "Do you want anything to drink or eat?"

Stonefaced, he shook his head. "No. I'm fine."

With nothing more to say, Tia moved to the

leather recliner and sank into it. She picked up the remote to turn on the television. Chris removed it from her hands and placed it on the glass-top coffee table. "Let's talk first."

That got her full attention. Those words and his action signaled the beginning of a serious conversation. "Okay."

Chris perched on the edge of the matching ottoman, close to her feet. He took her left hand in both of his, fingering her engagement ring. With an unnerving stare, Chris held her gaze with his own. "Sweetheart," he began, stroking her hand and speaking in a soft, comforting tone, "we don't have another three months. We've already used up the two additional weeks Reynolds gave us. He's expecting you and me to leave any day and for me to take over the France office immediately. That office won't run forever by itself or without supervision. There are items that need my attention."

Tia felt the edge of hysteria bubble up inside her and threaten to explode. Her question came out in a high, shrill tone although she tried hard to maintain her calm. "What am I supposed to do, Chris? My family needs me right now. I can't leave."

"Don't you mean you can't leave your mother?"

"Her, too." Her insides churned, but Tia's voice dropped an octave and added an accusatory note when she asked the next question. "What are you trying to say?"

In an act of surrender, Chris raised his hands, palms up. The expression on his face changed from concern to loving. "I understand how important your grandmother is to you. My family means the world to me, too. But we have plans and there are people expecting us. There are things that need to be done. I'm not trying to stir up any trouble or cause you more distress, but"— he paused—"I should have returned to France a month ago."

Her mother's worried and stressed features flashed before her. Didn't he understand how all of this affected and upset her life? "Chris, my grandmother is sick," she insisted.

"No, Tia." Chris placed a hand on her knee. "Your grandmother is on the mend and getting better. Dr. Ernst made that very clear today. She wouldn't be heading to rehab if he had any doubts about her health."

"You make it sound as if she got sick on purpose. Grandma Ruth didn't have a stroke to make life difficult for you. She got ill and ended up in the hospital."

"Yes, she did. But now Mrs. Wilson is getting better and will be able to get on with her life after her time in the facility. We need to do the same."

"That's just it." She linked her hands together to try and stop them from shaking as she spoke. "It's not over for my family or me. The real work has just started. My family will need me even more once Grandma Ruth is transferred."

"Not every second," he contradicted. "She'll be in a place that will provide all of the assistance she will require. Even if she did need twenty-four-hour care, it's not up to you to give it. You have four siblings and two parents willing and available to help. They all understand that you have other obligations."

She shook her head. "You don't understand. Everyone expects me to do my share, to help with my grandmother's care."

"No, they don't," Chris disagreed. "I've talked with Junior, Nia, and your twin brothers together and separately. They've encouraged me to get on the plane and go home and take you with me."

Stunned, her mouth dropped open. Tia couldn't believe Chris had done that. "I can't leave right now. You heard the doctor. We're at a critical point in my grandmother's care, and I need to be here."

"Who says that it's imperative that you be here, Dr. Ernst or any other physician? Your grandmother?" he asked.

"No." She felt trapped between loyalty toward her family and the man she loved. Why couldn't he understand and give her time to sort through her family's needs?

He shrugged in that French way of his and said, "Then I don't see the problem. We can leave next week."

"I can't," Tia countered. "Not now."

"When?" Chris shot back.

Tia gnawed on her bottom lip. "Maybe in a few weeks, a month at the most. Once Grandma Ruth begins responding to her therapy, then we can think about moving to France."

"We can't go on that long."

Those quietly spoken words hung in the room

like a scream. This time, her heart kicked into a gallop. She tried to calm herself, but fear grew inside her and ate away at her calm façade. "What are you really saying?"

"I love you, and I want you to come to France with me."

"I love you, too."

"I can't stay in Detroit much longer."

That was the second jolt to her system. An incredible sense of loss followed that question. *Would he leave me?* she wondered. *Of course not.* Chris loved her and wanted to be with her.

Deep down, she knew everything that Chris was saying was true. Reynolds had been generous by granting them additional time, but the move to the home office must happen soon. However, she wanted and needed Chris to understand her predicament as well.

Tia swallowed hard and asked, "You're planning on leaving?"

He ran a hand through his hair and let out a gush of hot air. "Yes."

The question and Chris's answer scared her. She didn't know what to say. Granted, she knew he needed to leave, but she didn't believe he would push her to make a choice. "Are you asking me to choose between you and my family?"

"No. I'm asking you to come with me like we planned."

The telephone interrupted her next comment. Tia decided to ignore it in favor of finishing their discussion. After the third ring, the answering machine kicked in, and the musical voice of her mother could be heard throughout the first floor.

"Hi, Tia-Mia. This is your mom."

Chris went still. He gazed at Tia with an "I told you so" gleam in his eyes while they listened without comment to Tia's mother.

"I know you're probably busy, but I wanted to let you know that I just spoke with Dr. Ernst. He wrote the script for your grandmother's transfer. Mother will be moved sometime tomorrow afternoon. Junior volunteered to be with her once she's been moved until after dinner. I'm going to the hospital and then follow the ambulance to the rehab facility. By the way, it's called Lexington Rehab Center. You can find it on Eighteen Mile and Orchard Lake roads. When you can get off work, I want you to meet me there."

Hissing out a hot breath, Chris stood. He shoved his hands into his pockets and paced the living room floor.

"Anyway, the twins will take the first few days. Your sister will do a couple of days in a row, and then it'll be your turn. But we'll talk about that tomorrow while the staff at the center gets mother settled." Tia heard the happiness and pleasure in her mother's voice. "I'm so glad you've decided to help. It will make the transition easier for everyone. I know this is a difficult time for you, and I really appreciate you helping me. Love you. See you tomorrow."

He loomed over Tia. "Your mother keeps hammering home how much she needs you. She won't give you a minute's break."

"Chris, that's totally unfair."

"No, it's not. I truly wish it was." He ran his hand through his hair. The blond locks stood on end in every direction.

Fed up with the back-and-forth, Tia decided to put all of her cards on the table. "Say what you've got to say, Chris."

He studied Tia for a long, silent moment. "I will."

Chris stared down at her. She got the impression that he was considering how far he should take this. The determination in his expression let her know that he was about to go all the way. "I'm saying you're allowing your mother to manipulate you and divide us. She's using your grandmother's illness to hold you close and keep you from leaving Michigan with me."

Enough is enough, Tia thought, jumping to her feet and practically yelling, "You're wrong. You will not talk about my mother that way. Momma wants me to be happy, for us to be happy. She'd never do anything to destroy that. I would never let her make my decisions for me."

"Prove it," he challenged.

"What?" She shook her head and shrugged. "How?"

"Our tickets expire on the thirty-first. I plan to use mine." Chris held out his hand. "Come with me."

Frantic and feeling cornered, Tia took a step back, shaking her head. "No. I can't do that yet. Can't you understand and be a little more considerate? I need more time to get my mother and grandmother settled."

Chuckling, he took a step closer to her. "Let's

say I agree, Reynolds is fine with the wait, and your grandmother gets better." The frustration and agitation in Chris's accent became more pronounced. He paced back and forth in front of her. "What happens when your mother comes up with a new excuse? Another reason why you can't leave yet? What am I supposed to do with that? How do I explain it to Reynolds or my family? There are many people involved in this situation, not just you and me. When will you be able to come with me?"

"Chris!" Tia replied, tossing her hands into the air. "I don't have an answer for you. Anything can happen and I need to be close until I feel more comfortable with leaving. We're crossing the Atlantic. I don't want to worry. You have a large family. I expected you to understand."

"I do, but my family and I both understand that I have a life of my own. There's a time when my job or something in my life may prevent me from being with them."

Tia recognized the hurt on his face, and her attitude quickly softened. Just as quickly, she thought about her mother's pitiful request to help her, and Tia hardened her heart against Chris and his demands. "I can't agree to anything right now. Everything is up in the air. I thought you understood that. My mother needs me."

"What about *our* life? The plans we made for *our* future. Are you willing to walk away from everything we mean to each other?" He sank onto the sofa next to her and took her hands. "Please don't let your mother destroy our future."

Bringing his hands to her lips, she kissed them. "You've got the wrong impression of my mother. She would never, never deliberately destroy my happiness."

"Then come with me."

Every fabric of her being wanted to say yes, to pack her bags and get on that plane with him. But she had made a promise to her mother and she couldn't leave. Not yet. Maybe soon. "I can't. Not yet."

Nodding, Chris dropped her hands and rose. "I see."

Worried, Tia stood and tried to touch him. He sidestepped her. "You understand, don't you?" she asked.

Chris stared at the carpet and then shook his head. "No. I don't. You know where I'm headed. Give me a call if you change your mind."

Chris leaned closer and kissed Tia. He poured all of himself into that kiss. Tia found herself caught up in the moment, trying to get closer to him and rubbing herself against his warmth. Moaning, Chris broke away from her. He caressed her cheek. "Good-bye, Tia."

He stepped around her and headed down the hall to the front door. The slamming of the door was the next thing she heard.

Shocked and confused, Tia dropped back onto the sofa. He'd left. This was the last thing she expected. They should have yelled, fussed, and then worked through some sort of compromise.

Chris was angry. After he calmed down and

thought about their situation, he'd give her a call and then they could talk.

He'd call. Tia felt certain of that. Chris would never cause her that kind of pain. Tia strolled down the hallway and entered her kitchen. She was hungry. After eating, she planned to give him a ring and see if he'd like to talk.

28

Two weeks later, Tia sat watching television with Grandma Ruth at the Lexington Rehab facility. As they chatted quietly, a young, perky nurse entered the room and whisked her grandmother off to physical therapy. Pushing the wheelchair, the nurse promised to bring Grandma Ruth back within an hour. Weary from thinking about Chris, Tia completed a series of small tasks. She took the mustard-colored water pitcher in the adjacent bathroom to refill it. When she returned to the room, a lone figure stood in the doorway.

Nia Edwards struck a pose, placing a hand on her hip, and asked, "What are you doing here?"

Shaken by Nia's abrupt arrival, Tia nearly dropped the water pitcher. "Helping our grandmother."

Nia waltzed across the floor with the daily newspaper in her hand and placed it on the nightstand next to the bed. "What about Chris?"

Please let my voice sound normal, Tia begged

silently. "What about him?" Tia shot back, trying to hold herself together so that her twin wouldn't know how much her question affected her. She didn't want Nia to see her cry, and she didn't have the strength to continue a discussion of her former fiancé for very long.

"I thought you two had a deadline from the boss? Needed to get out of the country right away." Nia moved away from the bed and peeked out of the room's window. A gazebo stood outside in the courtyard. It provided pleasant scenery for the residents.

At the mention of Chris, all of the anguish and pain Tia had been suppressing pushed forward and the flood of tears she was holding back threatened to fall. Tia fumbled, almost tripping over her feet and dropping the fresh pitcher of water. She recovered at the last moment with all the dignity she could muster, headed across the tile floor, and placed the plastic pitcher on the nightstand next to the bed.

Nia sank into one of the two tan vinyl chairs facing the bed, linked her fingers, and studied her twin with narrowed eyes. Nia didn't miss a thing. Tia knew what she saw: tired dark spots under her puffy eyes from lack of sleep, a shaky voice that she couldn't control, weight loss and listless movements.

Silence stretched between the sisters. Moaning softly, Nia shook her head.

Finally, Tia couldn't stand it anymore. She yelled at her sister, "What?"

Shrugging, Nia answered, "Nothing."

Spoiling for a fight, Tia replied, "Oh, yeah. It's something."

"Don't take your frustration out on me," Nia snapped, crossing one leg over the other. "I haven't done a thing to you. But since you asked, I'm wondering why you're here and Chris took a plane to France."

Tears sprung to Tia's eyes. She turned aside hoping Nia hadn't seen them. It was a battle Tia lost miserably. Nia's sharp gaze had seen what Tia wanted desperately to hide. "We agreed to disagree."

"Did you now? Which means what?"

"He's gone to France and I'm here to help with the family."

"Mmm-hmm. Sounds interesting. I'm going to propose another scenario." Nia leaned back in her chair. "Or, you let Mother win."

"Win? Win what? I don't have anything she wants."

"Au contraire," Nia muttered in bad French.

"Look, I've got a bit of a migraine." Tia brought a shaky hand to her forehead. "I'm not in the mood for your bad imitations and smart-ass remarks. Say what you have to say or be quiet."

"Don't get all snippy with me. It's not my fault you wimped out."

Furious, Tia whipped around to face her twin. She speared the identical eyes with her own and moved closer, sticking a finger in her twin's face. "I don't wimp out."

Nia raised her hands, palms up to her twin. "Hey, I don't judge."

"I didn't wimp out," Tia answered with more force.

"Then why have you let Mother destroy your future?"

"Momma doesn't control me. I made a choice to be here. You guys need my help."

Snorting, Nia replied, "No, we don't."

Tia opened her mouth to contradict her sister.

"Hush." Nia shut her up with a wave of her hand. "If you were pregnant and going into labor, we'd handle Grandma Ruth. There are four of us and then add in Mother and Daddy. That's enough people to be available. This is no different. If you weren't available, we'd handle our business without you.

"Mother doesn't need you here. If you remember anything I said to you a few weeks ago, I mentioned the fact that you did have four siblings who can handle anything that Granny puts out."

"Momma asked me to stay."

"Sure, she did. Now she's got you where she wants you—in Detroit while Chris is in France. I'd say she got everything she wanted."

Nia linked her hands together and rested them against her forehead. She sat that way for a minute and then lowered her hands and stared directly at her sister.

"Tia, when are you going to grow up and stop letting Mother manipulate you?"

"I am grown. No one controls me," Tia snapped.

"You're not acting that way."

"Momma was upset. She didn't expect me to move," Tia defended her parent.

"I can understand that, but don't you have the right to a life? To be able to enjoy the fruits of your labor?"

"Of course."

"Well, sister-dear, if Mother had her way, you'd never leave home or have a boyfriend. She wants you right next to her."

"If that's the case, why did she treat Darnell so well?"

"Mother didn't care about Darnell. He didn't interfere. Darnell went along with whatever went on in our family. So Mother was fine with that."

"Oh, come on. She's not that way about any of you guys."

"Mmm-hmm. Mother took to her bed like the heroine in a Victorian novel when you first moved out. It took Daddy a week or two to finally coax her out of it. He had to take her away for a few days to get her mind right."

Exasperated, Tia threw her hands in the air. No matter what she said, her twin had an explanation or reason.

"What are you saying?" Tia demanded. "Spit it out."

"If Mother lost her mind when you moved into your own place in the same city, what do you expect her to do when you plan to move to a different country? Tia, she's fighting back. Mother is finding ways to keep you here with her."

Tia shut her eyes against the blinding headache pounding at her frontal lobe. Would her mother go to those lengths to keep her in Michigan? Losing Chris and now Nia's accusations. This was painful. She missed and needed Chris. Nia was making it almost impossible to think.

"You can't hide from it. Junior told me that when you told Mother about your engagement, she had a whole boatload of reasons why you shouldn't leave with Chris. Come on, girl. Mother made it clear each and every time you brought him to one of our family functions that she didn't like him."

"They didn't hit it off."

"Please. What's not to like? Chris is handsome, fun, and crazy in love with you. I could see her having a problem with him if he was abusive or treated you badly, but everybody can see how much he loves you. It was in his eyes and the way he talked to you."

Tia couldn't stand it anymore. "If Chris is all of that, why did he leave me?"

"Chris got tired. Didn't want to fight with Mother anymore. Needed to get to work. Take your pick."

"I think you're painting Momma as a villain here. Chris has to take the blame for what he did. Momma wouldn't do that to me." Tia folded her arms across her chest. "She wants me to be happy."

Nia scoffed. "Yeah, right. She wants you to be happy as long as it keeps you close to her and gives her what she needs."

Making the time-out symbol with her hands, Tia said, "Stop. I know you and Momma have your problems, but I won't let you stir up trouble between Momma and me."

Snorting, Nia added, "You are right. Mother

and I have never been close. We probably never will be. You know I love you, and I don't want you to miss your window of opportunity."

"Window of opportunity?"

The door opened and the nurse pushed Grandma Ruth into the room in a wheelchair. Tia jumped up and headed for the door, ready to help her grandmother.

The nurse waved Tia away. "I've got it. Besides, she needs to learn how to get in and out of the bed without help."

Tia and Nia stood as Grandma Ruth climbed into bed with the nurse's help. The nurse fluffed pillows and straightened the bed. After a few minutes, she left with the promise of returning the next day.

"Do you need anything?" Nia asked.

Grandma replied, "Water."

"Okay." Nia picked up the pitcher and a cup and then turned to her twin. "Why don't you leave? You've been here all day. I'll take over."

"I will." Tia picked up her purse and fished around the bottom for her keys. "Is there anything I can do before I go?"

"No."

Nia glared at her sister. "You have to make up your mind what you're going to do with your life. Chris won't wait forever."

"He didn't wait at all," Tia reminded.

"Why should he? Generally, when you tell someone you love him, it means you want to be with him. You sent that man away without a kiss or a promise."

No, I didn't, Tia thought, remembering the final kiss between her and Chris. A kiss filled with so much passion and love it made her hesitate over her next move. She glanced at her bare ring finger, feeling fresh stabs of pain. When she took the ring from her finger, she saw the disappointment and hurt glittering from his beautiful eyes. It took everything in her to push that ring into his hand.

Chris tried to talk her out of it. Adamant, Tia refused to listen to anything else he had to say. If they were over, then he should have his ring. She insisted and after a moment he took the ring and shoved it into his pocket.

Nothing had worked out the way it should have. Chris was gone and she was alone. Her family was the only thing left to her and she planned to be there for them no matter what.

29

Determined to talk some sense into her mother, Nia Edwards opened the front door to her child-hood home, used her key, and entered. "Mother? Daddy?" she called, waiting in the hallway for some-one to answer. They must be home.

"Back here," Mrs. Edwards called.

Not sure where her mother was calling from, Nia started for the kitchen.

"Nia?" Her mother strolled from the rear of the house and stopped in the hallway. She tilted her head as she studied her daughter for a moment. "What are you doing here? Aren't you supposed to be with your grandmother?" Alarmed, her eyes widened. "Is everything all right?"

"I was there," Nia explained, pulling the strap of her purse more securely on her shoulder. "Grandma was asleep when I left. Everything's good. If you have a few minutes to spare, I'd like to talk to you."

Frowning, her mother's forehead crinkled and

her eyes appeared concerned. The older woman studied Nia, trying to figure out this turn of events. "Sure. I'm in the family room."

Nia knew her mother was wondering what she wanted. They never talked. It was an unspoken rule that they went their separate ways and only came together for family functions. Nia learned very early that she was not the chosen member of this family, and she understood her position in the family hierarchy.

"You hungry?" Mrs. Edwards asked, heading to the back of the house. She hovered outside the kitchen door.

"No. I'm fine."

Her mother nodded and continued to the family room. Oprah Winfrey's theme music could be heard on the television as they moved down the hallway and entered the room. Her mother dropped down onto the sofa and picked up the remote. Instantly, *Oprah* became a nonverbal program. For a moment, Nia hesitated, standing in the doorway as she watched the talk show host move around the stage without sound. Refocusing on her reason for being there, she stepped across the threshold and sank into the spot next to her mother.

"Is everything all right with Mother?" Mrs. Edwards asked again, moving her latest romance novel from the couch to the coffee table.

"She's good," Nia answered.

"Then what is it? What brings you here?"

"Tia."

That got Mrs. Edwards's attention. "What's wrong with my baby?"

"Mother, I don't mean to upset you," she explained as her hands fluttered over her slick bob and then dropped to the edge of the cushion. Intruding into someone else's life was not her way of doing things. Normally she let friends and family handle their own business. Unfortunately, Tia needed help. She didn't know how to deal with their mother. "Tia is falling apart; she's miserable. Breaking up with Chris has left her totally lost. It was the wrong thing to do. She doesn't know what to do without him."

Mrs. Edwards waved a dismissing hand at her daughter and smacked her lips, stating, "She'll be all right. I thought something was really wrong."

"Tia's not all right."

"I know my daughter. Tia-Mia made her choice. It'll take a few days before she settles down."

"No. She didn't make any decision." Nia pointed a finger at her mother. "You did."

"Don't be ridiculous."

"I'm not," Nia responded. "Things won't ever go back to normal. Tia truly loves Chris and he loves her. She needs to be with him."

Pressing her lips together, Mrs. Edwards turned the remote over and over in her hands. "I think you're making far too much of this situation." She slapped Nia's hand playfully. "Don't be a drama queen. Besides, how would you know?"

"I sat with Grandma today. Tia and I visited for a few minutes. Mother, have you taken a minute to look at Tia?"

"I've seen her. Tia's fine."

"She looks sick. She's lost weight, and I don't think she's sleeping. You need to talk with her."

Mrs. Edwards stared back at her daughter in horror. She gazed at Nia as if she had announced that she planned to have a sex-change operation. "What about?"

"Chris."

"No. That's not my place."

"But it was your place to make her promise to stay here with you?"

"That's none of your business." Jackie Edwards's expression hardened, becoming distant, and her voice dropped warningly.

"That's where you're wrong. It is my business. This is about my sister. I don't want to see her hurt anymore. Darnell hurt her enough."

"He didn't mean much. Darnell was just a passing phase," Jackie Edwards answered, shifting around on the sofa. "I don't need you to tell me about my child."

Okay, Nia thought. *I don't want to do this, but I have no choice. Mother will ignore the obvious because she got what she wanted.* "Somebody should."

"Nia Edwards, who do you think you're talking to?"

"My mother. The woman who can make this all right. The person who needs to let go of my sister and let her have a chance at life. Tia is staying because you put her in a horrible situation. She couldn't leave you when you needed her or while Grandma is sick. You made her *promise* to be here with you. That wasn't fair."

"You don't know what you're talking about. Besides, it's none of your business what Tia and I do."

"Yes, it is my business. I'm here to ask you to let her go."

Sitting as regally as a queen, she turned to her daughter with a cool expression that should have had every item in the room covered in ice. Nia felt the chill, but she didn't plan to back down. "I don't want to fight with you or cause you any distress, especially with Grandma being sick, but I can't let Tia suffer like this. It breaks my heart to see my twin this way."

"You don't know what you're talking about. Mind your own business."

"It is my business when I see her so unhappy. Don't you care?"

"Of course I care. Tia is my baby."

"And your favorite child."

"Don't say that," Mrs. Edwards practically yelled.

"Why not? It's the truth. That's why you can't stand the idea of her moving to France with Chris. There are valid reasons to be concerned, but you went way over the top. When she first moved away from home, you almost had a stroke. There's no way you can handle Tia living abroad. Mother, please don't do this to her. Don't take her life away. Tia will eventually come to hate you."

Mrs. Edwards sat up straight and pointed a finger in Nia's face. "I would never interfere in my children's lives."

"Yeah, right. Is that why you made Tia promise to stay in town until Grandma got better? Or put it in her head that she needed to wait a while before considering marriage? Mother, you're in Tia's business all the time."

Mrs. Edwards wagged her finger at her daughter. "You are stepping over the line, young lady."

"So what else is new?" Nia wanted to laugh and cry at the same time. Stepping over the line was her specialty when it came to her mother. "You and I have always bumped heads. We've never gotten along."

Mrs. Edwards's hand fluttered around the shirt opening at her neck. She opened her mouth to deny the allegation, but then shut it without saying a word.

Nia continued. "Don't bother denying it. We both know the truth, but this situation isn't about me. Tia is the one suffering, and you have the power to put an end to it."

Head held high, Nia's mother replied, "Tia-Mia can leave any time she wants. I don't have a hold on her."

"Yes, you do. Mother, Tia found someone who loves and cares about her. Do you have any idea how rare that is?" Nia scoffed. "Of course not, you don't have a clue. You've always had Daddy. It's special and Tia deserves to be happy. Let her go."

"I don't have any strings attached to her."

"It's time to step up. Do the right thing for your daughter. You have the power to steer Tia in the right direction. Don't take this from her."

Jackie Edwards sat stiffly at Nia's side.

"Guilt is a powerful emotion. And, Mother, you use it well. Not just on Tia, but also on all of us. Tia feels it more than any of us because she's with you a lot of the time. You are a master of manipulation, and I can see it because it's not directed at me. I can't let you do this to my sister."

She reached out and laid her hand on top of her mother's. Jackie Edwards shook it off. Nia fought back tears. Her voice was firm and without hesitation. "I'm not Tia and I never will be, but I'm here. When you need someone to go shopping with, call me." Hope fueled her next words. When Nia made her way to her parents' home, she'd never expected for her conversation to go this way. Maybe she needed something from her mother, a chance to have a fulfilling relationship.

"I get lonely," Nia admitted. "I don't always like to do things alone. Maybe we can help each other. I'll be happy to drive and shop with you. You won't be by yourself."

"That's what this is about. You want to take Tia's place."

"I don't need to take anybody's place. I have a life of my own." Jumping to her feet, Nia stared down at her mother with contempt.

Jackie Edwards shrank away.

"I told you at the beginning this was not about me. I thought I could appeal to your motherly instinct. As far as I'm concerned, the way you've manipulated Tia is *very* unmotherly."

"Don't forget who you're talking to. I am your mother."

"When you choose to be."

"Nia Edwards, stop before you say something you'll regret."

"You mean before I say something that you don't want to hear." Nia shook her head. "I was hoping to help us both, but you don't want that. You want your world the way it is and nothing else. That's not going to happen. Get ready for some changes. I'm going to encourage my sister to follow her heart. You do whatever you have to."

With that, Nia turned on her heel and marched out of the room. She didn't stop until she was on the front porch. Breathing hard, she took a minute to gather her thoughts and fought back tears before getting behind the wheel of her car.

She glanced back at the home where she'd learned so much about love and even more about pain and rejection.

Nia took a deep breath. It didn't matter. She turned the ignition and the car hopped to life. After glancing out of the side mirror, Nia pulled into traffic. She'd gotten through her mother's rebuff just as she had all the rest.

30

Stunned, Jackie Edwards sat quietly on the sofa as Nia marched out of the room. The agitated click of her daughter's high heels faded as Nia marched down the hall. The slamming of the door punctuated her departure.

Minutes later, Greg Edwards peered into the family room. "Is it safe?"

Frowning, she looked up and focused on the man she married thirty-seven years ago. "What?"

"Can I come in?" he teased. "Is the coast clear?"

Nodding slowly, Jackie waved her husband into the family room. She had so much to think about and consider.

First, Nia never visited. She made a point of avoiding her mother unless something important came up. Her twin girls had always been close regardless of the relationship they had with their mother. Tia meant the world to her sister. Nia loved her twin and was completely devoted to her.

Jackie knew Nia would do anything to help her

twin. No matter the situation, Nia let things slide off her back and went about her business unconcerned, unless it involved someone in her family.

Nia's accusations hurt. It felt like someone had flashed a light into her eyes while she was suffering from a migraine. Had she been treating her children unfairly? Was she being selfish? Did she deserve the things that Nia had said to her?

Greg crossed the floor and sank onto the cushion next to Jackie. Silence reigned as he sat by her side. After a moment, he reached for her hand and laced their fingers together.

"You heard everything?" Jackie asked.

He nodded.

"Am I wrong?" she whispered.

"Do you want the truth?" he questioned.

Jackie snorted. "No."

He squeezed her hand. "But you need to know."

She nodded.

Greg took a deep breath and let it out in one big gush. "Yes."

Shutting her eyes, Jackie sat perfectly still. Greg was a constant who enriched her life. She couldn't imagine her household without this man. He never lied. No matter how painful, he always told her the truth. Before he'd tell a lie, he wouldn't say anything at all. Nia had always been a problem between them. Over the years, they had learned to live together, but Nia always presented the only real disagreement they had. Now, all of her problems with Nia were coming back to haunt her.

Guilt mixed with a hearty dose of pain made

her feel like crying. Unfortunately, tears wouldn't make things any easier or better. She needed to sort this situation out. It was time to talk. "How do I fix this?"

"Which problem?"

Her head pounded. She squeezed her eyes shut and rammed her palm against her forehead, muttering sarcastically, "Thanks, my loyal husband. You are such a joy to be with."

"You asked." Shrugging, Greg chuckled softly and leaned over to kiss her on the cheek. "You stepped into it. I'm trying to keep you from bringing the funky odor and the mess into the house. Otherwise you'll smell up the whole place."

Jackie rested her head against his shoulder. "Have I treated my girls differently?"

"Yes."

"I didn't mean to."

"You probably didn't. But, hon, you gave birth to two girls. You raised one and did what you needed to for the other. You put all the love into Tia. Nia got what was left. I never understood what was going on in your head, but I tried to compensate and make it up to Nia by being the parent she needed, the person she trusted and came to when things went wrong."

Guilt-induced tears slid down Jackie's cheeks. She wiped them away with the back of her hand. Greg pulled a handkerchief from his pocket and handed it to her.

"Thanks." She took the white linen from his hand and dabbed at the wetness sliding down her cheeks.

"You're welcome."

How did I allow this to happen? Jackie couldn't believe that she'd been so callous and uncaring. "I love all of my kids."

"Yes, you do. But you forgot to show that love to Nia. You've always treated Nia differently from the rest." He pressed his lips together. Jackie got the impression that he was considering how much to say. His face took on a determined expression and then he added, "Nia always came second. Tia was the one you put all of your time and interest into. Your heart went into anything dealing with her. You used logic when it came to Nia. You always had time for Tia no matter the situation. If Nia required anything beyond food and clothes, you left her to me."

"I didn't mean to do that."

"I know." Greg patted her hand reassuringly. "But you did it and Nia realized that you favored her sister. We were lucky that the twins didn't hate each other. If anything, it made them closer."

The feelings of confusion and anger swelled inside of her and began to overwhelm her. In a small voice she confessed, "Nia was always so hard to handle. She wanted to play baseball with the boys. She couldn't keep still. Always busy. It was like working with a wiggly worm. If I put a dress on her, she'd come back with it torn and dirty. She complained loud and often when I dressed her and Tia alike. Nia became too much to deal with. She'd never sit quietly; she always had so much to say and do. I didn't know what to do with her."

"Nia was never your typical little girl, that's for sure. One thing I do know is that all she needed, all she ever wanted was for you to love her. Baby, you gave birth to her. Your job was to accept her the way she was."

"I didn't do that, did I?" Jackie twisted the handkerchief around her hand.

"Nope."

"I feel like a bad mother."

"You weren't a bad mother. You just didn't give her what she deserved. God is good. He's given you an opportunity to fix all of that and help Tia at the same time."

"I don't want Tia to go," Jackie whined. The sense of loss that she had felt when Chris and Tia announced their engagement filled her once again. She was going to lose her baby to a life apart from her. More than that, Tia would leave the country. How was she supposed to have a relationship with her daughter when she lived thousands of miles away?

"That's okay. I understand your feelings. I don't want her to leave, either, but she's grown and deserves a chance at happiness, even if it means her leaving us to live in another country. We can't stop that. No. I didn't say that right. We shouldn't stop her."

"Greg! What if something happens while she's living in France?"

He patted her hand. "We raised her right. If it doesn't work out, Tia knows how to come home. She also knows that we're here for her."

"I don't trust him." Jackie scrunched up her face.

Laughing, Greg leaned back in his chair. "You don't trust anybody."

Sitting straighter, she pointed out, "I liked Darnell until he started messing around on my baby."

"No, you didn't," Greg contradicted. "You tolerated him because he didn't interfere with you and Tia. If he'd been a tiny bit more aggressive or demanding, Darnell would have seen the wrath of Jackie Edwards."

She shrugged and then admitted, "I really didn't like him that much. He needed to go, the dirty dog."

"I know. From the beginning, Chris was different. He loves Tia, but it's up to her to decide where she wants to be. It's her decision. He's not going to cater to you or beg. It's about his life with Tia. She's got to choose. I respect him for that."

"True, but that can make for a controlling man."

"Chris isn't controlling or demanding. He expects Tia to be the woman at his side." Greg stroked her cheek with his fingertips. As usual, Jackie felt the same love she carried for this man for almost forty years. "Just as you are for me."

"He's a white boy. We've skirted around all the issues, but we can't ignore that one. It's too huge."

"No, we can't," Greg agreed. "And I worry about how that one fact will change her life, but it's Tia's life, not ours. This isn't Romeo and Juliet. No one will commit suicide if things don't work out. She has a right to choose, and it looks as if she has chosen Chris. All we can do is support her and help her in any way that we can."

Jackie opened her mouth to comment, but Greg raised his hand and cut her off.

"You don't like or trust him. I get that, but feelings don't reflect the fact that he happens to be in love with our daughter. Jackie, baby, Chris is a good man. Sometimes I watched him when they were here. If we asked Chris to drink twenty gallons of her dirty bathwater, he would."

Giggling, Jackie agreed. "I know. I've seen that look, too. That's what clued me in on his feelings the first time he came to dinner. I knew something big was going to happen, and I wasn't ready for it."

Greg sobered and asked, "What do you need to do?"

"Talk to my girls. Let them know that they both mean the world to me. Make sure Nia understands that I love her as much as I do Tia."

Nodding, Greg said, "Excellent."

She folded the handkerchief into a neat square and handed it back to Greg. He shoved the cloth back into his pocket. Jackie asked, "Can we suggest to Tia that she think about the situation a little longer? Make her see the error of her ways?"

"No. Nia was right. Our daughter is miserable. We can't let this continue. Thanks to you, Tia believes she can't leave until your mother is back on her feet. That was wrong, baby. It's time for you to let her go. Tia has done all of the things you have expected of her. Now it's time to let her lead the kind of life she wants. If you need someone to spend time with, go shopping with Nia." He sighed heavily and added, "I'll even go with you, but I think Nia would be happy to be with you. It's past time for you two to get to know each other better."

"I think you're right." Jackie picked up the telephone and punched in a number.

Frowning, Greg watched his wife. "What are you doing?"

"This is the first step to making everything right."

31

Tia climbed the basement steps, lugging a basket of clean laundry. She turned down the hall to her living room and dropped onto the sofa. Worn out, she pulled a pastel green towel from the basket, shook it out, and then folded it. Once she finished this load, Tia planned to start dinner. Lately, nothing appealed to her. She thought a salad might perk up her appetite.

The doorbell rang. Tia groaned. She really didn't want any company right now. For the first time in days, she would have one evening in her home without family and friends. If she sat quietly and pretended no one was home, maybe whoever stood at her door would go away.

Someone jabbed the doorbell a second and then a third time. This person didn't plan to leave. Sighing, Tia rose. If it was a family member, she could hurry them through their visit and send them on their way.

Tia headed for the front of the house and opened the door. Surprised, she stared at her visitor.

"Hi, Tia-Mia."

"Hello, Momma." *What is she doing here?* Tia wondered. She glanced past her mother and saw only her car parked in the lot. "Is everything all right?"

"Mmm-hmm."

"What about Grandma Ruth?"

"Doing great."

"Oh." *Then why are you here?* Tia wondered. "Is Daddy with you?"

"No. He's at home." Smiling hesitantly, Mrs. Edwards's shaky hand brushed away a lock of hair. "Can I come in?"

"Of course." Tia opened the door wider and stepped aside.

If everyone was doing fine, why had she received this unexpected visit? Tia's forehead crinkled into a frown, and her belly cramped into knots. Something didn't feel right. Tia snatched a quick look at her mother. She'd never seen her look like this. Lack of confidence was not one of her mother's characteristics. Normally, Momma practically oozed confidence. If she could bottle it, they'd live in Malibu instead of Detroit. "I was in the living room folding up towels. Come on in."

Mrs. Edwards followed Tia down the hall to the living room. The older woman perched on the edge of the couch, tightly clenching the strap of her purse sitting at her side.

Tia studied her mother's hand clenching and unclenching the leather strap as she returned to her previous spot and resumed folding towels. "What's on your mind?"

"Chris," Tia's mother stated.

Tia dropped the towel she was folding. She reached down and picked up the square of terry cloth. "Sorry."

"How is Chris? Have you heard from him?"

She gazed at the striped fabric and muttered, "I don't know. He's in France."

"He hasn't called? Sent you a note?"

"No. Nothing." Why couldn't her mother leave things alone? Tia didn't want to think about him. It was still far too painful.

Nodding, Mrs. Edwards continued to question Tia. "What about work? How are things going there?"

Tia felt as if she were on safer ground, so she let her guard down. "Busy. I don't know if I told you this, but Adam and Wynn are going to have a baby."

That brought a smile to her mother's face. "Really? Was it a surprise, or were they trying to have a baby?"

"Definitely a surprise. I've never seen Adam happier."

"Good for them. And Chris's position? What's happening with that? Does Adam plan to fill it or leave it open until Chris comes back?"

Surprised, Tia blinked several times. How had her mother brought the conversation back to Chris so smoothly?

"I don't know," Tia muttered softly as she

concentrated on matching up the stripes
towel set.

Mrs. Edwards licked her lips and leaned clo
to Tia. "This is hard for me, but I have to do this."
She took a deep breath and let it out. "I'm sorry
for everything you've gone through since your
grandmother took sick."

Tia's eyes widened. Where had this come
from? "It's okay. Grandma needs me."

Studying the carpeting, Mrs. Edwards shook
her head. "No, she doesn't. It was never about
her. I needed you, and I used her illness as a way
to keep you near me."

"Momma, you don't have to—"

Jackie Edwards placed a hand on her daughter's arm. Her voice quivered as she spoke, "Stop.
I'm sorry. I haven't been very fair to you lately. To
be honest, I've been horrible. You didn't deserve
it. Tia, baby, I was selfish. I didn't want you to go.
I shut my eyes to how much it hurt you when
Chris left."

"That's between Chris and me. Don't worry
about it."

"I do. It's not just between you and Chris. I
made it our family's business. Truly, I never had
anything against Chris. He was nice, handsome,
and respectful. What worried me was the way he
looked at you. Almost from the beginning, I
could tell that you meant something very special
to him and it scared me. I also could tell that he
was no pushover, not like Darnell, who went
along with everything. Chris wanted you and
went about finding a way to have you."

Tia's head began to pound with the pressure of all this. "Momma, why are you telling me this stuff now? I don't understand."

"Your sister came by the house today."

"Nia? For what?" This situation was getting creepier by the minute. "What does that have to do with me?"

"It had everything to do with you. She wanted me to know how miserable you were and how you missed Chris."

Tia hid her expression by lowering her gaze. Yes, she missed Chris terribly, but she didn't want to upset her mother.

"Nia loves you more than anyone else." Mrs. Edwards ran her tongue across her lips. "Your happiness is important to her. Your sister made me acknowledge some hard truths about myself."

Tia smiled. Yes, she knew Nia always fought for her, but this battle was between her and Chris. It had nothing to do with her parents or her siblings.

Her mother cupped the side of Tia's face and said, "I'm sorry. I've been selfish. Nia was right. You do deserve to be happy. I want you to call Chris and tell him that you're on your way to France to meet him."

Her heart leaped for joy, and then reality set in. She wasn't sure Chris would want to see her. "I can't, Momma."

"Why not?"

"I'm not sure Chris wants to see me. Plus, my plane ticket expired a few days ago. I can't afford to buy another one."

"Is that all?" Jackie Edwards reached into her

purse and pulled out a computer-generated form. She handed it to Tia. "I think this will solve your transportation problem."

Tia gazed questioningly at her mother. "What is this?"

"It's a ticket to Paris, silly."

"I don't understand."

"I'm sorry. I was wrong. I don't know what's going to happen in the future. I don't have a clue about tomorrow. Hell, I could drop dead tomorrow. I hope I won't, but nothing is promised. I do know that I want you to be happy. Chris loves you and completes your world. So, I'm saying go be with him. Call that man. Tell him you're on your way and get on a plane to be with him."

She dropped the towel in her hands and reached for her mother. Tia held on tight to the older woman. "I love you, Momma."

"I know. And I love you." Jackie Edwards let out a shaky breath. "It's time for you to have your own life, family, whatever. Go pack. Your flight leaves in about three hours."

"Three hours!" Tia yelped. "Oh my God. There's no way I'm going to be ready."

"Yeah, you will. Whatever you don't have, buy it in France."

Nodding, Tia rose and moved around her mother. The older woman caught her hand as she passed. "Tia-Mia?"

Already planning her wardrobe, Tia glanced at her mother. "Hmm?"

"Always remember that your family is here for you. There's a lot of stuff that you've never encountered before. I wasn't joking about the race thing, the cultural thing, or even about his family. Be ready for a lot of changes in your life."

"I know, Mom."

"Actually, I don't think you do, but that's okay. Remember, I'm only a phone call away. If you need me, call because I'll be on a plane to get to you as soon as I can."

Tia grinned. The lioness was back, and she didn't plan on anyone betraying or hurting her cub. "Okay. Is that it?"

"No. You tell Chris that I'll be watching to make sure he treats you right. And if things go bad, he'll have to answer to me."

32

Will Chris be there? Tia wondered, staring out the window of the plane. White cloud formations and blue sky surrounded the jet. She shifted in the small, uncomfortable seat, feeling too keyed up and nervous to appreciate the beauty around her. Chris occupied all of her thoughts. Would he be at the airport when she arrived?

After Tia had packed at super speed, Mrs. Edwards drove her to Metro Airport. Riding along I-94, Tia tried to reach Chris, first on his cell phone and then at the France office. Neither attempt was successful. She left messages at both locations before trying his home number. Again, the only thing she got was voice mail. She left a message there, too. Would he come to the airport? Would Chris be happy to see her?

Throughout her flight, she waited, hoping he would get in touch with her. Her cell phone sat in her lap. Maybe he sent her a text. She reached for the phone and switched to text messaging. Nothing.

Sighing deeply, disappointment overwhelmed her. Frustrated, she felt like tossing the thing in the trash. *Please be there, Chris.*

A chime rang throughout the airplane cabin followed by the captain's voice. He made an announcement, first in French and then in English, that they were nearing their destination and to prepare for landing. Once the announcement concluded, the passengers began returning items to the carry-on bins and snapping their seat belts into place. Tia stared out the window and saw the outline of the airport and runways below. The plane shifted while the flight attendants hurried down the aisles, removing trash and telling passengers to buckle up. Tia shoved the magazine that was in her lap into the pocket in front of her, stuffed her cell phone in her purse, and placed it under her seat.

Once the plane landed and the passengers disembarked, forty-five minutes had passed. All the while, Tia's tension grew. Chris's silence made her feel as if things were unsettled. Unsure what the flight attendants were saying and where she should go, Tia trailed a family off the plane, through the airport, and to the baggage claim area. Arms folded across her chest, she stood near them.

Expecting to find Chris waiting for her, Tia studied the surrounding faces. Some were anxious and some were happy as they waited for loved ones. She scanned the unfamiliar hordes for Chris's handsome and reassuring presence. Again, disappointment filled her. She fought down a layer of hysteria. What was she going to do? Biting down on her bottom lip, she decided to try Chris one more time. Maybe he hadn't received any of her previous messages. For the fourth time, she dialed his home number with the same results. His answering machine picked up.

Arms wrapped around her middle, Tia studied her surroundings. Everything, the people and environment, were so foreign. She felt as if she'd stepped onto a movie set. Was this how Chris felt when he had moved to Michigan—out of place and conspicuous? She gained new understanding and respect for the situation he had faced, leaving his home and settling in a foreign country.

What if he didn't come to meet her? What if none of her messages had reached him? She would have to come up with plan B. There were plenty of hotels. There had to be a Hilton, Hyatt, or Sheraton near the airport. She could stay a night and visit the Gautier home office tomorrow. Chris would be there, and maybe they could spend a little time sorting out their future—that is, if they still had a future.

Tia looked on one of the information boards to search for a list of hotels. She needed to be logical. She couldn't hang out at the airport all night.

Her heart wanted to believe that he would come. She half expected to turn around and find him standing right behind her. But the logical side of her brain knew she had to fend for herself and make provisions, no matter what happened with Chris. *No. Don't think like that,* she warned silently. *Chris will be here. He won't let me down.* She took another quick peek around her, but no one came forth.

Finally, a light flashed and a buzzer blared to announce the arrival of the passengers' luggage, which spilled from a small opening at the top of the carousel. She moved closer, studying the items as she waited for her bag to appear. All the while, Tia stole quick glances around her, hoping to see a familiar, welcoming face that would make her feel less like a foreigner and more like everything would soon be perfect.

As Tia waited, she switched between calling Chris's home and cell phone. Her efforts resulted in his answering machine and voice mail. Suddenly, her black bag came into view. She slipped the phone back into her purse and moved forward. She tugged at the handle of her bag, but it disappeared around the bend of the carousel before she could lift it. She waited for it to come around a second time. When it reached her again, Tia grunted and used all of her strength to pull the heavy luggage off the carousel. It barely budged. Without warning, the bag was lifted off the metal machine and placed on the floor.

Tia smiled, certain that Chris had arrived without her noticing and had helped her when she needed him. She turned, expecting to gaze into his beautiful pale blue eyes. Instead, green eyes the color of peas glanced back at her. Swallowing her disappointment, she said, *"Merci."*

"No problem," he answered with a salute of his hand. He turned to his family and strolled away.

Nibbling on the corner of her bottom lip, Tia realized that she was out of time. She had to decide what to do. With a nod of her head, she made an executive decision. Chris hadn't shown up, and she needed to find someplace to stay for the night. She noticed a man exiting the building through a sliding door down the hall. A taxi stand stood beyond the exit. Pulling her bag by the handle, Tia headed for the exit, praying that the cabbie spoke English.

She intended to be settled before nightfall. The doors slid open, and she moved through them and stood curbside. She stepped up to the taxi just as he pulled off. *Dang!* she thought. *I'll have to wait for the next one.*

A black sedan pulled smoothly into the cabbie spot and stopped in front of her. Mindful of crime against tourists, Tia took a step back, remembering all the horror stories about tourists being robbed and left for dead. The door opened and a blond man got out. "Tia!"

Her eyes widened in surprise and pleasure. She grinned like a fool, but she didn't care. "Chris." She dropped the handle of her bag and ran toward the love of her life.

Arms open, Chris waited for her. She flung herself at him. "I thought you didn't want to see me."

"Never!" he proclaimed, raining kisses on her face. "I missed you so."

Tia reached up and stroked his cheek. "I missed you, too." She ached for his lips on hers. Tia didn't have to wait. Chris leaned in and pressed his lips against hers. She wrapped her hands around the strong column of his neck. She inhaled, reveling in Chris's unique scent. Less than twenty-four hours ago, she was certain she'd never experience these sensations again.

Lips pressed against hers, he whispered, "Tia, I love you."

Tears sprang to her eyes and she answered, "I love you, too, Chris."

He nibbled on her bottom lip, pulling it into his mouth and sucking on it. He deepened the kiss as his tongue slid across her lips, getting his first taste of her. Eager for the taste of him, Tia moaned, rubbing herself against him. Chris cupped her cheek, gently stroking her skin. The gentle touch of his fingertips caressing her throat made her tingle all over.

Angry French words that Tia didn't understand were punctuated by tapping on the hood of the car. Groaning, they broke apart, ending their private reunion. "Give me a minute, man," Chris said in French.

Tia grinned up at him. "Maybe we should go."

Nodding, Chris backed away from her and waved at the cop. He hurried around the car, grabbed her bag, and placed it in the trunk. The cop closed his ticket book and returned his pen to his shirt pocket.

Chris saluted the cop. *"Merci."* He offered Tia his hand and said, "Let's go home."

She nodded as she took his hand. Always the gentleman, he helped her into the car before taking the driver's seat.

"I left you a ton of messages. Why didn't you answer?" Tia asked.

Chris took one hand off the steering wheel and laid it on top of hers, squeezing it as he answered, "I was at one of our factories, but I forgot my cell phone. I didn't call the office until I was ready to go home. That's when I got your messages. I hurried right over here and prayed that I would catch you before you left the airport."

Chris pulled away from the curb.

Tia studied the passing scenery and then turned to Chris. "Where are we going?"

Grinning, he looked at her and placed a hand over hers. "You and I are going to my mother's. Everyone is there and they expect to meet you."

Her heart galloped. Meet his family? She didn't feel she was ready for that.

"Don't worry," Chris said, driving them toward their future. "They're going to love you as much as I do."

Want more romance in your life? Don't miss
What Love Tastes Like

Available now wherever books are sold.

Here's an excerpt from *What Love Tastes Like* . . .

Could anybody possibly be that fine? That's what Tiffany Matthews asked herself as she fastened her seat belt, took a deep breath, and clutched a teddy bear that looked as frazzled as she felt. The bear had an excuse—it was almost twenty-five years old. And so did Tiffany—she was exhausted. Graduating from culinary school and preparing for a month-long overseas internship had taken its toll.

There was yet another draining aspect to consider: Tiffany was terrified of flying. But after taking the anxiety pill her best friend had given her, she brazenly endured the curious stares of fellow passengers as they watched the naturally attractive, obviously adult woman sit in the airport, enter the Jetway, and then board a plane with a raggedy stuffed animal clasped to her chest.

Tiffany didn't care. During a childhood in which her mother worked long hours and her grandmother loved but didn't entertain, Tuffy the teddy bear had been her constant and sometimes only friend. No matter what happened, Tuffy was there to lend a cushy ear, an eternal smile, and wide, button-eyed support. This stuffed animal was also the first present she remembered her father giving her, when she was five years old. Unfortunately, his gift stayed around longer than Daddy did, a fact that after years of not seeing him still brought Tiffany pain. They were estranged, and while Tiffany would never admit it, having her father's first gift close by always felt like having him near. Tuffy brought comfort—during her childhood of loneliness, her teenaged years of puppy love and superficial heartbreak, her college years of first love and true pain, and now, while pursuing a dream her parents felt was beneath her. As the plane began its ascent into the magnificently blue May sky, Tiffany squeezed her eyes shut, praying the pill would stave off an attack. She knew she'd take any help she could get to make it through this flight, even that of a furry friend.

It wasn't until the plane leveled off and her heartbeat slowed that she thought of him again— the stranger in first class. Their eyes had met when she passed by him on the way to her seat in coach. Tiffany had assessed him in an instant: fine, classy, rich. *And probably married,* she concluded as she finally loosened the death grip she had on Tuffy and laid him on the middle seat next to her. *Clearly out of my league . . .* Still, she couldn't help but remember how her breath had caught when she entered the plane and saw him sitting there, looking like a *GQ* ad, in the second-row, aisle seat. His close-cropped black hair looked soft and touchable, his cushiony lips framed nicely by just the hint of a mustache. But it was his eyes that had caused Tiffany's breath to catch: the deepest brown she'd ever seen, especially set against flawless skin that not only looked the color of maple syrup, but she imagined also tasted as sweet. This information was absorbed and processed in the seconds it took the man two people in front of her to put his carry-on in the overhead bin and step aside so the people behind him could continue. The stranger had glanced up at her. Their eyes had held for a moment. Had she imagined him giving her a quick once-over before he resumed reading his magazine?

Tiffany tilted back her seat and placed Tuffy on her lap. Perhaps it was the medication or the lack of sleep the prior night, but Tiffany welcomed what she hoped would be a long slumber that would take her over the Atlantic, all the way up to the landing in Rome. If she was lucky, she thought, she'd wake up with just enough time to pull her seat forward and place her tray table back in its upright and locked position. And if she was sleeping, she wouldn't be thinking about how much she hated flying, and she especially would not be thinking about Mr. First Class. She knew she was kidding herself to think she made any kind of impression as she passed by the sexy stranger. How could she, dressed in jeans, a Baby Phat T-shirt, and clutching a tattered teddy bear? *No need to sit here fantasizing. If I'm going to dream, might as well do it in my sleep!*

* * *

Dominique Rollins, or Nick as he was known to friends, put down the magazine and picked up his drink. After staring at the same page for over five minutes, he realized he wasn't reading it anyway. For some inexplicable reason, his mind kept wandering to the woman back in coach, the sexy siren who'd passed him clutching a teddy bear as if she were five instead of the twentysomething she looked. His guess was that she was afraid of flying and the toy was some type of childhood relic, like a security blanket. But to carry it openly, in public, holding it as if it were a lifeline? *Too bad, because that chick is as fine as chilled wine in the summertime.* Nick appreciated the stranger's natural beauty, but he liked his women successful and secure. Not that he was looking for women on this trip, he reminded himself. He wanted a carefree few days without any complications. Nick knew all too well that when it came to the words *woman* and *complication*, one rarely appeared without the other.

Her eyes . . . Nick tilted his seat back and sipped his Manhattan. That's what intrigued him about her. In them was a curious blend of trepidation and intelligence, of anxiety mixed with steely resolve. The combination brought out his chivalrous side. A part of him wanted to walk back to where she was, sit her on his lap, and tell her that everything was going to be all right. His rational side quickly shot down that idea. One, she was a stranger; two, she'd hardly appreciate being treated like a child—clutched teddy bear notwithstanding; and three, Nick wasn't in the market for a woman—friend or otherwise—he reminded himself for the second time in as many minutes. He was grateful for his work and the newest acquisition that had helped to take his mind off Angelica, the woman who'd dashed his dream of them getting married and having a family together . . . and who had broken his heart.

Nick signaled the flight attendant for another drink and reached for his iPod. He didn't want to think about Angelica on this trip. He wanted to enjoy this mini-vacation in Rome, one of his favorite cities, and dine at Anticapesa, one of his favorite restaurants and the inspiration behind the upscale eatery in his newly acquired boutique hotel.

Thinking about the quaint, thirty-four-room property he and his partners had purchased in Malibu, California, and were transforming into a twenty-first-century masterpiece brought a smile to Nick's face. Following the global economic collapse, the men had outwitted their corporate competition and had gotten an incredible deal on the 1930s Spanish-style building. The group, four successful men with diverse and various corporate and entrepreneurial backgrounds, all agreed that it was the good looks and sexy swagger of Nick and another partner, Bastion Price, that sealed the deal with the sixty-something, hard-as-nails Realtor who'd handled negotiations. This trip was the calm before the storm of Le Sol's grand opening, less than one month away.

Nick pressed the button that reclined his seat to an almost horizontal position. He tried to relax. But every time his eyes closed, he saw the short-haired, chocolate brown, doe-eyed beauty who'd passed him hours before, with those hip-hugging jeans and bountiful breasts pressed up against a tight, pale yellow T-shirt. *You're flying to Rome for pasta, not pussy,* he mentally chastised himself. Even so, his appetite had been awakened, and the dish he wanted to taste wasn't from anybody's kitchen.